LACE FOR A LADY

Recent Titles by Eileen Ramsay

BUTTERFLIES IN DECEMBER
HARVEST OF COURAGE
WALNUT SHELL DAYS

NEVER CALL IT LOVING *

* available from Severn House

LACE FOR A LADY

Eileen Ramsay

severn House

This first world edition published in Great Britain 2002 by
SEVERN HOUSE PUBLISHERS LTD of
9–15 High Street, Sutton, Surrey SM1 1DF.
This first world edition published in the USA 2002 by
SEVERN HOUSE PUBLISHERS INC of
595 Madison Avenue, New York, N.Y. 10022.

British Library Cataloguing in Publication Data

Ramsay,   Eileen
    Lace for a lady
    1.   Love stories
    I.   Title
    823.9'14 [F]

    ISBN 0-7278-5846-7

Typeset by Hewer Text Ltd.,
Edinburgh, Scotland.
Printed and bound in Great Britain by
MPG Books Ltd., Bodmin, Cornwall.

For the Balmossie set with love and laughter.

Skip awa.

Acknowledgements

Thank you to Graham McNicol who provided information on smuggling in the Arbroath area; to Miss Naomi Tarrant, Curator of Costume at the National Museum of Scotland, and to the Regency Loop – especially Dee Hendrickson.

One

'Twas the soap that did it, or rather, the lack of soap. One could make do with last year's gowns and – if the truth be known – the one she was wearing was, at the very least, three seasons old. A respectable toilet water could be concocted from the flowers of the garden or the woods – Miss Rattray was a veritable genius in that line – but to be reduced to using soap made in one's own kitchens, that no matter how dear Rattles tried to disguise it, was the selfsame used to launder the household linen, just would not do.

The Honourable Lydia Carpenter examined herself in her pier glass and sighed. 'You are not vain, Liddy,' she assured herself, and then, with the familiarity of the closest of acquaintance, went on, 'Of course, there is little for you to be vain about: mousy brown hair, mousy brown eyes, mousy brown skin . . . you must spend less time in the glare of the sun, my girl.'

She turned her attention to the miniature of her late brother that stood on her dressing table, and surveyed with love – and not a little chagrin – the most golden of curls, the bluest of eyes and the sweetest of smiles. She laughed. 'You will agree, dear Harry, that I have ever asked little, but now I ask, nay, I *demand* soap. Delicate, perfumed and, *bien sûr*, French.'

The ancient purse hanging from her waist contained a very large, masculine handkerchief, two keys, one to her jewel box, the other to the wine cellar, a hair ribbon that must surely belong to the youngest Carpenter daughter, but not even the smallest coin of the realm.

Why do I bother to protect these keys? mused a disgruntled Lydia Carpenter. My jewel box contains only Mama's wedding band, for Papa has sold everything else of value, and the cellar holds nought but cobwebs.

There was a light knock upon the heavy oak door and the door flew open to reveal the Honourable Charlotte Carpenter. She was dressed more as a maidservant than a daughter of the house, but even the rather too short pale blue muslin morning dress could not disguise Charlotte's undoubted beauty. Tendrils of golden hair, fine as silk, escaped from the unbecoming mobcap that she wore, for Miss Carpenter had been engaged in dusting the public rooms of the house.

Her sweet nature matches her beauty, thought Lydia with a smile as her sister, duster in one hand and an embossed envelope in the other, hurried into the room.

'Liddy, the most wonderful thing . . . you will never guess,' began Charlotte.

'You are in the right of it, dearest, I will never guess unless you sit down and tell me . . . but first take off that dreadful cap.'

Charlotte removed the offending article allowing her hair to tumble down in luxuriant waves around her shoulders.

'It is singularly unfair that when my hair escapes its pins it resembles nought so much as a witch's, and when yours escapes it is a thing of beauty.' She smiled lovingly as she looked at her younger sister whom she knew saw nothing special in her looks and indeed took them for granted.

'What nonsense you do talk, Liddy,' said Charlotte, 'but be serious and do look at this. I opened it. I should have brought it to you first but it was addressed to both of us, you see.'

'Indeed, I behold an extremely expensive envelope. Smuggled, I shouldn't wonder, for 'tis unlikely to have been made here.'

'Oh, silly. Look, it's from *him*, from London.'

Liddy took the proffered envelope and would have denied that her heart was beating rather faster than its wont. Only one signature could have made her gullible young sister react so. She would show that she was made of sterner stuff.

'Hurrah, at last one of Scotland's absentee landlords is deigning to visit his humble home and we are summoned to a dress party; such condescension on Lord Pittenmuir's part, I swear I am quite undone.'

Charlotte gazed at her sister and Liddy saw puzzlement and distress in her lovely eyes. Charlotte could not know why Liddy had grown to hate the dear friend of her childhood days. Keir Galloway had shared lessons with Liddy and Harry before the boys had been sent south to school. During the holidays she had ridden with them, fished and sailed and even, to Miss Rattray's undisguised horror, swam on occasion. Indeed Papa, on his infrequent visits, had blamed Keir for his eldest daughter's unfeminine, even hoydenish behaviour.

'Liddy,' reminded Charlotte, gently. 'Lord Pittenmuir was Harry's friend.'

'Friend.' Liddy turned on her sister. 'Friend, you say, Charlotte. Not one word did he pen when our dear brother lost his life, nor did he bestir himself to attend the funeral service.'

She collected herself, seeing how she had upset her younger sister. 'Forgive my wicked temper. We will repine no more on His Lordship's insincerity and abominable ill manners, but we will, if you wish, attend his party and you, Charlotte Carpenter, shall outshine everyone. Quickly, let us find Rattles and beseech her aid.'

Miss Rattray, the governess, was not difficult to find, for each morning took her to the old schoolroom where she tried to instil some learning into the heads of the youngest Carpenter girls. She had come to Balgowan House first when Lydia and Harry were small and she had remained to teach Charlotte and Lord Pittenmuir's younger brother, Jamie, and then later the rest of the Carpenter girls. Often Liddy asked her old mentor if she would not prefer some more lucrative position, but Rattles stayed, as Liddy well knew, out of love for her charges and not, as she said, because she was waiting for Lord Balgowan to pay her the salary so oft forgotten since the death of the girls' mother.

The little girls were dismissed to take a walk in the gardens while Miss Rattray perused the invitation. 'This is a secretary's hand, Liddy. I would have expected you to know that. I can only assume that Jamie caused this to be delivered in his brother's name. He is always most punctilious about the dignity of his brother's position and would ne'er overstep himself.'

'You believe that Lord Pittenmuir has asked these to be sent?' asked Charlotte anxiously.

'No, dear child, but I assure you that he has taken his brother's advice that a visit to his Scottish seat is sadly overdue and that a small party to reacquaint himself with neighbours is quite *comme il faut*. No doubt, upon his arrival in Scotland, His Lordship will make haste to visit here where, after all, he did learn his first lessons.'

'Dear Rattles, you have the right of it. We may expect a visit any moment.' Charlotte was once more in alt and seemed not to notice that her sister had shown none of the excitement one would normally have expected.

Keir Galloway was not only an old family friend but also – and more importantly – the most eligible bachelor in the county, if not the country.

'How do you bear these uncomfortable chairs, Rattles?' Liddy rose and moved away to the narrow barred windows of the old schoolroom, thus hiding her face from her sister and her former governess.

'Why, I am at once not so tall and better padded than you, my dear,' answered Rattles calmly. 'You will not be so foolish as to refuse this invitation, Liddy?' she added with a frown.

'Refuse? Dear Rattles, shall I confess to Lord Pittenmuir that a Jacobite flame yet burns in my heart, and that it would be anathema for such as I to darken the door of one who has willingly forsaken all the ideals of our shared childhood?' Had Miss Carpenter been more kindly endowed by nature, her bosom would have heaved with the strength of her emotions. Countless passions, long damped down, had been stirred by the simple receiving of this invitation, but she must control them.

'Don't fret, Charlotte, my love. Naturally I shall attend His Lordship's party and mayhap I will even simper with all the other old maids of Forfarshire.'

'Dearest Liddy, you have such a strange sense of humour,' laughed Charlotte uneasily. 'Jacobites indeed. Did you and Lord Pittenmuir used to play at Jacobites?'

Lydia thought of the secret meetings in the old castle where she, Harry, and Keir had sworn fealty to the line of Stewart kings; the kings for whom her grandfather had sacrificed wealth and position. Had they been childish games? Never. ''Twas Grand-père, Charlotte. He had but lately returned from exile in France. Papa, you remember, had been born there and our own dear Mama was French. Grand-père used to tell Harry and me the story of how he took his family and left with his Prince—'

'Closing the gates behind him,' broke in Charlotte.

'Leaving everything. Forbidden to return to the country he loved almost as much as the Stewart cause. Miss Rattray added our family's story to our knowledge of history,' continued Liddy with an air of wistfulness.

'I never romanticized the Jacobite cause, Liddy. You children did that for yourselves.'

'We did not make it glorious,' said Liddy, simply. 'It was.'

'It was an appalling waste of life, my dear, but let us repine no more upon it and turn our energies to finding new gowns for you and Charlotte. You must wear white, Charlotte, but it suits you so do not despair, and even though you have never been formally presented, Liddy, I do think we can say that you are "out" and therefore we may choose a colour more flattering.'

'Do not fret, Rattles. I daresay my dove-coloured crêpe will do adequately.'

Since the crêpe was the one gown Liddy had caused to be made since she had put off her blacks for Harry, both Miss Rattray and Charlotte made a simultaneous resolution that Lydia should have a new dress for the occasion.

Miss Rattray muttered something about crêpe being such a serviceable material, and Liddy, knowing full well the tumultuous thoughts racing around in her old friend's head, pretended to take the remark for a compliment. When Charlotte had returned to her dusting and the younger girls had been set a task by their governess, Liddy and Rattles retired to the shabby old library where Lydia conducted the business of the estate in her father's absence. She rarely sat in the yellow drawing room that should have been the ideal setting for the daughter of the house. It had been the favourite room of Lady Balgowan, the daughter of French aristocrats, and Liddy hated to see the beautiful brocades on the once exquisite walnut sofas so shabby. She had all but closed off the room acknowledging that the less wear and tear the materials received, the longer they would last, there seemed no way of ever renewing them.

She unburdened herself to Rattles with whom there was no need to pretend. 'Charlotte must have a new gown for the party. I would like her to take her proper place in society, but where is the money to be obtained? My housekeeping box is quite empty until the next quarter; indeed there are some pressing accounts that must be paid before we think of such fripperies as new gowns, slippers and the like.'

'You will not approach your father?'

5

Liddy rose as she always did when she found it difficult to find the right words. She walked to the window and stood there for a moment before turning again. 'I had hoped that Papa might be persuaded to finance Charlotte's coming-out. He was only ever interested in his son . . .' Liddy flushed delicately, feeling that it might appear she was reproaching her parent. 'I do believe that is often the way with gentlemen, and he does hold us in regard, whatever appearances may shout to the contrary.'

'If he could but recover from dear Harry's death . . .'

'I believe that if Harry had died in a hunting accident, Papa might have been brought to bear it, but to die for a cause in which Papa cannot bring himself to believe—'

'Harry believed in it, Liddy. He was no Jacobite drinking toasts to some long lost dream. King George is his king; this United Kingdom is . . . *was* his country and for its safety he died and you are wrong to demean his death.' Miss Rattray stopped, conscious-stricken, as the confiding young girl disappeared and a veritable giant towered over the governess.

'You are wrong to presume, Miss Rattray, that I demean my brother's death,' and with that parting shot Liddy hurried from the room. Out, she would go out. Burdens seemed easier to bear outside the house and walking or riding furiously seemed to help her solve problems. She was quite shattered by Miss Rattray's attitude and it was only after the words had been uttered that Liddy realised how much it had meant to have Rattles as a confidante. Lady Balgowan had died when baby Alice was scarce two years old and through the years it was Rattles who remained steadfast. Papa had stayed more and more in London once Harry had gone to school, and after his son's death, Lord Balgowan had returned but once – to bury him. The friends of their childhood had grown up and gone away. Keir, no, she would refuse to think of him. Even the death in the Iberian Peninsula of his best friend had not brought him back to the beliefs of their shared childhood.

Some twenty minutes later as she stood on the headland looking out to the estuary, Liddy was able to laugh at herself. The Stewart line was gone; it had left over sixty years earlier and really there was little wrong with poor old George, apart from the fact that he was no Scot and those children of his were a sorry bunch. God help us all when Prince Florisel ascends the throne.

She stood watching a boat being rowed towards Arbroath. Fishermen – or French spies? Would Napoleon send spies through Scotland since he was having such a sorry time invading from the south? The boat had disappeared and Liddy found herself wishing that she had changed her clothes and ridden for she would dearly have loved to see where that little boat had gone. Not for a moment did she really entertain the notion that it carried spies from France, but she knew well that the cliffs were riddled with caves and it would have been interesting to learn which caves were still frequented by the children of the district.

The craft appeared again and the fishermen, for so it was, saw Liddy on the cliff and waved to her. She waved back unmindful of the fact that they mistook her for some fisher lass and not the daughter of Balgowan. She saw the unmistakable shape of lobster creels in the bottom of the boat. Someone would eat well tonight.

She turned and looked inland. Trees prevented her from seeing the manor house in which she had been born and where her family had lived for over a hundred years, but standing stark against the skyline were the ruins of Balgowan Castle. It had not been so much destroyed in warfare as simply allowed to fall down. Too large and inconvenient to be lived in comfortably, bits had been breached by foes and in latter years by farmers looking for good stones for their walls or dykes. It was Liddy's dream to restore it; she had issued instructions that no more stones were to be removed, but as yet no money had been found to begin essential repairs. If funds were not forthcoming the ancient seat of the Carpenters would simply crumble away.

As a ruin it was beautiful. It must once have been breath-taking. Rhododendrons, unknown in Scotland when the first stone was laid, now rioted over some of the low walls, and roses, once cultivated, now ran wild, rearing their heads through the roof of what had once been a chapel.

Liddy knew every inch of the castle, from what remained of the battlements to the escape tunnels that ran beneath the ancient walls to the sea. There were local legends of the nefarious purposes to which those tunnels had been put and Liddy had spent hours exploring them with Harry and Keir. The explorations had died a natural death when the boys went south to Eton College. Exploring dirty caves and passages had been no fun alone and there was no way in which the little Charlotte could have been prevailed upon to join such expeditions.

Thoughts of Charlotte brought back the overwhelming problem of how to finance her sister's unofficial debut into the limited society of the area. No doubt Lord Pittenmuir would bring some attendant satellites in his wake and those with pretensions of being 'anyone' would certainly leave no stone unturned in their efforts to shine in the glow reflected from the London luminaries. Charlotte's natural beauty would be unsurpassed, but she was very young and quite unsophisticated. Gentlemen used to the painted ladies in town might well not recognize a diamond in their midst. Charlotte must shine brighter than any. Liddy turned again towards the sea. Out there lay Norway, Denmark and, if one sailed far enough south, France. France with its silks, its perfumes, its *soap*.

After dinner she repaired as usual to the library, but instead of occupying herself with schemes to make one shilling do the work of three, she sat poring over an ancient history of the nearby town of Aberbrothock together with the plans of Balgowan Castle. These confirmed much that she already knew. Once there had been a large structure where now lay ruins. However, for once Liddy was not so much interested in what had been above the ground, but in what lay hidden beneath the jumble of stones. With a slim finger she traced the tunnels; the Lords of Balgowan had needed several methods of unobserved departure from their stronghold in the past.

She was puzzled. 'I could have sworn . . .' she mused looking at little black lines on the faded parchment. 'First thing tomorrow I will look for myself.'

No one would have been surprised had they seen her stride out towards the castle next morning. Even Rattles had stopped bemoaning the fact that the Honourable Miss Carpenter had no chaperone and that there was no longer even a gamekeeper on the property to lend her some protection. Liddy herself never gave her dignity a thought.

She reached the castle but did not enter and wandered off instead among the outbuildings and the old gardens.

'I wonder.' For a while she poked and pried among the ruins until, with a joyous cry, she uncovered the entrance to a tunnel.

'Just where I remembered,' she congratulated herself, and without considering her gown, she plunged inside.

A very dirty but exultant young lady eventually found herself in what had once been the great hall of Balgowan Castle. Three tall slit-like windows, stretching almost from floor to ceiling, stared sightlessly across the estuary. At one end of the room stood a massive carved stone fireplace. Liddy rememberd that there was another entrance to the tunnel under the roasting spit, but not even Harry and Keir together had been able to move that.

'Lawks, how dirty everything is. When I was last here . . . surely it's scarce ten years since Keir . . .'

She stopped and looked at the fireplace where somehow it seemed that the ghost of a slender blue-eyed boy laughed at her from the shadows. *Come on, Liddy, let's be bears roasting on the spit.* How angry Rattles had been at the condition of her dress that day.

As it happened, they had never played together again. Lord Pittenmuir had decided that it was time his son started understanding the management of the estates he would one day inherit, and Lord Balgowan, on a trip home to fetch Harry, had ordered Rattles to 'do something about that gel'.

'And behold me, ten years older and even dirtier than I was then.' Liddy's words echoed around the building and suddenly she shivered. It was cold and damp in the great hall. It was doubtful that even a huge fire burning at one end of the room could ever have warmed it. Liddy tried to picture the room as it had been once, tapestries on the walls, rushes on the floor, and later rugs, and braziers in corners to help the fire. How smoky and dark it must have been with those narrow slits allowing scanty light either in or out.

'Lights in these windows must surely have guided smugglers.' A nonsensical thought intruded again in her mind and ruthlessly she pushed it away. It would not be denied, though. 'Nonsensical,' she told it. 'I am a woman and hampered both by convention and skirts. To ride unescorted on our own land is hardly reprehensible, but anything more would be unforgivable.'

Smugglers, smugglers.

The area had once been a hotbed of smuggling activity. Every farmer, every fisherman, even the minister of the local church had been involved, if only to the extent of turning a blind eye to the activities of the community. From the windows of the castle, the Lord of Balgowan had most assuredly watched the approach of the smugglers' vessel. Did they then sit before that huge fire carousing with their smuggling band or did they have genteel parties where only the host knew for certain that the claret was but newly arrived from France?

Liddy remained at the window and watched the farmhouses and cottages. Were any of their inhabitants engaged in smuggling, or was it true that it had died out before the war had begun? The daughters of Balgowan, so sheltered and isolated as they were, would be the last to know. Why should that be so? What if Miss Carpenter rode down into the town and made inquiries? Who would answer Miss Carpenter? No one. They would smile and pull their hair and bow and act the humble, lowly fisherman and, more importantly, say nothing.

Things were different when the Honourable Harry had ridden in to the town . . . but Harry is dead. Suddenly, reason flew with the wind out of the windows of the castle and Liddy turned and hurried back to Balgowan House. Unobserved, she hurried up to her bedchamber, looked around very carefully and then hurried on to her late brother's room. Everything was as he had left it. Quickly Liddy rifled through his wardrobe, extracted some riding attire and held it against her. Liddy was tall for a woman and Harry had not been particularly so for a man.

With the suit still held against her she looked into his mirror. 'You are insane, Lydia, all lost to proper sentiment,' she said aloud and hurried, with the suit, from the room.

Two

The sun had scarcely lifted its head above the horizon when it saw a horse and rider. Perhaps the horse was not the finest of its kind but he and his rider were as one. The horseman was crouched high above the shoulders as the little brown mare galloped as fast as her brave little heart would allow along the sand. Then the rider reined her in and turned her towards the sea. Such fun, such joy to splash through the waves.

'Hey, lad, over here.' The loud voice was one that was used to being obeyed.

The horseman hesitated and looked over his shoulder. A group of red-coated militia were filing down the cliff and it was their leader who had hailed the young horseman.

'Oh, heavens, just what I don't need,' said the rider in very unmasculine tones.

The Honourable Lydia Carpenter, wearing her dead brother's second-best riding clothes, looked around wildly, assessing her chances.

'What price my reputation if I am taken before the colonel and unmasked?' said Liddy as she dug her boots into the pony's rather plump sides and horse and rider leapt forward along the beach away from the redcoats. 'Sorry, Amber,' Liddy whispered. 'Please, please, do not let me have misjudged . . . Just about here . . . yes . . .'

The troupe of militia was now on the beach. 'Fan out and find him,' ordered the sergeant. 'Obviously up to no good or he would have stopped when I called.'

The soldiers did as they were ordered, but all they found was a row of hoof prints leading into the sea.

Keir Galloway, Lord Pittenmuir, stifled a yawn and turned the full gaze of his brilliant eyes on his secretary.

'Enough, Henry. Surely it is sufficient punishment to be doing one's duty, as seen by one's heir –' he bowed across the room to where his younger brother lounged in a chair – 'and one's secretary, without having to hear the life history of each one of Jamie's guests.'

'They are not my guests. As you jolly well know I have invited these people in your name,' answered the Honourable Jamie Galloway, huffily, 'and I don't know why you are yawning because you retired last evening before eleven.'

With both brother and secretary looking at him like whipped dogs, His Lordship repented. He could not, of course, confess that it was hours after eleven before his head finally touched his pillow. He stood up and stretched to his full splendid height.

'You are unkind, Jamie. At my advanced years that horrid journey from London is dashed fatiguing.'

'Deuce take you for an incorrigible rogue. You contrive to dance all night, hunt all day – I've even heard tell that you listen for hours to those prosy old bores in the House – and doing the polite in your own house sets you atremble. Strap me if I don't envy you your stamina.'

Jamie laughed, but his brother, attuned to his character and moods, could sense the jealousy that troubled him. Where he himself was over six feet in height, Jamie barely reached his shoulder. While his eyes were a deep brilliant blue that could sparkle like diamonds or glint like ice depending on his mood, Jamie's were smaller and paler. Lord Pittenmuir had agility and physical strength to match his height, whereas Jamie had inherited their mother's more delicate constitution.

The Honourable Jamie was a very attractive young man. Even his brother could see that, but Keir still worried that the youngster felt inferior when he compared himself with his older brother. Was that why he refused to move to London during the season to take his rightful place in society? Jamie preferred, he said, the company of such of his peers as chose to remain in Scotland attending to their estates.

Keir supposed, too, that his brother enjoyed playing Lord of the manor. While he, of necessity, remained in London, Jamie managed his Scottish estates conscientiously. No doubt many of the tenants had begun to think of Jamie as their landlord. Was it not he who answered all their questions and commiserated with them over lost beasts and poor harvests?

'I promise to recoup my strength by the day of the party,' said His Lordship. 'You were telling me whom I might expect to see.'

'Company is dashed thin this time of the year, but old General Fairweather is sure to come and the Carpenters, of course, Charlotte is quite the most ravishing creature.'

'Sits the wind in that quarter?' teased his brother.

'Charlotte may look higher than a younger son.'

'The Carpenters are poor as church mice,' began Keir cruelly. 'When His Lordship sticks his spoon in the wall they won't even have a roof over their heads.'

'Good gracious, Pittenmuir, you sound as if you positively dislike the Carpenters, and yet you were always such friends. Charlotte may be poor, but her lineage cannot be faulted, nor her sweet nature. Miss Carpenter has already hinted that their father expects Charlotte to make a brilliant marriage.'

'Then he'd best bestir himself to bring her out lest she end an old maid like Liddy. Who does he expect to wed her, General Fairweather?'

'His Lordship may entertain hopes of an earldom?' suggested Major Fordyce, Keir's secretary.

'An earldom? Me? I have known Liddy all my life,' – for some reason His Lordship had forgotten that they were discussing the Honourable Charlotte's chances – 'and she hit me with a play-thing she wanted at my fifth birthday tea. Hardly the stuff of which romance is made. The last time I saw her she had grown as tall as Harry and almost as gawky.'

'How does their father in town, Keir?'

His Lordship frowned and for a moment the brilliant eyes were sad. 'Harry's death has all but destroyed him. When he chooses to honour a gathering with his company he seems set fair to drink away what little is left of the estate. How those girls will survive, I know not. Perhaps you should offer for Charlotte, Jamie. In that way you'll be in a position to give them shelter.'

'Great heavens, do you tell me that should I have the great fortune to win Charlotte, I should be saddled with the terrifying Lydia and all her sisters?'

'Not to mention the indomitable Rattles.'

Keir laughed and his face was that of a boy again. Severely

wounded at the battle of Vimiero in August of 1808 – that same battle that had taken the life of his friend, Harry – he had laughed little of late. The thought of his brother giving house room to the governess who had ruled his early years filled him with mirth. So, too, did the horrified expression on Jamie's handsome face.

'Enough of your matchmaking, Keir. Methinks I'll return to town with you, see for myself what you find more attractive than Scotland.'

'Do, brother, but in the meantime I may ride over to Balgowan to see this vision for myself.'

In no time at all he was changed into riding clothes and trotting across the fields of his estate. His landlord eyes noted the crops and animals and, for his tenants' sake, he hoped for a good harvest. Several bad ones had placed a severe strain on many Scottish farmers. Lord Pittenmuir thought, too, about Harry's death. There was so much that he needed to explain to Liddy and some things that could not yet be explained. Memories flooded him of the hundreds of times he had visited Balgowan House, entering as often as nought, through the servants' or tradesmen's entrance, and, more often than they should, he and Liddy and Harry through the casements. What fun they had had, what adventures.

'Help.' A faint voice called out and broke his reverie. But, there was nothing to be seen but grazing animals. Had he heard anything? Had there indeed been a genuine cry for aid or was it perhaps a trick? He felt for his pistol but, naturally, on such an errand he had brought none. Deuce take it, he said to himself, you are seeing French spies everywhere.

There it came again, a faint cry, more a moan, and with no more thought of spies Keir put his horse in the direction of the sound. He dismounted at the edge of the wood. The stallion would accept no other rider and it would be a brave man indeed who would try to drive him away until his master returned.

'Are you there?' he called. 'Speak if you can.'

Nothing. There was no sound at all in the wood, not even a bird sang in the trees. Keir backed towards his horse, but just as he was about to vault into the saddle there was a slight rustle in the bushes and a piteous moan.

'For pity's sake, sir, don't go.'

A boy of perhaps no more than fifteen or sixteen years lay huddled in the undergrowth. His blood-soaked breeches were evidence of his inefficiency with the axe that lay at his side. In an instant Keir was kneeling beside him, his long fingers delicately exploring the extent of the wound, and finding that it was not near as bad as the amount of blood shed had caused him to assume, he bound it up with his neckcloth, sparing not a single thought for his valet's shock at this cavalier treatment of the lovingly starched and ironed material.

'Your name, lad, and direction?' He had by now helped the lad, wincing, to his feet, and it was obvious that help would be needed to get him home, so weak was he from loss of blood.

'John Reid, sir. I live with the fisher folk down Auchmithie way.'

'You have wandered far in your search for wood.'

'Miss Carpenter will vouch for me, sir. She lets me cut wood to sell in exchange for jobs about the place. I do not lie, sir.'

'I am sure you do not, lad, but you will never make it to Auchmithie without the attention of a surgeon. I had best take you to my house. From there I will send a message to your people.'

John was about to explain that he had no people when he realised that his rescuer expected him to approach the magnificent horse which had been grazing peacefully, but which now threw up his head and snickered alarmingly.

''Tis the smell of blood, lad, but fear not. Calaban is no monster. I will put you up and climb up behind.'

The fear that young John felt about being transported to a castle – the home of he who, to all intents and purposes, owned him body and soul – was writ plain upon his face and Keir laughed. 'I promise not to eat you, lad, but you must have a physician see that wound and, no doubt you can make your way around a hot meal.'

There was no complaint from the injured boy during the long ride to Pittenmuir Castle. Keir tried to make the stallion's gait as smooth as possible, but he could tell from the occasional groan that his young passenger was not so comfortable as he pretended.

'You do not believe the tales then, John?' he asked to keep the boy's mind from his pain.

'The ghosts of the Danish warriors, m'Lord. Naw, them are tales to scare children. But, when you loomed up so big and black against the sky, I near believed. That's why I failed to answer your first call.'

'Pain and loss of blood do strange things to a man,' said His Lordship reflectively.

And so Keir Galloway, Lord Pittenmuir, did not make an afternoon call on the friend of his youth, Miss Carpenter. Naturally, had Miss Carpenter known that her old friend had spent the afternoon and most of the evening – for Dr Inglis felt that it would be foolhardy to move the patient – at the bedside of a sixteen-year-old boy, she could have forgiven, nay, applauded him, but she did not know and was therefore judgemental.

'Lord Pittenmuir is grown so used to the sophistication of the ton that he quite despises his old friends. Well, we shall show His Lordship that we are none of us so rustic as he supposes.'

Therefore, while Keir sat and attempted to put young John – obviously struck almost dumb at the enormity of being waited on by a *Lord* in his own castle – at his ease, Lydia spent anxious hours trying to think how she could possibly compete with all the beautiful women His Lordship was used to flirting with, and wondering miserably why she should even want to dazzle him. After all, had they not been perfectly comfortable together when her hair was in bunches and her petticoats hoisted up about her knees? However, Lord Pittenmuir was now a star in the London firmament and had shown he cared little or nothing for old friends.

Liddy looked out of her windows and the sea called to her. Dare she answer? Dare she dress again as Harry and ride astride on the beach, revelling in such unaccustomed freedom and allowing the music of the waves to lull her unhappy spirit?

It had not been easy to evade the militia and only her knowledge of the coast and the cliffs had allowed her to escape them. She had ridden into the sea and then hugged the coast for a little way until she had come to an outreach of volcanic rocks. The rocks concealed a cave so deep beneath the cliffs, that the old smuggling tales swore that at the right tide a boat could slip in there and hide. The intrepid young heirs to Pittenmuir and Balgowan had tested the tales and found them to be true. Too many drenchings, however, had caused their tutors to forbid any unsupervised trips to the shore and so the caves had been left inviolate, until Miss Carpenter had remembered them in her mad flight.

Safe in her bedchamber, Liddy laughed. Why not? She would dress and slip out for a breath of good clear air, but this time she would look carefully for red-coated soldiers before she ventured onto the beach. Miss Carpenter pulled on Harry's breeches and slipped her long legs into his riding boots. Then she lowered an old gown – one she used when working in the garden – over the whole and nonchalantly went to the stables.

'I'll take Amber out on the cliffs for a while, Tom.'

'You should ought to wait for John, Miss Liddy. ''Tain't fittin'.'

Liddy smiled. If he only knew. She allowed him to help her into the saddle and trotted sedately out of the stable yard. When she was well away from the house she took Amber into the thick bushes growing along the carriage way, looked around carefully and pulled off the dress, tied her hair back with a ribbon, and a few minutes later a slender youth might have been seen cantering along the path that led to the beach.

This time no cries of 'Stop there' disturbed her gallop.

I must not become complacent, decided Miss Carpenter, as once more in her old gown and with her hair tumbled about her shoulders, she slipped from Amber's back and gave the pony over to old Tom.

Later that same evening a letter was despatched to London assuring Lord Balgowan of his daughters' continued affection, but reminding His Lordship, oh so gently, of his obligations. Liddy, who placed no trust in princes and even less in mere barons, did not sit idly by waiting for her papa to answer her missive, but instead bent her not inconsiderable energies to finding the wherewithal to provide the fripperies Charlotte would require if she were truly to outshine the stars in the London firmament.

For hours Liddy closeted herself in the library. Her reading material would have surprised any member of society who happened to be in a position to look over her shoulder. Her father would have been unsurprised, but then he had always been disappointed in the maidenly charms of his eldest daughter.

For Miss Carpenter was not reading the *Ladies Monthly* magazine.

Her plans had come to her with breathtaking suddenness as she had stood relaxed on the beach and looked towards the ruins of Balgowan Castle that stood gaunt against the skyline. However, she was no longer the little girl who rushed headlong into all manner of ill-advised pranks, dragging her brother with her. She had to consider very carefully; there was too much at stake for undue haste.

'Rattles, it is clear that Papa is not going to answer my letter in time for Pittenmuir's party. *Sans doute*, he is out of town. I do believe that all people of wealth and birth desert the city at this time of year – do we not see even Lord Pittenmuir able to tear himself away – but I have wracked my brains and I cannot find it in me to purchase furbelows with money that should, by right, go to the honest tradesmen who serve us so well.' As she talked Liddy moved restlessly from sofa to window seat. 'I did so want her to have a gown to remember for her first grown-up party.'

'Indeed, my dear, 'tis a very small party and Charlotte is very beautiful. No matter what she wears, she will outdo the other girls. We will contrive something with what we already have. Come. We will all look through our wardrobes and through your dear mama's boxes; assuredly there will be something there we may use.'

Charlotte was not at all distressed at the measures that had to be taken to find her a gown. Naturally, like all young girls, she would have been thrilled to call upon the local leading modiste, but all her life there had never been enough money, and so she had not expected a new gown. Now, she insisted that their little sisters come with them to the attics to dress up in all the strange clothes that Liddy assured them their mama had worn.

The pile of discarded gowns on the attic's wooden floor did not inspire Liddy who was no needlewoman, but Charlotte and Rattles pounced on the piles with cries of glee. Rattles was adept with her needle and, although the fabric from which the late Lady Balgowan's clothes were constructed in no way resembled the current fashion for the lightest and most revealing of gauzes, they were rich in ornamentation. Valuable lace was there in plenty, as were underskirts that could assuredly be put to good use. Rattles and Charlotte exclaimed and snipped, and snipped and exclaimed again. One gown, a court dress made and worn in Paris, yielded a treasure trove of real pearls around the neck, and carefully Rattles unpicked the minute stitches that held them in place.

'See, Charlotte, my love, for your debut you really will wear your mama's pearls.'

Abruptly Liddy rose and left all four of them to the delights of the boxes. Miss Charlotte Carpenter to be wearing the trimming from an old gown as a necklet. It was not to be borne. She hurried upstairs to her room and unearthed her jewel box. In solitary splendour reposed the wedding ring of the late Lady Balgowan.

'I have held on to this for eight years, dearest Mama.' To give him credit, although her father had sold all of the unentailed properties, he had never asked for the ring. 'It's in a good cause,' Liddy whispered as she changed into her walking dress. 'You would wish her to go as befits her station.'

Outside she found Old Tom, the gardener and their only permanent outside helper, weeding his sheltered asparagus beds.

'Morning, Miss Lydia,' he said with a welcoming smile.

'Tom, I must go to Arbroath. Will you get the gig for me?'

Tom straightened slowly and even more slowly scratched his bald pate. 'Well, Miss Lydia, I could leave these here weeds or I could tell young John. He was here earlier.'

Liddy's gloom brightened immediately. They had not seen young John for a few days and, for the journey she was about to undertake, the boy's company would be preferable to that of the old man.

'Do that, Tom,' she said and the gardener shuffled off to find John.

Young John was tall, broad and freckled and had a shock of bright red hair. His face usually wore a wide grin. He lived among the fisher folk with an old woman he called 'Granny', but he knew nothing of his history. He could handle a boat and, though none too fond of horseflesh, had forced himself to handle a horse.

'Afternoon, Miss Lydia.'

'Good afternoon, John. I had wanted you to drive me this afternoon, but if I'm not mistaken, you are limping.'

'It's nothing, Miss Lydia. I hurt myself a few days back, but it do be mending.'

Liddy well knew that the cost of medical care was beyond the boy's means. 'Shall I look at it for you, John?' she asked. She and Rattles were used to dealing with minor aches and pains.

'Been seen to, Miss Lydia, and my granny put a poultice on it. Shall us go then?'

'If you are up to it,' she said. 'I will be away some hours and would not take you away from more gainful employment.'

'No indeed, Miss Lydia. I were going to wash tatties for Balmossie, but he won't say nothing if I wash 'em tonight.'

'Then let me tell you that I am on an errand of some delicacy. Take me to Watson, the jeweller. Luckily I am unknown in Arbroath.'

'Ach, Miss Lydia. Everybody do know the Carpenters.'

Liddy was astonished. 'Why, how can that be? I have not been in the town above five times in my life.'

'What an innocent you are, miss, if you'll pardon my presumption. Never mind, I'll take you if you are of a mind to go.'

He was quiet for a moment and Liddy almost smiled so obvious was it that he was thinking deeply. 'If you be selling somat, Miss Lydia,' he said at last, 'Strachan'll give you a fairer price.'

Liddy looked down at the honest sunburned face and saw anxiety and concern writ there. 'Thank you, John, and when I am come to an arrangement with Mr Strachan, you may drive me to Miss Petrie's Emporium. The *Abbey Times* tells me she has taken delivery of some exclusive materials.'

'Dresses,' snorted the boy and set the horse atrotting.

The journey there and back passed very pleasantly with interesting conversation. The subjects were such as should not have interested the eldest daughter of a baron, and were, in the main, matters that, had John been older, he would never have dreamed of discussing with a sheltered young lady, but since he was young and she was fascinated, they parted company three hours later on the best of terms.

Not only had they discussed Viscount Wellington's successes in the Peninsula, and his brother, the Marquis's chances of leading the Tory party, but whether the Regent would keep his promise not to change Perceval's government while it seemed even remotely possible that the King might recover his sanity, and they had stopped on the way home to share a Forfar Bridie. Rattles would be wondering where she was as the family meal would have been over long ago and since she had given the boy the larger part of the meat pie, she was ravenously hungry, but she had a heart as light as her growling stomach for she had material for Charlotte's new dress.

Three

The Honourable Lydia Carpenter did not take particular pains to look her best for Lord Pittenmuir's party. She was a long time in her room because a petticoat required sewing, and if she had taken down her hair twice and rearranged it, well, the eldest daughter of Lord Balgowan could hardly attend a party looking like a milkmaid, no matter how charming.

'We will contrive an air of quiet refinement,' said Miss Carpenter to her reflection in the pier glass. She did wear her new gown. How many hours must poor Rattles and dear Charlotte have laboured over it? They had taken her best green silk chemise gown and refashioned the bodice so that it was daringly low. Crossed with dark green ribbons, such bosom as nature had given her was emphasized but, no matter how rigorously she followed the regimen of exercises suggested in the *Ladies Monthly*, there was still too little there.

'You are too tall,' the image in the glass told her, 'you will tower over every man present.'

Her sisters were not so hard to please as Miss Carpenter. 'Oh, Liddy,' breathed the little girls. 'You look splendid.'

'In the manner of Boadicea,' complimented Miss Rattray.

'How well Harry's combs become you,' said Charlotte, which was, of course, the best compliment.

'Rattles, you were wont to say that Boadicea must have caused terror in the hearts of the Romans,' teased Liddy, 'and I assure you there is no one I wish to terrify this evening,' she added somewhat mendaciously, 'but let us turn our attention to Charlotte.'

Charlotte's gown was very simple. The material purchased by Liddy for the ridiculously frugal amount she had been given for her mama's ring, was not near so grand as she had hoped. Rattles's clever needle had, however, added a pale blue petticoat

21

fashioned from the under dress of a ball gown originally worn by their mama. The same gown had yielded yards of the most exquisite lace that now formed the deep scalloped hem and little cap sleeves of Charlotte's first 'real' dress. The palest of blue slippers – sewn by her own hands – and white kid gloves, rescued from the depths of a trunk, completed the ensemble and Miss Charlotte was pressured to admit she did indeed look 'quite nice'.

'Come, girls, we must not be too late,' scolded Rattles. 'Your dear mama was used to say that the timing of an entrance is a hard-won skill: never too early, but not so late that, although one is noticed, one is thought to be ill-bred.'

The old coach had been burnished until it gleamed, and Tom and John had groomed the horses as they had never been groomed before. They were an ill-assorted pair but would pull well enough together, John assured Liddy as she came down the steps flanked by Charlotte and Miss Rattray and waved on by the schoolroom party.

From some attic above the stables, coachmen's uniforms, from an earlier era, had been unearthed, brushed and aired.

'How splendid you look, Tom,' Liddy lied bravely, for in his wide-skirted coat and cocked hat, Tom looked as out of place as one of the late Lady Balgowan's gowns would have been at the soirée. 'You too, John,' she added as the boy, now footman, helped her into the elderly vehicle.

The weather, which had been kind all summer, did not let them down. The evening was balmy, heavily scented with gorse and honeysuckle. The light was that perfect light found, Liddy was sure, only in Scotland, and added to the delights of the evening ahead.

Miss Rattray, in her best brown bombazine, enlivened by a five-tier Betsie collarette of lace salvaged from the trunks in the attic, looked forward to her first party in years. Betsie collarettes were slightly passé, but Rattles had been unable to afford one when they were 'in' and was delighted to sport one now. She looked at her charges. 'Charlotte, your excitement is writ large upon your face for the world to read. Control, my dear.'

'To look excited is terribly bad form,' chimed in the equally excited Liddy. 'One must cultivate an air of boredom, or better, insouciance.'

Another girl might have asked her sheltered sister how it was that she had become such a fount of information, but Charlotte did not. 'I shall try, Liddy,' she began earnestly, 'but I fear everyone will know how delighted I am. Do you think Lord Pittenmuir has houseguests? Rattles, just think, mayhap there will be ladies of the ton in the latest modes. How very exciting.'

Both Liddy and Rattles sent up devout, though silent prayers, that the assembly would be graced by no London fashions. Gowns put together from outmoded relics and out-of-date fashion magazines might shine in the kinder smile of Forfarshire society, but would scarce show to advantage beside Bond Street.

The castle of Pittenmuir was a fairytale of lights. Huge tubs of flowering bushes stood on every step up to the entrance hall where a crystal chandelier winked and glittered in welcome. A most superior housemaid took them upstairs to a withdrawing room to leave their wraps and tidy any curl that had dared to escape from its pins.

'Why, Miss Carpenter, and you too, Charlotte, how are you both? I had not looked to see you here tonight.' The vision who thus addressed them did not deign to notice Rattles who removed her serviceable old cloak and then contrived to blend into the wallpaper. Although the Carpenter ladies, while still polite, did not respond to her greeting with any degree of affability, the lady continued. 'Is it not wonderful that Lord Pittenmuir is come home. Grandfather, the General, was adamant that I leave town and sample the delights of the country for a few months. "Fresh air, Leonora," he said, "fresh eggs, fresh cream, early nights," but do you know, I swear I am likely to become as jaded here with gaiety as ever I was in London.'

'Then do not let us keep you from the party, Miss Fairweather. I believe I hear a country dance.' Liddy replied, with a laboured smile.

Thus dismissed, Miss Fairweather shot a glance of dislike at Liddy and left the room, almost slamming the door behind her.

'Lydia,' expostulated Rattles. 'There is no excuse for ill manners. Why do you dislike that girl so?'

'Harry was one of her victims, but the heir of an impoverished baron was not good enough, although she kept him dangling while she made her casts.'

'Mrs Harper says she had an offer from a baronet but rejected him because she was hoping that the Earl of Edgeware might come up to scratch.' Charlotte blushed with shame as her sister and her governess stared at her in astonishment. 'Is it bad form to say such things?'

'What Mrs Harper says to you in the stillroom, Charlotte, should remain within those four walls. Really, my girl, gossiping with, oh . . . don't cry,' Liddy finished as great tears welled up in the beautiful eyes. She resolved to have words with her housekeeper on the morrow. 'We will refine no more upon it, goose. Let us join the party. Does not that music order you to dance?'

Charlotte was completely taken in by her sister's gaiety and needed no urging to descend to the ballroom. Rattles, however, sensed that for some inexplicable reason, Liddy was nervous and she feared that her headstrong mistress would do something she would later regret. She followed the girls to the top of the staircase. Liddy stood poised there, looking down at the throng below. There, in the entrance to the ballroom, Lord Pittenmuir and his brother were welcoming the guests.

'How thankful I am to be no longer a young woman,' thought Rattles as she saw a smile light up His Lordship's handsome face.

At that moment, Liddy and Keir's glances met and locked and he smiled again, his eyes lighting with intimate tenderness and warmth. Liddy allowed herself to be dazzled. This is Keir, my friend. Was I wrong about him?

But then some imp of mischief caused Miss Carpenter to wipe the hesitant smile from her face and to return his smile with a cold, formal bow. Was it the golden vision who appeared at his side and slipped a proprietary arm through his, or was it rather that he turned to greet the vision, his smile still in his eyes?

Above them Miss Carpenter stood, as if, for a moment she knew not what to do. Rattles saw her half turn to the shelter of the retiring room and then turn again proudly and sail down the staircase.

'Boadicea,' groaned Rattles and went after her.

Lord Pittenmuir disengaged himself and walked towards her. 'Liddy, my dear,' he began.

'Thank you for inviting us, my Lord,' said Miss Carpenter coldly. 'Ah, I do believe I see Sir Thomas Inglis,' and seeming somehow not to notice her host's outstretched hands, Miss Carpenter swept past him into the ballroom.

For a moment Lord Pittenmuir looked shaken as he examined

his hands and then he saw Miss Rattray. 'Dear Rattles, how good in you to come. Jamie, do look who is here.'

Jamie bowed after exchanging a smile with his brother that said he remembered their conversation of earlier. Lord Pittenmuir turned to Miss Fairweather.

'Miss Fairweather, I don't believe—' he began.

'Really, Keir,' said Miss Fairweather with an enchanting smile, that was at the same time somewhat cold, 'I did not make the tedious journey from town to share your reminiscences with your governess. Jamie will fetch her a glass of negus, won't you, Jamie.'

'What a perfectly lovely idea,' smiled His Lordship. 'Jamie, you two young people dance while my dear Rattles and I enjoy a comfortable cose.' He turned his back on the dazzling Miss Fairweather and extending his arm to Rattles, led her into an ante-room.

'Your manners always were excellent, my Lord,' smiled Miss Rattray, 'but you must go and attend to your guests while I search for Charlotte.'

'Who has grown into quite a beauty,' said His Lordship ignoring her request and sitting beside her.

'Yes, she is very beautiful,' sighed Miss Rattray. 'My Lord, Miss Carpenter—'

'Has other fine qualities,' Lord Pittenmuir finished for her. 'Charlotte is in the ballroom, Ma'am. Will you be happier there?'

Rattles looked into his eyes but could read nothing. She stood up. 'Miss Fairweather is not the only one of your guests who would object to associating with a governess. Should your Lordship call on the young ladies while you are in residence, I should enjoy hearing of your adventures then.'

He smiled again. 'Dear Rattles, life was easier when Liddy and I were small enough to smack, was it not? Let me take you to Charlotte.'

She took his arm and he led her into the ballroom where he stood casually by her side watching the dancers. The grand lady who had greeted him frostily and then bowed to him like some veritable dowager had taken him aback, but His Lordship had not been several years in the ton without learning a little about women. His friend Liddy, his own – he admitted to the silence of his heart – once and forever friend, had grown up and must not be taken for granted. And he had done just that. When Harry was killed he had assumed that she would understand when he had not appeared.

He wished he had been able to visit before; no use to say that he had tried. He had fully expected that he and Liddy would begin where circumstance and parental decree had left them. He smiled, indeed laughed at the vision of Liddy as a young tomboy climbing down a cliff face with her petticoats in her drawers. Miss Carpenter, who, regretting her bad temper, was walking across the floor towards him, saw him laugh. He could only be laughing at her hairstyle, copied from an old magazine and slipping from its combs. She drew herself up to her five feet and ten splendid inches, turned away, and left him once more observing her back.

He frowned, shook his head, and went off with commendable fortitude to renew other old acquaintances. The hand of the ethereally lovely Charlotte must be sought for a dance.

Meanwhile Liddy accepted a dance and a glass of punch from Captain Ogilvie-Fenton and wished her head did not ache so.

'Glad to see you out of mourning, Liddy old thing. Harry would not have had you grieve, y'know.'

'Of course he would,' snapped Liddy. 'It would have been extremely unnatural for me not to grieve for a dearly beloved brother.'

'No need to be cross-grained, old thing,' said the captain looking somewhat pained.

Liddy was possessed of the most shocking desire to hit the captain over his handsome head with the first weapon that came to hand. She had never, she decided judiciously, looked so elegant, and still he addressed her with the familiarity of a brother. 'Old thing', indeed. No one would ever address Charlotte so.

'I have a headache, Captain. It is such a crush in here.'

As she had foretold, everyone who was anyone, and quite a few who were no one at all, had accepted Lord Pittenmuir's invitation.

Simon looked around. 'Crush, old girl? I was actually worrying that evening was set to be a dead loss. No one who's anyone is here. Need to get you to town, stand in a ballroom worrying about which oaf's going to step on your toes – that's a good party, Liddy, old thing.'

26

'We are more civilized in the country, Captain.'

'Come along, old girl, it is a lovely evening. Shall we take a turn in the gardens? That will assuredly clear your head.'

Liddy rose, gratefully. 'That would be pleasant. Do but wait while I fetch my wrap.'

Miss Rattray demanded her attention on the way to the retiring room.

'Fusspot,' laughed Liddy indulgently after listening to Rattles listing the reasons why she should not walk alone in the twilight with a man who was not an immediate member of her family. 'I am quite safe with the captain. No, dearest,' she added as Rattles gave every indication of her intention to join them, 'you need not chaperone me, it is Charlotte who requires your diligence, so hounded is she by my Lord's guests.'

While Rattles turned ready to scold anyone who might importune her charge, Liddy slipped out through a side door and found Captain Ogilvie-Fenton awaiting her.

'Shame to hide that pretty frock under such a dull shawl, Liddy.'

'La, sir, I shall take that as a compliment to my exclusive modiste.'

They walked among sweetly smelling roses.

'Look who's there,' chortled the captain suddenly. 'It's Pittenmuir and the maneater. Shall we bid him watch his step?'

'Do let us return to the house, Captain,' begged Liddy, but he had already started forward.

'Miss Fairweather, your servant. My Lord.'

Was the young lady annoyed to be thus interrupted? If so, she recovered quickly and, ignored Liddy's sour look at her gown. It was the most delicious confection of bronze silk with a chemisette of pleated cloth of gold (without which the gown would have been positively indecent) and worn with a gold ferronière from which an emerald was suspended. 'Captain Ogilvie-Fenton, and you again, dear Miss Carpenter. How well you look. Am I mistaken, but did you not wear a dress of just that colour last season, or was it perhaps the year before? My memory . . . Oh, my lamentable memory.'

'Indeed you are in the right of it, Miss Fairweather. I had the original dress fashioned just before Harry was killed. Miss Rattray has remade it, so clever as she is, and since, fortuitously, I am able to wear it still . . .'

Miss Fairweather, who was noted for overindulgence followed by almost penitential abstinence, hastened to change the subject. 'Dear Harry, we were speaking of him the last time we met, Keir. Do you remember, but of course you do?' She added archly, 'It was that grand ball in Lisbon . . . what, three months after Harry . . . well, you were still on crutches, and promised that, on the very first opportunity, you would waltz with me.'

A ray of hope flooded Liddy's heart. Had His Lordship been on active service he could not have been expected to attend a memorial service. 'You were still on duty, Keir, in Lisbon? I had thought you invalided out after Vimiero.'

Lord Pittenmuir heard the hope in her voice but it was too early to unburden himself. He could not tell her he had been requested by the Prime Minister to remain in Portugal as a spy.

'Why no, Liddy. I was but enjoying the undoubted beauties of Lisbon,' and he smiled down into Miss Fairweather's charming face. 'The elegance, wit, charm . . .'

'Special indeed, my Lord, if they are worth hobbling after,' interrupted Miss Carpenter. 'Captain Ogilvie-Fenton, shall we leave His Lordship to his . . . waltz?'

For the second time in the evening His Lordship was dismissed.

Liddy's headache was, by this time, almost insupportable. How she longed to return home, but Charlotte was so enjoying her first party that she could not, in charity, ask her sister to leave. She was spared the pain of watching His Lordship waltz with Miss Fairweather, though, because His Lordship had decreed that only a few uncontroversial country dances were to be played, and, no matter how Miss Fairweather pouted, he remained firm.

He asked Charlotte to dance. As host he felt it his duty, as a man he knew it would be a pleasure, and as an older brother he knew that it would annoy Jamie.

'Do the blighter good,' the big brother decided unkindly. 'Make him bestir himself a little.'

He could not know the spark that had been ignited in an unsophisticated girl's heart when the sophisticated, handsome, peer of the realm had smiled at her and unwittingly he blew on the flame by soliciting her hand for a reel. Captain Ogilvie-Fenton was prevailed upon to partner the nineteen-year-old daughter of Lady Johnstone-Carruthers. The third couple in their set was comprised of Miss Fairweather and Major Fordyce, Keir's secretary. Thankfully, Liddy sat with the dowagers and watched Charlotte, cheeks rosy with effort and excitement, flying up and down the room with her host.

'I do not see Anne, Mrs Wallace,' she remarked to the minister's wife. 'I trust she is well.'

Had she been less intent on her sister, Liddy would have been surprised by the expression on her companion's face. As it was Mrs Wallace hesitated a few moments before replying. 'Indeed, Miss Carpenter. Mr Wallace and I feel that she is quite recovered.'

Immediately Liddy was all concern. 'Mrs Wallace, do you tell me that Anne has been ill? Why have I not known? How remiss in me not to have called at the manse lately.'

'We did not wish you to know, my dear. Your own grief was so terrible.'

A cold hand clutching at her heart, Liddy looked at Mrs Wallace. 'Let me understand you, Ma'am. Am I to assume that Anne's illness was something to do with my brother?'

'Look at Charlotte, my dear. See how she glows, her heart shining in her eyes, as she dances with His Lordship. Young men's careless kindness. Surely our host cannot be unaware of his looks, his style, and his effect on our sex? Perhaps he is so used to his position, his appearance, that he is unaware of his power. Mr Carpenter had but to dance a strathspey with Anne. He smiled at her, told her she was in looks; careless kindness. She fell in love and so was devastated when he fell.'

Liddy was disquieted. Appalling. Poor Anne. 'Oh, dear Ma'am, I cannot believe my brother flirted with so young and unsophisticated a maid.'

'Nor did he,' answered Mrs Wallace at once. ' Out of kindness he took notice of the minister's daughter. It was Anne who misread his natural good manners. It is often so with unsophisticated young girls, and no doubt Anne's infatuation would have died a natural death but unfortunately . . .'

'Young men's careless kindness,' echoed Liddy looking at her sister who was smiling into Lord Pittenmuir's eyes. 'I wish we had known your daughter shared our suffering, Mrs Wallace, and I trust that her health has not been severely affected.'

'No indeed, a lack of appetite, for which her papa was wont to scold, led to a slight weakening of her recuperative powers so that an attack of influenza last winter laid her quite low. Mr Wallace and I decided, upon her recovery, to send her to her aunt in Edinburgh. Her uncle, my brother, is minister of St Giles. Now, I would not go so far as to say she is sunk in dissipation, but she is enjoying what I may modestly call a social whirl.'

The dance was ending.

'I believe Edinburgh quite leaves London in the shade, so elegant is the company,' answered Liddy automatically as she watched her sister's animated chatter and the way she was laughing up at Keir.

'There has been one good outcome of these dreadful wars. No one makes the grand tour and so they come to Edinburgh instead. I know Mr Wallace would scold me for vanity, Miss Carpenter, but I may tell you that Anne has met Walter Scott who is become so popular with his tales and ballads, and my brother writes that the great Catalina is expected to sing at a most select gathering to which our daughter has received an invitation.'

Poor Mrs Wallace. Liddy had hardly heard a word of the delights enjoyed by Miss Anne. It was not that she begrudged her either Walter Scott or Madame Catalina, but all her thoughts were concentrated upon her sister. Could Charlotte have become *bouleversé* over Lord Pittenmuir? She had gazed into his eyes with such a look of . . . what? Heavens he was quite ancient when compared with Charlotte. Surely she could not find him attractive when he had terrified her before.

Miss Carpenter decided to examine His Lordship quite dispassionately. Yes, there was much in face and figure to recommend him to any young lady interested only in the height of a man or the breadth of his shoulders. One might, with impunity, call him handsome and his eyes were, well, yes to be honest, a most attractive blue if, that is to say, one had a partiality for blue eyes. Some young ladies too might notice, though they should not, the strength of the muscles in the excellent thighs revealed by the skin-tight satin breeches and silk stockings, but other more discerning young women, like Charlotte for instance, would be much more interested in a man's character, his loyalty to his friends and to cherished ideals.

'Are you unwell, Miss Carpenter? Shall I summon Miss Rattray?'

'I do beg your pardon, Mrs Wallace. I was not attending. Truth is, I have had this headache all afternoon, so sultry is the weather, and should not have come.'

But the evening was not over until Miss Carpenter had been forced to listen to Charlotte prosing on all the way home about the exquisiteness of the castle furnishings, the skill of the musicians, the unbelievable delights of the evening, and above all, the appearance, manners, charms ad nauseam of Keir, Lord Pittenmuir.

Four

'There's the trees there, dead ahead.'

The captain of the little boat shook his head in dismay. There seemed to be nothing ahead but a solid wall of cliffs although he had been assured that if he listened to the directions of the boy, John, he would find safe harbour. He said a silent prayer and headed straight for the wall of crumbling rock.

'By Saint Roques, a hidden cove.'

'As sweet an anchorage as you could hope to find, Captain.'

The craft, the *Shuska*, ran up onto the shingled beach and swiftly and silently the strange-looking crew, strapping large-bosomed wenches, began to unload the cargo and hurry with it towards the cliffs. They disappeared, like magic, into the cliff face.

'Caves, Captain,' whispered the boy. 'Some so deep, if the tide be right, you could put your boat right in them.'

Captain Visieux was not so gullible as to believe that. 'Where is this leader of yours, this Euan Pate?'

'Watching us, I shouldn't wonder. Don't you worry, he'll be here, and with your money.'

'I must leave with the tide, comprenez? So, if your elusive Euan Pate wishes to see the *Shuska* again, I must see the colour of his money.'

He stopped as a slim figure slipped from the shadows and ran lightly down the beach towards them.

'Bonsoir, Monsieur Le Capitaine, and on time too. No trouble?' The young man spoke in perfect French.

'None, Monsieur Pate. The sea was like a pond for the duck. We may anticipate some profitable runs ere the weather changes.' He gestured towards the ship. 'Let us conduct our business over some good French wine, from my cut.'

'Excellent idea, mon ami.'

The light in the small cabin showed the smugglers' leader to be of average height for a man. His brown hair was tied back revealing a handsome face, perhaps a trifle soft, but his youth would account for that. For the rendezvous Mr Pate had chosen a brown coat and serviceable breeches, but the cut of the cloth and the superfluity of capes on his overcoat proclaimed to the veriest simpleton that Mr Pate, whatever else he purported to be, was very much the gentleman. So, too, did the authority evident in the way he moved and spoke and Captain Yves Visieux, who had hoped to prove himself smarter than his young client, was soon disabused of the idea.

'You are a good judge of wine, Monsieur,' commended the Frenchman as his young guest pronounced his finest wine 'tolerable'.

'My family has extensive knowledge of your country and its wines.' He finished the wine at a swallow and stood up. 'I must be off to see to the disposal of our goods. We shall expect you again at the next full moon. *À bientôt.*'

And he was gone, swinging lightly up the staircase and over the side to where John Reid was waiting with a rowing boat.

'Fine women those,' called the captain who had followed him above decks. 'Some fine sailors among them. Should you ever tire of their undoubted charms I would be pleased to sign them on. Adieu, mon ami.'

The young smuggler laughed and let himself down into the waiting rowboat and was swiftly rowed ashore to where his crew were assembled.

'Everything ready?'

They showed him their creels and he smiled. 'Good lads. Now be off with you, each man to his own bolthole. We meet in the designated place tomorrow night.'

'We had best take care, Euan. Miss Carpenter walks or rides there a great deal these days. It would not do for her to see us.'

'Never fear, lads. I have some ideas of how to keep all the overly inquisitive away from there. Rely on me.'

The men, for so they were, hurried off to their own cottages and Euan Pate and the boy, John, stayed awhile talking on the beach. John had set his creel out before leaving for France and inside were two fine lobsters.

'I will purchase those if your granny has no need of them,

John. There should be no one about at this hour, but if there is, then a sale of lobsters is nothing remarkable.'

'Is there no other way . . .' began the boy.

'Ah, John, don't you think that I have given hours of thought to this endeavour? Do you really think that if there was any other way to save my family that I would not have discovered it? Your kind heart does you credit, but I have no regrets about embarking on a life of crime.'

'Miss Lydia . . .'

Liddy, for it was she, turned quickly to glance about them. 'Ssh, John. You must address me as Euan, think of me as Euan, or you cannot help me in this.'

John nodded, his face grave. 'Take care . . . Euan. Shall I go part way with you? Best not, perhaps.'

'I know every inch of this area and will come to no harm. You had best be off to make peace with your granny. Until tomorrow.'

Only the curlews that cry plaintively across the dark moors saw them go.

Liddy, a woman disguised as a man, was well satisfied with the night's work. She laughed at the thought of her crew divesting themselves of their skirts and their bosoms. She whistled gaily as she sauntered jauntily up the headland and over the moor. If the curlews wondered at her sudden appearance they gave nothing away. Familiar with the terrain she most certainly was for she slipped like a fox behind a gorse bush and thus into the neck of one of the tunnels that honeycombed the area. It was dark and overgrown, but it presented no problems to her except when she forgot her height and bumped her head on a ledge of overhanging rock.

'Strap me if I don't conceal a lamp here,' she said, so deep into her charade that she spoke like the boy she was pretending to be.

The tunnel had become even lower and she walked more carefully as in some places she was compelled to bend almost double. Ugh. Some particularly damp and slimy vegetation dropped like a curtain over her face, but she pulled it away without a second thought.

The door must be quite near, she thought. Indeed, I should have brought a light. I make a demned inefficient smuggler.

She walked a few more yards, made quite loathsome by

constant drips of slimy water from the rocks. The walls, too, were awash with a viscous fluid, a combination of water and decaying fungi. At last a dead end. Was it indeed the door? As a child, the smuggler had run from the beach to the ruins of Balgowan Castle countless times through the old escape tunnels. It had been naïve not to realize that decay and damp over the years would only have accumulated and made the way unrecognizable. The door would not budge; the hinges were rusted tight. Liddy struggled with the bolt, even unwrapping the stock from round her neck to gain better vantage, but at last, when she was well nigh exhausted, the bolt was wrenched protesting from the safe house where it had nestled for years and screamed across the track.

She used all her strength and, thankfully, the old oak door, complaining heavily every inch of the way, opened outwards and she was able to step into the room. There were obvious signs of recent visitation: a lamp that was surprisingly free of dust, a flagon of water, a mug. She used some of the water to clean the worst of the signs of her journey from her face and hair. There was no mirror and so she was thus spared the full ignominy of seeing how dishevelled she was. Then she took the lamp and climbed through the trapdoor into what had once been the great hall of the castle.

It was the room least ravaged by age and vandalism, standing as it did at the centre of what had once been an imposing structure. The windows stared with sightless eyes at the sea on one side and farms and fields on the other. Liddy ran from window to window showing the light for a moment, no more. For a full ten minutes she remained still with the light covered while the silence drifted slowly around her before settling once more on the dusty floor. Then, like a demented firefly, Liddy ran again from window to window. Indeed, any naïve soul who sees the lights will swear the castle is haunted and warn their fellows to stay well away.

By a door, other than the one by which she had entered, she left the castle and went to the ruins outside. Up and down the steps as only one vastly familiar with the terrain could have gone at such speed she ran, and then, dousing the light, she disappeared through the hanging door of an outbuilding. The castle was riddled with tunnels and she had found the opening to another, as ten minutes later she reappeared in the grounds of Balgowan House. She waited until the moon slipped obligingly behind a cloud and then she disappeared among the trees. When the moon showed her face again, the gardens were quiet and still; not even the large rhododendron bushes stirred to show that someone had passed.

Inside the house, Miss Carpenter crept like a cat up the back stairs towards her bedchamber. She reached the door of her sanctum and listened a moment in the hall. Nothing; the house slept. With a sigh of relief she opened the door.

'Really, Lydia, I thought time had cured you of this non-sensical dressing up.'

Lydia's hands leapt up to restrain her wildly beating heart. 'Rattles,' she gasped. 'You scared me half to death. How are you here?'

'How could I sleep with you out in that absurd garb? Liddy, dear child, I know I have no right—'

'Of course you have the right, Rattles, earned by years of unstinting work and sacrifice – but I think the less you know the better. How did you find me out? I thought myself to have been most circumspect.'

'Too circumspect. Indeed that was what made me suspicious in the first place. Quickly, take off those dreadful breeches. Do but look at yourself in the mirror and all pretentious vanities will fly out the window.'

Liddy laughed and submitted to her governess's administrations. Her mind worked at top speed. How much did Rattles suspect? How much would be good for her to know? If she, Liddy, played 'lady of the manor' and said nothing, the old lady would be hurt and would worry, perhaps unnecessarily. By the time Rattles returned from the nursery with two mugs of hot chocolate, Liddy was tucked up in bed.

'Rattles, have you heard rumours to the effect that the Aberbrothock smugglers are abroad once more?'

Miss Rattray nodded. 'Aye and that boy you are so thick with, the gardener's lad, tells me there are ghosts,' she ended with an unladylike snort.

'The ghost was me – or should it be I?'

Rattles ignored the attempt at humour. 'The smugglers?'

'That's me, too.'

Rattles sat down rather heavily on the blanket box at the foot of the lady's elegant four-poster.

Liddy put down her mug and crawled to the end of the bed. 'Dearest Rattles, I have upset you and indeed I do not mean to do so. I am in no danger, Rattles.'

'A ghost, Liddy. That sounds like the ploys you were used to engage in with Harry and my Lord Pittenmuir, and you should have grown out of it, but smuggling . . . Tell me you are jesting, you do not participate in such illegal doings.'

Liddy stood up in her bare feet before her former governess. 'Behold Euan Pate, their leader.'

Miss Rattray did not appreciate the levity of tone employed by her erstwhile pupil and Liddy sat at her feet as she had done as a naughty little girl. Miss Rattray stood up, the embodiment of dignity in her shabby old dressing gown. 'Mayhap you should tell me nothing, Miss Carpenter.'

'I have hurt you, dearest Rattles, and nothing was ever further from my mind.' Liddy clasped the governess's hands in hers. 'Sit down please, dear friend, and I will reveal all.'

Miss Rattray allowed herself to be led to a sofa. Liddy wrapped her robe about her and began. 'As you know, I have been a supporter of the Stuart cause since childhood. King George, harmless though he may be, does not command my loyalty nor does the Regent deserve it. Our former Prime Minister, Mr Pitt, instituted heavy taxes on imports as a way to finance this ridiculous war with France. My mama was French; ergo, I will not war with France.'

'Do you desire France to invade us then, Liddy?'

Liddy brushed aside the question. 'The upstart, Napoleon, will not invade Scotland. There is the Auld Alliance, our friendship with *La Belle France*.'

'And Harry?'

'We will not speak of Harry.'

'Liddy, my dear child,' began Miss Rattray.

'Rattles, if you love me, I beg you desist. Papa has no more the wherewithal to finance a coming-out for Charlotte. It was those German upstarts who took his fortune, and now, by killing his son, have broken his heart. I am responsible for my sisters and I swear I will not have Charlotte throw herself away on the first man to offer for her. She will go to Edinburgh – London even –

and will make a dazzling debut. There will be none to outshine her.'

Liddy looked triumphantly at the governess who gazed back complacently.

'What of Charlotte? Is she to have no say in this? Will she desire her sister to defy convention –' she gestured to the discarded raiment – 'to lower herself to mix with all manner of riff-raff, to run into danger, not to forget the slight matter of contravening the law of the land?'

'She will know nothing. Rattles, if you cannot bring yourself to believe that I am in the right of it, at least you will admit that I have been most careful in my planning.'

Observing that Rattles had folded her hands, Liddy launched eloquently upon her explanation. 'Smuggling has been a way of life in this area for centuries. When harvests were bad farmers took to the sea – not to fish but to trade: Scottish salmon for French wine, grain for oranges or lemons. Today with taxes on soap and writing paper, hand mirrors and playing cards so extortionate to pay for their war, it is positively patriotic to avoid import duties. I have, as you know, an acquaintance with several of the fisher lads and the farmers around here, so it was easy to start the Aberbrothock smugglers again, and here lies the supreme jest . . .'

'How many know you for the daughter of Balgowan?'

'None save John. Someone had to know; you must see that. You remember that you used to tell us that the smugglers were wont to dress as fisherwives so as to walk boldly under the nose of the tidewaiters? Well, so too do my men – as pretty a bunch of damsels as you would wish to meet – and I – the only true female among them – must dress as a man.' Miss Carpenter thought this a merry jest.

A spasm crossed Miss Rattray's face and Liddy hurried on. 'Would you have me, Miss Carpenter, sit in the great hall of the castle with my smugglers about me? I thought not. I shall ape my dear grand-père and wear a small sword – I would not wish to be totally unarmed. I planned the trip; with my knowledge of the French tongue it was simplicity itself, and then I sat here calmly mending collars while my men were at sea. It's a long voyage from France to Arbroath . . .'

'And may I ask why you choose to rendezvous in such a potentially dangerous place as the castle?'

'It's quite safe. We have put it about that ghosts walk around there. I have played the part several times lately. It is from your tales of the old Danish warriors.'

'My attempt to educate you has redounded upon me.' Miss Rattray almost smiled.

'Every child hereabouts has heard how the Danes raided this coastline. They buried their dead on hillocks looking out to sea and planted trees about them. Now there stand fine copses and each one on a direct line to a safe anchorage. Our tidesmen, however, are not so well read and know few of these safe anchorages. This lack of historic lore and a superstition that the dead walk at night near their burial mounds, should keep us safe.'

'But must you associate with these men? Could John not be your deputy?'

'It is much too onerous a charge for so young a lad. I know the castle and its secrets better than any. After our business there tomorrow has been transacted, and my smugglers otherwise engaged – she felt it prudent not to elucidate further – I will slip away. I have checked all the tunnels. All is quite sound, Rattles. You need not fear for my safety, or my reputation.'

'Rash girl. And what of your papa?'

Lydia laughed. 'I am of age, and besides, Papa always said I was more boy than girl – not enough to take Harry's place,' she finished quietly.

'Lydia, desist. You will be caught.'

'I will not be caught,' said Liddy with the supreme arrogance of youth. 'It is not for myself, Rattles. I swear to you that it is only until there is enough for Charlotte. If indeed, the profits are such as they must be from this one trip, then I vow I will not long be engaged in a business that so distresses you. I am in the right of it to contravene the law.'

Miss Rattray stood up and kissed the girl. 'I will say goodnight, though dawn is almost upon us and the household will be stirring before you sleep. I cannot agree with you but will do all I can to protect you.'

After she had gone Liddy found herself unable to sleep, still stimulated by the events of the evening. Goodness . . . she had downed a glass of wine alone in a room with a man unknown to her father. How the gossipmongers would love such a morsel.

She had stood on the beach in the early hours alone, but for a young boy. Was John too young to compromise her or was his estate too humble? Such stupid conventions. Was John not worth ten of the pimply youths who abounded in her own level of society?

She stood at her window, that to her commanded the finest view in the whole shire, and tried to calm her thoughts. Slowly, the sky began to lighten and to stretch long, pale fingers from the estuary across the fields, kissing the tops of the trees, bathing the farm cottages in a soft warm light. Some day someone else would stand at this window admiring the beauty spread out before her. Would she love it as she and Harry had loved it? She must not think of Harry and the waste of his young life, nor of what that death would, in the long term, mean to them. Papa surely must make some provision for the little girls, and if Charlotte were to make a brilliant marriage, then all would be well. But, this would no longer be hers . . .

'You are a sentimental fool, Liddy,' she scolded herself. 'Can the sea not be seen from a thousand windows, and the trees, are they not like other trees?'

Be that as it may, a nasty little voice whispered, were it not for an accident of birth that made you female, you could, in the fullness of time, look forward to inheriting them.

She drove the voice away and, at last very weary, climbed into bed and fell instantly into a dreamless sleep from which she was awakened six hours later by Charlotte.

'Are you unwell, dearest? It is so unlike you not to be the first awake. Rattles said your sleep was disturbed and to let you rest.'

Liddy looked at the clock and was scandalized. 'Eleven o'clock. How could I sleep so late? The day is half-done,' she exaggerated. 'Have you forgotten we are to call upon Mrs Johnstone-Carruthers this afternoon? What is it, Charlotte? Something is wrong?'

'No,' answered Charlotte sitting down upon the bed. 'At least I hope it is nothing. See . . .' From the pocket of her apron she drew a letter that she offered to Liddy. 'Jamie sent it over this morning. His brother included it with estate letters.'

Liddy regarded the missive just as she might have regarded a coiled serpent and hesitantly stretched forth her hand for it.

'Struth, Charlotte, this is Papa's hand,' she exclaimed, with both relief and chagrin in her voice.

'Of course. Why, Liddy, who did you think . . . oh, you thought it might be from His Lordship? Jamie says he is quite fixed in town although he thinks his brother may be on some visit since he has not heard from him.'

Liddy had not been attending to her sister so busy had she been in reading the unexpected letter from Lord Balgowan. 'What a nuisance,' she blurted out, but stopped at the look of amazement on Charlotte's face. 'Here, read for yourself. It seems we are to expect a visit from Papa.'

Charlotte perused the letter while Liddy dressed.

'He was out of town at the races.' Charlotte's sweet face was aglow. 'That is why he did not answer your letter. Is it not wonderful, for now I may confess to you, dearest of sisters, that my heart was sore that he did not write explaining that he could not finance a new gown for Lord Pittenmuir's party. I always knew that he loved Harry the best, did not we all, but was I not foolish to fear he did not care for me at all?'

'Yes dear,' said Liddy automatically for she was feverishly trying to work out how she could possibly keep her new double life from even the most indolent and least interested of fathers.

'Papa has had such a run of luck, Liddy,' continued Charlotte disregarding the fact that her sister had already read the letter. 'He has gifts for all of us, a gown from Bond Street for me, but Liddy, I cannot love it more than the gown you procured for me. He has materials for you, for you must leave off mourning and think to come out in the autumn. Her Grace of Gordon has agreed to sponsor us, but the Lennoxes and the Montagues are all so beautiful that none shall notice us beside them.'

Liddy, aware of her unusual height, laughed at the picture in her mind, and told Charlotte to go and tell their sisters of the joys that awaited them. She would attend to estate business. Everything must be *comme il faut* for the return of the absent Lord. There should be no reason for complaint over the way she had managed his house or his younger children.

In the afternoon, old Tom brought the gig round to the front of the house and Liddy and Charlotte went off to take tea with their near neighbours, Mrs Johnstone-Carruthers and her daughter, Amanda. Mr Johnstone, for so had been the title of her husband, a fabulously wealthy East India merchant, had very obligingly died several years before leaving his wife in possession of his fortune. Since her own birth, though not noble, was good, she had spent the last years and quite a large part of his fortune in trying to establish her daughter, Amanda.

Amanda, dressed in an exorbitantly expensive afternoon gown of palest pink together with a delightful chip-straw hat, was in the garden when they arrived.

'Miss Carpenter, Charlotte, how do you do? Mr Galloway has called. Is that not gracious of him. He is such a gentleman, do you not agree, Charlotte, and most unlike the other gentlemen who call. Do you know I never have the least difficulty in talking with Mr Galloway. But let us go in. Mama will be wondering why I am delaying out here in the garden and I know she wants to hear all you have to say.'

Chattering all the way and scarce leaving space for them to insert the briefest of answers, Miss Johnstone-Carruthers led the way into a prettily furnished drawing room where they found, not only their hostess and the Honourable Jamie Galloway, but also Mrs Wallace and her son, John, who turned quite pink with pleasure upon seeing Charlotte. If the Honourable Jamie was also happy to see her, he did not show it, and Miss Charlotte frowned for a second and then smiled at the company.

The tea table was loaded with an abundance of the finest examples of the pastry-cook's art and Mrs Johnstone-Carruthers encouraged her guests to sample as much as possible. She encouraged her plump daughter too, taking pride in her healthy appetite.

'If I remember rightly, Mrs Wallace, the last time your dear daughter was here it was well nigh impossible to coax her to eat a mouthful and behold how rundown she became. Best watch out for Charlotte too, Miss Carpenter, so thin she is. This fashion for young ladies to starve themselves in an effort to emulate these poet fellows ruins the constitution.'

'Miss Rattray watches solicitously over Charlotte, Ma'am. You need not fear for her,' said Liddy quietly.

'And what of Anne, Mrs Wallace? Talk is like to arise in a small community when a gel is absent from home so long.'

'I met Miss Anne at the Assembly Rooms,' said Jamie. 'You knew that I travelled as far as Edinburgh with Keir on his return south, but that's by the by. Anne was looking and dancing delightfully and I besought her to return to us soon to teach us all the steps she has learned.'

Mrs Wallace smiled at him gratefully. 'Indeed, Mr Galloway, Anne finds the capital's society so agreeable that her father and I feel we are selfish to wish her to return.'

'Nonsense, Ma'am,' said her hostess brusquely. 'A daughter's place is at her mother's side.' Luckily this rude remark reminded Mrs Johnstone-Carruthers of her own daughter whom she summoned to her side so as to be nearer Mr Galloway, and he, with his customary politeness, drew Amanda into the conversation.

Liddy's heart was already beginning to thump alarmingly and her stomach to feel decidedly queasy at the thought of the masquerade she was so soon to undertake, but she managed to keep up her part in the general conversation. She was surprised, however, to be asked whether or not Lord Balgowan could be expected to entertain upon his return north, and if His Lordship were bringing some part of his London circle with him.

'Indeed, I know not. He is not fond of Scotland, Ma'am, and speaks of removing us all to town.'

'Charlotte,' breathed Amanda ecstatically, 'a London debut. Is it not wonderful?'

'It is, my love,' interrupted her mother, 'but let me point out to you, my dearest child, that envy should never find a home with my daughter. We shall give a party to welcome home His Lordship; that would be unexceptionable, you would agree, Miss Carpenter, so close has been our intercourse all these years.'

Liddy was struck dumb at the thought of her papa, who would find difficulty recognizing his own daughters, being claimed as close acquaintance by someone he had probably never met. Luckily, Mrs Johnstone-Carruthers expected no answer and went on, 'Is His Lordship to return soon, Mr Galloway?'

'I think not, Ma'am. He appears to be fixed in town and wishes me rather to join him, which, if all our friends here – he looked particularly at Charlotte as he spoke – are to travel south for the season then, no doubt the autumn will find me in London also.'

This seemed to be a fitting end to the tea party and, waved off by many protestations and promises of a welcoming fête for the return of the prodigal, Liddy and Charlotte were driven away.

43

'I hope you had some tea, Tom?'

'Aye, Miss. Grand scones that fancy Frenchman makes. Mrs Johnstone wants to ape the old Duchess of Gordon.'

'Tom,' said Liddy sternly, feeling that she had sadly allowed too much familiarity in such staff as they had. 'Lord Balgowan is to return soon.'

Not a whit abashed Tom continued, 'Like he'll bring some staff with him, butlers and the like. About time too.'

He drove home in his usual phlegmatic way and Liddy and Charlotte abandoned their usual habit of talking freely and chatted of the progress of the crops.

Dinner was taken at its usual early time so that the nursery party might join them, and Liddy inspected her little sisters' dining room manners severely and decided that, thanks to Rattles, His Lordship would find nothing of which to complain in the conduct of his daughters.

'Lord Balgowan may elect to bring town ways with him, Liddy, in which case dinner will be much too late for Alice and Marie-Louise.'

'Mr Galloway says it is the custom in some Edinburgh homes for the nursery party to be set in chairs around the room while their elders eat,' said Charlotte.

'Barbaric,' said Liddy. 'They must fall off their chairs with exhaustion so long do formal dinners last.'

'Should your dear papa bring such customs with him, rather we must ensure that the babes are well fed before coming down else the smell of all the good forbidden things will be harder to endure than fatigue.'

'Just think, Alice, if you had bread and milk for supper and were then forced to sit quietly watching your elders eat poached salmon or roast lamb,' teased Charlotte.

'With gravy,' added Rattles for Alice more than any of her sisters enjoyed her food.

'I should ask Papa for some,' said miss composedly and set her eldest sister to wondering if she could possibly remember their father whom she had not seen for three years. It was quite possible that the babes had been kept strictly to the nurseries during their papa's last stay so great was his grief at the death of his son that he had taken no pleasure at all in the company of his other children, not even Charlotte, who so closely resembled her brother.

But at last the little ones were in bed and Rattles and Charlotte were busy with their never-ending needlework. Liddy could see that Miss Rattray was amused by the predicament in which she now found herself. She could hardly say, I must away to rendezvous with some smugglers, or if she begged to retire early, Charlotte would be sure to come to see what was amiss. How was she to get out of the house?

At last the tea tray was brought in and Liddy forced herself to pour calmly and to hand round the cups.

'Liddy, my dear, why do you not retire early this evening? You look quite peaked and must still be exhausted from last night. Charlotte and I will see to the lamps and locking up.'

'Indeed, you are not quite yourself, Liddy. A good night's rest will make you feel better,' added Charlotte.

'Yes, you are in the right of it.' It was hardly a prevarication to agree that the benefits of a night of restful slumber could not be overestimated. Liddy kissed them both and hurried off to her room.

Singly and in twos or threes her men would soon begin making their way to the castle. John, her fierce protector, might even be there before she arrived. Dear John, he was quite as appalled as Rattles at the idea of Miss Carpenter in breeches.

Once in her room Liddy drew Harry's clothes out from the deepest recesses of her clothes' cupboard. Miss Carpenter, or rather Mr Pate, examined himself critically in the glass and decided that, although a little old-fashioned – young gentlemen were now sheering their locks and curling them in the Brutus style in fancied imitation of the Roman emperor Lucius Brutus – he was still a fine figure of a man.

She hung up her dress and drew the curtains round the bed lest Charlotte peep in and, quiet as a cat, slipped out and down the stairs leading to the kitchens. Mrs Harper and Bessie had already retired. The kitchens, pantries, and other offices were lit only by the moonlight stealing in through the windows. The kitchen door was locked and bolted.

'Forsooth, why must we use so many locks and bolts when there is nothing of value to steal? I hope Mrs Harper is a light sleeper.'

Liddy gently turned the heavy iron key and slid back the bolts. As with everything else in Mrs Harper's province, the bolts were well oiled, and, for Liddy, letting herself clandestinely out of her own house was a simple matter. She stood for a few minutes in the shadow of the door and then, sure that there was no one around, bolted into the shrubbery like a rabbit pursued by a fox.

Her passage through the tunnel was a deal more comfortable this time since she had had the foresight to equip herself with a lantern. Less than fifteen minutes later, Mr Pate was entering Balgowan Castle. As she had supposed, John was already in the great hall.

'All well at home, John?'

'Aye, Miss, I mean Euan. My granny's off on her travels again and like as not I won't see her before the bad weather.'

Liddy said nothing for it was well known that John's grandmother, if so she was, was one of the tinkers who preferred to travel around and sleep under the stars rather than to remain in one place. She had often left a young John for weeks at a time. The wonder being that she ever came back at all.

'I have been around our customers. Ready money, I told them and every one of them has paid me and some have offered advance payments, too.'

'Splendid. Once the men are here we will match what has already been bought against what we have, and then we will split the rest among them or hide it safe until we find a buyer.'

'Best not be too generous, Euan, stick to what you agreed. You can rely on old Charlie Spink, but there's one or two others I would trust no farther than the end of my nose, so you best be careful and . . . watch how you sit. Why they are unable to tell you be a lady, I do not know. You move like one, you look like one, you speak like one . . .'

'John, John, I promise to mend my ways. Behold my demeanour.' She sat down, as her brother used to sit, legs thrown out in front and crossed at the ankle. 'This Charlie has been useful already.'

'He has run contraband all his life, knows the business.' John hesitated and then plunged in. 'Miss Liddy, you do not intend to . . . to . . . drink with them.'

'Assuredly. It would look most odd if I did not. I'll not drink brandy or rum – I misdoubt me I could stomach rum – but a gentlemanly glass of claret . . .' She saw that her champion was shaking his head and she laughed. 'Why, what a puritan you are. I have shocked you.'

John was not to be mollified. 'It don't look right, a lassie drinking—'

'I promise not to become inebriated and disgrace you.'

There was a muffled oath and a sound as if someone had stumbled in the dark. 'Quiet,' whispered Liddy needlessly, 'someone comes.'

A few moments later and the first of the smugglers, Charlie Spink, had arrived and in less than fifteen minutes those of the band who had been able to leave their hearths were assembled, each man seated on a keg of brandy in the absence of chairs.

'Let us drink to success, lads. To your hard work and skill.'

'And to your planning, Euan,' inserted John who felt that it was vitally important that the men realize that their leader did much more than merely receive a share of the profits.

'Aye, that too,' said Charlie, 'but first we had best look at what we have here and what is on order for next time.'

'Starch?' There was disbelief in the voice that echoed the item read by Spink from the list he had been asked, discreetly, to supply.

'Aye, lads, starch, pays as well as brandy, and the same customer wants some fancy French windowpanes too.'

'Blow me down if I thought I was to be going marketing like some witless kitchen maid.'

'Gin ye get paid, what's your worry, Tam?' Asked Charlie.

'Damn sight harder to carry glass for some gentry's bit o'muslin.'

Liddy felt that it was time she asserted her authority or the smugglers would soon be ranged into two camps, one on the side of the older, more experienced Charlie and the other on the side of the more hot-headed Tam.

'Come, men, cease your arguing and let us look to the pleasanter business of dividing our spoils and looking to our profits. On this first excursion our margin is low, yet there is still sufficient that every man may have his own keg as we agreed, and a few shillings in his pocket.' She waited while John filled mugs and continued. 'Charlie and John have not been idle and with the orders they have brought in today, we may confidently look forward to greater profits.'

These were the words they wanted to hear and they set to work happily dividing the cargo according to its eventual destination.

'Those of you who have a horse or mule must bring them next time. We land at Maiden's Cove and with horses hid in the Mason's Cave—'

'That's Pittenmuir land, Euan.'

'Aye and him safe in London with his fancy English friends. We will use the cove for we have but whetted the appetites of our customers and, if you are to undertake the dangers of such a voyage, it would be sensible to bring in as much as the *Shuska* can hold. I myself take no profit from this first trip.'

'Aye, go on, Euan,' said the burly Tam, mellowed by liberal doses of brandy. 'It's only fitting that you have your share. After all, we are no good without you there to set things up.'

At this there was a general murmur of agreement.

'Best you be going . . .' whispered John.

Miss Carpenter, who had only the haziest notion – culled from the pages of the romantic drivel which adorned her shelves – of how men behaved when in their cups, would dearly have loved to have stayed, but her sterner self and John's surprisingly steely hand upon her arm brought wiser council, and seeing her men engaged she rose and moved back into the shadows of the great stone walls. A few minutes later she was outside, standing perfectly still and quiet, listening. Small sounds of revelry did float to her on the night air and devoutly she prayed that any honest citizen of Pittenmuir or Balgowan would not be on hand to hear it.

Five

W hether it was in any way due to the claret she had
consumed the evening before – the veriest thimbleful,
she assured herself – or the lack of sleep from the preceding
night, Miss Carpenter did not wake until very late the next
morning. For some unaccountable reason she felt happy. Was it
due to the fact that her papa was so soon to return home and to
remove the burden of the household from her shoulders? No, she
could not, with any honesty, say that she was looking forward to
that gentleman's return. Having been reared in conditions of the
strictest propriety she knew perfectly well that it was somewhat
unfilial of her not to be counting the hours until his arrival but,
no matter what she said to Rattles in defence of her papa, she did
feel that Lord Balgowan had treated his daughters most shab-
bily. Her happiness came from quite another source; she had
organized a smuggling ring that looked to become successful.
The only way in which her happiness could be increased was if
she were to accompany her merry band on one of their expeditions, but that would not do. It was not that she wished to
emulate those enterprising young ladies of a previous century
who had become pirates, although being possessed of a plank
from which one might suspend one's worst enemy did have a deal
to recommend it!

Liddy, you are become unhinged, she admonished herself
sternly, and banishing a delightful image of Lord Pittenmuir
jumping into a sea swarming with maneating reptiles, Miss
Carpenter rose docilely and dressed for the day.

She found her sister dusting the breakfast parlour; a housekeeping chore Charlotte was more than pleased to abandon.

'Liddy, are you quite rested? I did carry some chocolate to you
at eight o'clock last night, but you were sleeping so deeply I had
not the heart to wake you.'

'I am quite rested and ready to put all my energies to work.' Since the laborious task that she intended was the working out of a date for the next smuggling trip so that it would not coincide with her papa's arrival, she was glad when Charlotte took herself off to prevail upon Mrs Harper to make some toast for the mistress of the house.

She must find out, too, if there was any murmuring from the villagers about spooky goings on at the castle. Tonight ghosts would walk again in the vicinity of the old ruins. Would she ever seek her rest at a reasonable hour? Her light breakfast over, Liddy took herself off to the gardens to see old Tom.

'Is the asparagus finished, Tom?' she asked by way of greeting.

'Aye, it's a short season and over long since. Pittenmuir grows it out of season in his succession houses. Mayhap he has extra. I could talk to—'

'No, indeed, Tom,' said Liddy quickly. 'Papa is used to fine vegetables in town. Here he will enjoy what we can provide. You sleep well, Tom, since you seem able to work such long hours?'

'Ain't much as would wake me, Miss Liddy, not even ghosts and such.'

'Ghosts, Tom?' Liddy laughed lightly although even to her ears her voice sounded strained. 'Surely you do not believe in spectres.'

'Not me, Miss, although there's some as do. That boy John were up here with tales of sights and wailing from the castle.'

Liddy looked round. 'John, was he here?'

'Aye, he was, and shaking in his boots about Danish warriors or some such nonsense. It's that old granny of his – she don't believe in God but ready to believe in any old superstition.'

'Mayhap I can set his mind at rest, Tom.'

'Isn't he eating his mutton at Balmossie. If His Lordship is looking to hiring, Miss Liddy, he won't do better than that lad; there's room above the stable. I'd soon rid his head of nonsense like ghosts.'

Nothing would have pleased Liddy more than to give a home and regular wages to John, but a lucky run at cards would scarce give Lord Balgowan sufficient funds to put his house in order. Bond Street dresses could perhaps be financed by the throw of a dice, but it would take more than lucky chance to set a neglected estate in profit again.

'We must all of us await Lord Balgowan's arrival before we make plans, Tom,' said Liddy and took herself off to the stables.

There she was forcibly struck by the amount of work their overburdened staff accomplished in a day. The stable was swept and tidy, the mangers full of clean, sweet-smelling hay, and the coats of the horses shone from grooming. Together with the gardens, Tom managed the stables and, with John's help, the supplying of wood for the fires.

'At least I have always managed to pay Tom,' thought Liddy humbly. 'Little though it is.'

They were not left long in anticipation of their papa's return for scarce a week after the reception of the letter, a coach and four rumbled up the carriage sweep and disgorged one superior butler, a modestly but elegantly dressed female who was his wife – and hired as maid to Miss Carpenter and Miss Charlotte – and several trunks and boxes needed by His Lordship to sustain life so far from civilization. Close upon the coach came a stylish phaeton driven by a groom, who could hardly have been other than a retired soldier so straight was his carriage, and reclining against the squabs an elegant figure whom they had no difficulty in recognizing as their papa.

Lord Balgowan was not tall, but he had a broad athletic figure enhanced by the excellence of his tailoring. There were no fobs or seals dangling at his waist for, like his late son, His Lordship did not emulate the dandy set, but it was obvious to even the untrained eyes of his daughters that His Lordship was dressed with style and taste. His hair was brown like Liddy's and cut à la Brutus, but where Harry's blue eyes had sparkled with mischief and charm, there was no light in those that calmly surveyed his ancestral home. The coldness in them sent a shiver through his eldest daughter, but she reminded herself that her papa was yet heartbroken and rushed forward to greet him.

It was a most delightful reunion. No one could have doubted the warmth in Lord Balgowan's eyes as he sat in the yellow drawing room, a little girl perched happily on each knee. He would stay, he told them, for some months, and was conscious of his neglect of his daughters. He threw himself on their mercy and begged their forgiveness.

'Dearest Papa,' sobbed Charlotte, 'there is nothing to forgive.

We share your grief and only wish that our love could have helped you bear it.'

The contents of the trunks and boxes had been unpacked and exclaimed over. For Charlotte there were lengths of spider-gauze that could be made into a gown that would strike jealousy into the heart of even Miss Fairweather. For Liddy, a celestial blue crêpe trimmed with puff muslin, as well as leather, calico, and silk gloves from Green the glovers in Little Newport Street and silk stockings from Churtons. The two little girls had not been forgotten, for apart from the charming printed cotton dress lengths that Charlotte promised to make up for them immediately, there was a doll for each of them, almost life-sized with eyes that opened and closed! Rattles had her present, too; a shawl, not unfortunately from Kashmir, since the war had stopped trade there, but from Paisley and if Rattles thought it interesting that a shawl made scarcely sixty miles from where she sat should be exported to England and transported back to Scotland at exorbitant expense, she was too polite to say so. Discreetly, when he had an opportunity to see her alone, Lord Balgowan pressed upon the governess her accumulated wages and charmingly begged her not to leave them now that she had become a wealthy woman. Miss Rattray laughed at the witticism.

The new servants were introduced. The butler, Etienne, was a Frenchman who had been in service with a family well known to His Lordship's father. Unfortunately, every member of the family had perished in the Terror and when Etienne had finally managed to reach England he had been delighted to find employment with one who had known his late employer. Madame was an Englishwoman, a very superior dresser who would be honoured, she told the young ladies, to look after them. Madame did nothing so vulgar as boast, but she too had been in service in the finest households and she was certainly *au courant* with the latest styles. Charlotte was ecstatic.

Liddy was not so enchanted as she foresaw difficulties to which she gave serious thought. Her first worry, that the new and sophisticated servants would disrupt the ordered regimen of the house, proved needless. Mrs Harper was to reign supreme in her kitchens and was delighted to have a butler of such evident superiority and Frenchness as Etienne to answer the door for her, to wait table and, no doubt, to look after the wines. Now, with

His Lordship in residence once more, it was unthinkable that Balgowan House should not take its proper place in county society.

Liddy well knew that Mrs Harper longed to sharpen her skills. She went down to the kitchens after the carriages had been unpacked and saw Mrs Harper looking with pleasure at her shelves – well stocked for the first time since the death of the heir.

The housekeeper turned with a smile to her young mistress. 'Pardon me, Miss Liddy, I were daydreaming of the old days. When your dear mama were alive such dinners I produced, not like these economies we been practising. The Duchess of Gordon was used to come to dine and once her Ladyship says to me, "Harper," her Grace says, "Lord Balgowan's home chef is the equal, if not the master, of my own imported and exorbitantly expensive chef." Her very words, Miss Liddy, "exorbitantly expensive". Not that I'm puffing up my own consequence, Miss Liddy.' Carefully she changed the alignment of her splendid new vinegars before continuing. 'To my mind fine feathers don't make fine birds nor fine ingredients fine dinners, but to see you at the foot of a well-provisioned table with all the young people of consequence about you . . .'

Emotion clouded her speech and Liddy took advantage of the break. 'Dear Harper, your meals have always been delicious, and I am glad that all goes well in the kitchens.'

'Oh, but Miss Liddy, a butler only adds to your consequence, and I'm sure Miss Rattray would be the first to agree with me that your dear papa is right to employ a dresser for our young ladies. Made poor Bessie quite weep. Just imagine, Mrs Harper, she says to me, our darling treasures at last in their rightful place. I were suspicious of Madame . . . so different and sophisticated, but I took to her right away, I did. "Your Miss Charlotte is the most beautiful young lady it has ever been my pleasure to attend, Mrs Harper," she says, which shows that she has good feeling as well as judgement, but . . .' She stopped talking for a moment to better align some bottled cherries on a shelf. 'Pray don't get in a miff, Miss Lydia, but Madame says as how although you are not what society terms a beauty, with the proper gowns and hair-style, you will be distinguée whatever that means, for, she says, Miss Carpenter has *presence*.'

Miss Liddy was touched and not a little amused. So, she had

presence, had she, and with Madame's attention would be distinguée, would she? She wondered idly at the skill of the woman to so quickly recognize and lull the jealousies stirring in the bosoms of these old family retainers. Harper and Bessie had no need to be told that, but they were ready to welcome into their midst anyone who so quickly saw the attributes of their darlings.

I need to persuade her to devote her energies to Charlotte ruminated Liddy, for the truth is that to me a personal maid will be more hindrance than a help. How can one hide one's brother's breeches from the eagle eyes of one's dresser? How will I be able to slip away to meet my 'ladies' with an abigail waiting to see me to bed?

Liddy's bedchamber, too, was not best placed for stealing out in the dead of night without arousing the house. She would have to creep out tonight, for the *Shuska* was expected at Maiden Cove. Once again John had sailed with her and he would not know of the return of Lord Balgowan. She would have to get out of the house.

Dinner, to which Rattles and the schoolroom party were also invited, was a *tour de force*. There was soup, followed by a loin of veal and then a brace of partridges, accompanied by artichoke hearts and mushrooms stuffed with Stilton and deep fried. Tom's early plums accompanied a syllabub. Monsieur Etienne had consulted with Mrs Harper and had provided the wine for which was begged His Lordship's pardon since the finest wines needed time to rest after their gruelling journey.

'Claret does not travel,' commented Lydia winning a gesture of approval from her papa who would have been horrified to find that his daughter was thinking of the indifferent claret she had hidden at the castle.

Thankfully, like his eldest daughter, Lord Balgowan had no desire to prolong the evening. He knew that there was much to discuss; they had scarcely touched upon his plan to remove the family to town and had not discussed the estate at all, but his bones ached from the prolonged jolting over abominable roads, and the inadequate hostelries between London and Arbroath. He would have a night's rest, for if Mrs Harper's housekeeping was ought like her cooking, his bed would be dry and warm, and then he would be fit to examine the books, the state of his younger daughters' learning, and to drive around the estate with his elder daughters, for he had forgotten the extent of it.

'You have not mentioned your valet, Papa,' said Liddy. 'You were used to have one.'

'Clever puss, you would remember Stefan. I regret that I commanded his talent and affection only when I was in funds. Not that I bear him ill will; a man has to look after himself first.'

'He has left you, sir?'

'A year since. He found employment with a vulgar man in Yorkshire. Of a surety they deserve one another.' Thus casually did His Lordship dispose of one who had served him well, as Liddy remembered.

Dutifully Liddy kissed the offered cheek of her father as he retired for the night. Liddy was concerned though. She had felt several times during the evening that she did not know this man, and that was ridiculous. He was her father, but she had never really known him, for she had previously loved her father, but did not feel that particular emotion for the Lord Balgowan who had just bid her goodnight. Harry's death had changed him intolerably.

Her bedchamber was a haven; she sat down in the shabby chair by the window and looked towards the estuary. Very soon Monsieur Visieux would be charting his way towards Maiden Cove. She did wonder though, that with her father returned home, what need would she have of the services of such as Euan Pate? The rights and wrongs of the question would have to wait upon the morrow for it was almost time to leave for the meeting place.

A genteel knock heralded the arrival of Madame. 'You are awake, Miss Carpenter. I was in terror lest I spend too much time with Miss Charlotte, but such lovely hair she has. I could not resist giving it a good brushing.'

Since Miss Rattray had given Charlotte's hair one hundred strokes every night for as many years as she could remember, Liddy did not feel this statement augured well for the continual tranquillity of the household, but she said nothing, hoping that Rattles' continued good sense would dissolve the problem. She allowed Madame to fuss over her and to help her into a night-dress, but she refused to have her hair brushed, assuring Madame that she was too exhausted by the day's excitement. Madame agreed that she should sleep and went off carrying Liddy's lilac crêpe that had a drawn thread.

A few minutes later there was a discreet knock and the door opened to admit the governess. 'What a good dinner we have enjoyed, Liddy, my love,' said she seating herself by the bed and pulling her tatting from her dressing gown pocket.

Liddy was most forcibly aware of the number of times Rattles had sat in the same place wearing the same serviceable old dressing gown. 'You do know that no one could ever take your place with us, do you not?'

'Please, not another Cheltenham tragedy,' begged Rattles with a smile. 'I have but reassured Charlotte and I expected better from you. I am delighted to welcome Monsieur and Madame. How our consequence is raised. Now, had Madame been French it would have been above all things great.'

Liddy laughed and then grew serious. 'You must see, Rattles, that the arrival of Madame presents a difficulty. Help me dress for my ship is due this very night and I should be there. I must saddle Amber for I ride to Maiden Cove. We will talk tomorrow,' she finished, forestalling the questions and remonstrations hovering on her governess's lips.

With Rattles's efficient, though disapproving aid, Liddy was soon in her brother's clothes and stealing down the staircase to the kitchens. It seemed as if every stair groaned in an attempt to alert the master of the house to his daughter's iniquities, but no one stirred.

'The servants are yet awake, Liddy,' whispered Rattles and then, showing an amazing facility in subterfuge, 'Creep out and I will make myself hot milk. Should Monsieur come to investigate, I shall stay here drinking it until he returns to his quarters.'

Leaving her partner-in-crime, Liddy opened the kitchen door as quietly as possible and then with a glance up to assure herself that no one looked out from any window, she hurried to the stable. The old garron whickered welcomingly and she thanked the fact that Tom was a sound sleeper. Soon, she had Amber saddled and bridled. Lights yet showed in the rooms allotted to the butler and his wife, and not at all gratefully, Miss Carpenter berated Madame for sitting up to mend the broken thread.

'I must risk them hearing Amber's hooves, for there is no time to wrap them even if I could find sacking.'

Begging Amber to be quiet, Liddy led the mare from the stables and risked hurrying across the yard to the welcoming shadows. She led the pony out of the yard to a grass verge where she mounted. The lights, except in the kitchen where Rattles stood guard, were all gone out, and taking this for a good omen, Liddy cantered through the woods towards the road leading to the beach.

Once on the beach she broke into a gallop and enjoyed the exhilaration of flying along the waterline. She dismounted among some caves a distance from Maiden Cove, for many, if not all, of the smugglers would recognize her mount, and then, agile as a mountain goat, she scrambled across the caves and rocks. Monsieur Visieux, Pete Smith, Charlie and John were supervising the unloading and Liddy watched for a while, noting the deep grooves the hogsheads of brandy cut into the ground. She moved so quietly that she was upon the men before they noticed her.

'Good evening, gentlemen,' she said from behind them and enjoyed the childish satisfaction of seeing Monsieur jump.

There were several horses and at least two carts in the cave that stood a full hundred feet deep and with a great yawning entrance. The men were filling the panniers on the horses with bounty and Liddy noticed a great flat parcel, wrapped round with sacking and rope, which must have been the windows for the Arbroath merchant.

'All well, Monsieur?'

'*Bien sûr*, Mr Pate. What caves these are. One could hide an army inside.'

'Or a ship's cargo.'

'*Vraiment*, this is a paradise for a trade such as ours. Do the tidewaiters not suspect?'

'Smuggling has been dead on this coast for nigh on fifty years,' answered Mr Pate, who was become an authority on the 'gentlemen' and their activities. 'In its heyday fortunes were made. Tidewaiters were used to patrol the cliffs above looking for ships, but they could scarcely watch every cove between Dundee and Arbroath, and there are hundreds. Political pressure put an army detachment right in the town and that effectively put a stop to the trade,' finished Mr Pate regretfully.

'And the tidesmen?'

'They sit in the harbour and examine the cargoes of ships that dock there, so behold us, almost under their collective noses.'

This seemed a time to drop his bomb. 'Indeed, as it happens, we may not make any more trips.'

The men turned, aghast. 'This ain't time for jokesmithing, lad.'

'I do not jest, gentlemen. Lord Balgowan is come home and how we are to run right under his bedroom windows, as it were, is beyond me.'

'You know His Lordship?'

'Well enough to know no tales of ghosts will frighten him.'

'If you know so much, lad, you know that he won't stay long,' said Charlie. 'We'll lie quiet as ghosts are supposed to be and His Lordship will sleep sound in his bed.'

'He will stay long enough to inspect the castle and rumour says he intends repairs. We dare not leave contraband there.'

Obviously this thought had not occurred to the smugglers. 'Devil take him. He had little interest in the estate even when his boy was alive. What brings him here now? We be hard pressed to find safety for them hogsheads, big as they are.'

John had been looking from one to the other speaker. 'There be a great barn at Balmossie where we could stash them awhile. We could roll bales in front to make it look like the barn be full of hay.'

'And what of Balmossie?'

'One of our best customers, Charlie, and not averse to a little extra for services. Right fond of spruce beer, if you get my meaning.'

'Let us discuss tactics at the hall,' Liddy said sternly, quite sure that for tonight, at least, the castle was safe. Balmossie was on Pittenmuir land and nothing would induce her to become involved with that family. Besides, Lord Pittenmuir was Lord Lieutenant of the county, an arduous task which had heretofore been too much for His Lordship to undertake, but no doubt that would change when and if he heard of the rebirth of the lady smugglers.

Six

It was not long before Lord Pittenmuir was apprised of the activities of smugglers near his Scottish seat. If the truth be told, His Lordship laughed a little when his astonished secretary revealed that it appeared to be members of the weaker sex who were heavily involved. Keir had enjoyed his lessons with Miss Rattray and was aware of the old tales.

A picture of a nine-year-old Liddy came into his head. *I'll be the smuggler, Keir, you and Harry be tidewaiters.* Where had that little Liddy gone?

He should have spoken to her long ago, but she had avoided him, never being at home after that party that Jamie had arranged. They had been like brother and sister once; she should have known that something must have prevented his appearance at Harry's memorial service. He would not sink so low as to seek her sympathy by informing her that the cannonball that had killed Harry had tried hard to do away with him too – and nearly succeeded. He had begged Jamie not to tell her of his injuries, believing that the death of her beloved brother was more than enough to bear and then, when he might have spoken, the Prime Minister had demanded his help on that other matter. He was a fool to have expected his relationship with Liddy to remain the same. They had grown up and apart. He laughed harshly. It was of no import now; there were always other little matters and one of them was this smuggling business.

There were those besides Liddy who knew the old stories; others who also knew how to disappear like wraiths into the caves that proliferated in the area. Every fisherman and every farmer had his bolthole in a barn or under the hearthstone of his very home. To find the leader of a band of smugglers could mean searching every cottage or fisherman's shack along the length of Scotland's Golden Mile.

Truth to tell, he had sympathy for the smugglers and were he to return to Scotland he would be only a half-hearted figure of justice. He would leave it awhile – Jamie could act in his stead.

'You rang, sir?' His butler, Chalmers, was in the doorway, stolid and calm as usual.

'I am expected at Downing Street. Be so good as to ask Major Fordyce to dine with me this evening and have Tregarth attend me in my dressing room. And Chalmers –' Lord Pittenmuir accompanied his orders with the particular smile his attendants, but few others, were privileged to see – 'would you send the proper instructions to the stables for me.'

So it was that, fifteen minutes later when His Lordship, attired in prime doeskin pantaloons, the most fashionable of severely starched and unruffled cambric shirts, a neat grey waistcoat worn under an exquisitely fitting black coat, and a pair of leather boots, found that his town chaise was at the door.

'Walk the horses, Thomas,' he said upon arrival at 10 Downing Street, the home of the Prime Minister, Spencer Perceval. 'I do not expect to be above twenty minutes.'

Perceval, a Tory politician, had championed the cause of the Princess of Wales, which had infuriated the Prince, now Regent, who was the candle round whom all the Whig moths flew. It could not have been easy during these first few months of the Regency to conciliate the Prince, but Perceval with tact and dignity had managed to do so and it was even said that their royal master had been seen to dine at Number 10 – an accolade indeed for the Tory minister. The Regent still remained critical of Viscount Wellington's operations in Portugal and it was known that many of his Whig friends, who were being encouraged by the Regent to accept posts in the administration, wanted a negotiated peace and the return of British troops from the Iberian Peninsula. It was of the war that Perceval wanted to speak.

'We have heard that Napoleon plans an attack on Russia. The best of our generals and incidentally the 10th Hussars, the Regent's regiment, are still in the Peninsula and the news is not good. Here in the United Kingdom we have food both scarce and expensive with wheat costing three times its pre-war price. The great textile centres of Yorkshire and Lanarkshire are without foreign markets. What good is our new industrialism if we cannot sell what we make, if our skilled workmen are unemployed?'

'Surely a march into Russia would be an act of unmitigated folly?' asked His Lordship returning to the main issue.

'You know his ambition, Pittenmuir, better than many, but like you, I believe that an attempt to bring the might of Russia to its knees is the act of a madman. Go to France, Keir, and discover if this is shade for a more sinister threat. Does Bonaparte intend drawing our strength to the east while he spreads west? We have been at war with France since 1793, more than half your life, my Lord, and it must stop.' He stood up and walked around the room and turned again to his visitor. 'Go to France. Find out Napoleon's plans so that we may foil them and save our sadly overburdened little island.'

The Arbroath smugglers would have to wait.

Much later Major Fordyce asked with the ease born of long comradeship. 'Are you ill, Keir, that you dine at home?' He watched his employer help himself to beef. 'Your appetite belies my fears.'

Lord Pittenmuir gave a crack of laughter. 'You are as fine a trencherman as I, Henry, and so have no cause to comment so rudely on how well I load my plate. I am not ill and have refused several invitations. I have a letter from Jamie,' he tossed the missive across the table. 'He expects action but I must needs go abroad.'

'Spain?'

'France.'

Major Fordyce was in his employer's confidence and knew of his recent activities. They had fought together throughout the Iberian Peninsula from which campaign the major was the only one of the triumvirate, consisting of Pittenmuir, Harry and himself, to emerge unscathed. He had sold out and with Tregarth, His Lordship's servant, had nursed Pittenmuir back to health.

The secrets of the Prime Minister, however, were of a different nature, and His Lordship deliberated for a while deciding how much was needful for his excellent secretary to know.

'The smugglers, Keir?' asked Major Fordyce at last.

'I cannot blame them, Henry, but as Lord Lieutenant am duty bound to stop them. Be so good as to write to Jamie asking him to set inquiries in motion. After all, the boy knows these farmers better than I and will have some inkling of who the smugglers might be.'

'Have the military been apprised of the presence of the "Gentlemen" or is it the "Gentlewomen of Arbroath"?' Henry asked as he refilled the glasses.

Keir gestured to the letter. 'You have as much information as I do. I would surmise that as yet all is rumour. Once Jamie has clear proof . . .' he shrugged eloquently.

They applied themselves again to their rare roast beef accompanied by inelegant quantities of roasted potatoes.

'Picture the consternation were I to ask my Aunt Eugenia and her starchy friends to sit down to such a meal,' Keir commented, wryly.

'Since Mrs FitzGeorge writes that when she dines with her crony, R,' replied Henry, 'there are at least thirty dishes on the table at one course and some of them out-of-season, I ask if you are bold enough to defy convention.'

'Never. Behold me quaking in my shoes.'

Lord Pittenmuir rang the little bell that stood just beside his wine glass and servants appeared, replacing all evidence of the entrée with an array of creams which were one and all rejected.

'Strawberries, Chalmers, and put some cognac in the library and, if you please, Chalmers, attempt to mollify Jean-Christoffe.'

The butler smiled as he withdrew. 'Yes sir,' he told the tray he was carrying. 'I will, against my will, try to mollify that ridiculous frog. I've told him time enough that you're a man of simple tastes. Damn, when was there last a good party in this house? Master Jamie's coming-of-age, and even then His Lordship was weak from wounds, and Master Harry and too many other friends gone. Isn't one upstart Frenchman not causing enough trouble?'

His spiteful monologue had changed to a voice of honey when he reached the kitchen. 'Milord is *désolé* that he finds himself unable to eat even *un morceau*. I believe no one in England is capable of appreciating your art, Monsieur. Perhaps you may wish to return to France,' he finished hopefully.

Unaware of the battle of the titans below stairs, Pittenmuir and his secretary were talking. Lord Pittenmuir held out a beautifully shaped manicured hand to his secretary. 'Is that the hand of a gentleman?'

'Of course,' Henry answered in some puzzlement.

'Is it not also the hand of a spy? You appear at a loss, my dear Henry. You see my hand and see the hand of a gentleman because, *mon brave*, that is what you expect to see. In a few days someone will see this hand and know it for the hand of a spy.'

'With permission, my Lord, you speak nonsense. Anyone seeing you knows you for a gentleman.'

His Lordship rose and blew out all but one of the candles. He pulled off his coat and his exquisitely arranged neckcloth, rumpled the cloth and tied it loosely around his neck. His hair received the same rough treatment as his linen and bending down towards Fordyce he spoke to him in a guttural, unrecognizable voice.

'Good God.'

'Gentleman or spy?' asked His Lordship in his own well-modulated tones. He returned to his chair and sat down, every inch a gentleman. 'It would be better were I shorter, but sometimes I stoop, oft times I limp, and at times I try to appear taller and thinner than I am. Change my hair, go without shaving – even a day makes me look disreputable – and naturally, Schultz does not make my coats. Gentleman or spy, Henry?'

'May I suggest your Lordship wear gloves.'

Pittenmuir laughed. 'Dirt under the nails, Henry. Let us repair to the library. I am toying with an idea and I hope that a few glasses of my – I fervently hope – unsmuggled brandy will help me think.'

The library was His Lordship's favourite room in this house, a house not part of the original estate. He had bought it just after his father's death primarily as a convenience for Jamie who had just gone up to Oxford. No matter what Liddy Carpenter thought, he loved his Scottish home and would allow nothing in it to be altered or modernized, but in this attractive, tall, narrow house he was able to buy the more modern furniture as suited his fancy. The library was not panelled and such wall as appeared between the tall narrow windows was hung with light watercolours. The rosewood sofas, while elegant, were strong enough to support the weight of a man. Lord Pittenmuir was tall and so liked the design of this particular example of the carpenter's art that allowed him to rest his back against the padded arm at one end and dispose his legs along the length. He made himself comfortable as soon as he had poured some brandy.

'Good smuggling weather,' commented His Lordship looking out at the gentle rays of the setting sun. 'I believe I can with a little dissembling, become a ruffian. Methinks I shall try my hand at smuggling.'

Henry choked and lost most of his brandy. 'You jest,' he managed at last.

'No, indeed. It has become quite difficult to get into France. One can hardly sail one's yacht to Calais. I have taxed my brain and voilà – I join the Arbroath smugglers, unmask them and get to France, both.'

'One problem. They are women.'

'Fie, Henry, you must know them to be men dressed as women. What think you? Shall I look charming in sprigged muslin?'

Major Fordyce did not deign to reply.

'There was an old man among my pensioners who taught Harry and me to sail,' His Lordship continued. 'No doubt he will help.'

Henry interrupted the flow. 'Keir, I beg you to rethink. What manner of man becomes the leader of a band of cutthroats: a ruffian, a blackguard, the worst type of malefactor? What mercy would he give you, Lord Lieutenant of the county, if he discovers your imposture? If he does not dispatch you, the French certainly will.'

'Then I must ensure they do not unmask me.' He rose from his couch and strode around the room, working out his plan as he walked. 'Speed is of the essence. My yacht? No, I cannot leave her at the harbour. My racing curricle.'

'Damned uncomfortable for a journey of three days.'

'As if that signifies and 'twill be a dashed sight more comfortable than the Peninsula.'

'The roads in Scotland . . .'

'I will hire a saddle horse if they be too bad. Come, I must be off at first light.'

Three days later a very tired horse and rider could have been seen making their way along the top of the steep cliffs that led from Arbroath to the fishing village of Auchmithie. The elements were against them and a driving rain slashed at them as they picked their way in the gathering darkness until at last the rider was forced to dismount and lead the poor brute, lest it lose its footing and send both of them over the cliffs.

'You are a fool, Keir Galloway,' His Lordship chastised himself, 'and on a fool's errand. Less than two miles away is the home of your heart: food, hot water, dry clothes and unimagined luxury for this poor brute and here you are, likely to catch your death trying to find a house you have seen but once and a man who saw you last when you were twelve years old.'

They plodded on, the horse now even too tired to show his hostility to the twigs and leaves that were thrown against his face by the wind, but at last they reached a track that Keir thought he remembered. He was relieved to see the shuttered cottages that made up the one street. He knew where he was going now. Almost fifteen years ago he had been in this same spot, on his way to see old Charlie. Defiantly, for he had assumed rightly that his father would disapprove, he had gone and shared a pot of soup – even now he could smell it, rich with fish. Later he had confessed the whole to his papa who had merely suggested mildly that perhaps it was better always to let him know where his son was going. Liddy had been furious, he remembered, not because the cottage was so humble but because he had gone without her, and Keir laughed in the darkness at the memory of that mutinous little face.

He was there but no light showed. It was late and he could not read his timepiece. What if the old man was deep asleep, or frail and ill? How old must he be? He had seemed old then. His knuckles had barely touched the heavy wooden door when it opened a crack as if the occupant had been waiting beside it for just such a summons.

'Who be there on such a night?' asked a gruff voice and a lamp was thrust almost into Keir's face. A gasp of surprise and the door fell open. 'Is it indeed you, my Lord? Enter.'

'Thank you, friend, but first I must find shelter for my horse.'

'Wait,' came the order and the door was shut only to open almost immediately to reveal the oilskin-clad fisherman. 'Get in, lad, and throw a log on the fire. I'll attend to the nag,' and Lord Pittenmuir found himself thrust unceremoniously into the cottage. For a moment he leaned against the door, savouring the delight of being out of the rain. Then he pulled off his dripping greatcoat and hung it on a nail behind the door.

Unconscious of the track left by his boots, he crossed to the fireplace and tossed a log on the embers. He stirred them with the toe of his boot until small flames began to dance.

'Sit down, lad, and I'll fetch something to take the chill out of your bones, and you won't say no to a bowl of my stew.'

The voice behind him was so unexpected that Keir jumped. Damn it, what kind of spy was he to so easily let slip his guard. 'You yet move like a cat,' he said with a laugh that barely disguised his annoyance.

'Can't hear a thing against that wind,' said Charlie dispassionately.

Fifteen minutes later His Lordship waved away the offer of a third bowl. 'I must talk to you before I fall asleep on my feet.'

'You be safe here, m'Lord, you should know that.'

Keir looked at him for a moment in complete astonishment and then, as realization dawned, he laughed. 'Of course, it must look like that. Did you think me escaping from justice? Fie on you, was it not always Harry you said would grow up to evade the law?'

'I'm sorry about the lad.' For a moment they both stared at the fire seeing their own memories. 'He were a good boy. It was that rag-mannered little sister who caused mischief.'

Instantly Keir was twelve years old and ready to leap to Liddy's defence, but in time he remembered his business. 'Miss Lydia is somewhat changed, but enough of that. I need your help. I must find a reliable route to France.'

'I no longer have a boat, lad.'

'I thought not, but you know who does. Look, I must put all cards on the table. Some secrets are not mine and so I may not divulge them, but what I can tell, I will. I am here at the behest of the Prime Minister. There is disturbing rumour from France; it seems Napoleon is set to invade us.'

'Them fellows have been saying that for years, lad. Boney won't dare show his nose near these shores.'

'A French spy was known to be busy on the south coast, Charlie, but we lost him. I have been assigned to apprehend him ere he causes trouble. Maybe he is here. The colonel of the local militia sent reports of a young man who evaded questioning by his men and who seemed to disappear into thin air. Why would an honest man avoid the militia?'

'An hundred reasons: guilt, fear, sheer bravado.'

Keir nodded. 'Possibly. There is talk of the re-emergence of the "Arbroath Ladies". I think to join them. What cover for a spy, you agree?'

The old man stood up and stretched. 'You're all about in your head, lad, but I put that down to exhaustion. We'll talk after you have slept. Take my bed; it's not what you're used to, but will suffice tonight.'

There was no denying him and Keir was exhausted. He found himself swaying towards a truckle bed in the corner of the room. He wanted to ask Charlie where he was to sleep but the words deserted him. Instead he gave up the struggle and fell into a deep sleep from which he did not waken until the storm had blown itself out and a weak sun was invading the little room.

Of his host there was no sign, but bacon sizzled on the fire and he could smell coffee. He stood up and stretched, for the bed was considerably shorter than himself and it was fatigue rather than comfort that had kept him unconscious. He took stock of his surroundings and felt a pang of shame for the luxury that usually surrounded him. The main room in which he found himself contained a handmade table with a wooden chair beside it, a dresser on which reposed a few cheap dishes and some candlesticks, the bed on which he had slept and a more comfortable, but extremely shabby chair by the fire. No rugs lay on the floor and no pictures adorned the walls. It was as he remembered it – a plain house for a plain man. He went across to the curtain that divided the two rooms and looked in, but just as quickly dropped the curtain. The room, more an alcove, contained barrels that he was sure contained smuggled brandy.

'I was in the right,' he smiled. 'Charlie certainly knows at least one smuggler.'

He moved to pull on his boots which were by the fire and was touched to find the toes stuffed with paper. Charlie must have removed them as he slept and the realization brought home to him how naively he placed trust in those who had befriended him in boyhood.

'Awake, lad?' Charlie had entered, his arms full of brushwood that he threw into the bucket by the fire. 'Come on, wrap yourself round them rashers and we will talk.'

'I trust you slept as well as I did, Charlie,' said His Lordship sitting himself down at the table.

'Don't need much when you're my age.' Charlie replied as Keir lifted the bacon onto a platter, filled two mugs with scalding coffee, and carried all to the table.

'Your horse be fine; he's in a shed across the road. Not from your stables?'

'I bought him just north of the border. Grand staying power; better than he looks. My brother won't know him, if that worries you.' Lord Pittenmuir finished his bacon and pushed his plate aside. 'Have you considered my proposal?'

'You made no proposal, lad. You did talk nonsense about smugglers—'

He was interrupted.

'You could help me if you will. You used to be the most important man here. All looked to you for advice. Introduce me . . . please, as the son of an old friend, perhaps. I can disguise my voice. I have been at this game before. My own brother will not know me, Charlie.'

'Even if I do know some of these smugglers – which I have not said I do – would I set the local justice among them?'

'You know me better, Charlie. I give you my word I will lay no evidence against them. Methinks Mr Perceval will be grateful if they get me safe to France. Take me to their leader, I vow you know him, and let me speak for myself.'

Charlie stood up and walked over to the tiny window bending over to look out. 'I cannot, lad, for I know not where to find him.'

Lord Pittenmuir finished his coffee slowly. 'Will you help me? I feel sure that, though perhaps not a smuggler yourself, you know who they are.'

'Too old or too honest, lad?' His keen eyes raked His Lordship's face and he, to his chagrin, found himself flushing.

'I beg pardon, sir. I know you to be honest . . . I thought you too old.'

'You have not changed, lad, though you be a yard taller. I do know the gentlemen, all but the leader. Only John Reid knows him.' Lord Pittenmuir's eyes lifted from their contemplation of the coffee grains in his mug. 'You know John?' asked Charlie.

'I met him some months gone. He would know me as I am. How come that such a callow youth knows the leader of your band?'

'Never thought on't. It was John approached me about the smuggling. Said this Pate had heard o'me from some friend as preferred not to make hissel known. Asked me to get a gang together – fine sailors, and some farm boys, too. Pate does the organizing. Speaks the lingo like a frog.'

Keir was immediately alert. 'Is he from here? I do not recall a Pate among my tenants or Lord Balgowan's either.'

'Where he comes from, I know not. The boy knows and I doubt he be a tenant. He be a gentleman, lad.'

Keir stood up and took the place at the window Charlie had vacated. The leader of the smugglers is a gentleman who speaks French. Mayhap I have so easily stumbled on my spy.

'This gentleman of yours, Charlie, how long does he spend in France? Come man, be straight with me; you are one of them, are you not?'

'Aye, lad. But it is Euan Pate who is the brain. I will tell you no more m'Lord, until I have spoken with him.'

Keir laid a restraining hand on the old man's arm. 'Charlie, your smugglers are safe from me. I will do nothing, if you aid me to entrap them, but a French spy is another matter. I cannot, will not, turn a blind eye. Tell me of Pate. Does he leave the boat long? What contacts does he make? Is yours a French ship, Charlie, and with a French captain?'

'You're on the wrong track. It ain't easy to catch a spy. Young Pate never boards at all, never mind get off in France to spread sedition.'

'Damn. It seemed so perfect.'

'Nothing is in this life, lad.'

'Very well. I confess I retain hopes of your Pate, but you can tell him that you need another hand or someone good with pistols. I care not. I must get to France, and whatever this sprig of the nobility is, he too is safe if all he has in train is a little honest smuggling.'

'He had me bring a gown, would you believe, and some soap and notepaper.'

'Damned unusual spy, but if he is buying a lady's affection with goods from France he has my sympathy. Will you help me? And not a word to the boy.'

At last Charlie agreed, but reluctantly. 'You have an air that can't be hid, lad.'

'Chop off my hair without regard for style, some soot, and I swear I will not know myself.'

With his hair cut in a ragged line, Pittenmuir did look somewhat different. He affected a slouch and to Charlie's surprise, the beautifully modulated voice was gone.

'I doubt me Master Jamie would recognize his brother in that shirt.'

Keir swept him a bow that destroyed the effect. I thank you, sir,' he said in his own voice. 'Now, look your last on Keir Galloway. Have you a relative who would lend me his name?'

'Nay. I've lived here too long to suddenly sport some kin. You are the son of an old friend, down on his luck and wishful to make a copper or two.'

'Tut, tut, Charlie, nothing illegal – except smuggling. As a child I found the thought vastly exciting.'

'You'll feel different with a man o' war breathing down your neck. Come, your name, for we meet tomorrow.'

His Lordship considered. 'Ian. It's common enough, and Scott, for that's what I am, whatever anyone else thinks,' he finished somewhat enigmatically.

Seven

Miss Carpenter was well pleased. Sometimes, she felt like a juggling man at a country fair; a ball in each hand and yet two more in the air, but, all in all, intuition told her that she had her affairs under some vestige of control. She had persuaded her papa not to inspect the castle and since he was none too anxious to spend money on such low priorities as restoring the home of his ancestors, this had not been too difficult. On the pretext that she wished her bedchamber to undergo transformation, she had installed herself in an ancient apartment a considerable climb from Madame's rooms, but possessed of a spiral stair leading to an outside door. Why she had not removed there when she began her adventures, she was at a loss to comprehend.

The key of the outside door now reposed in the pocket of Miss Carpenter's gown. She could feel it bumping against her leg as she walked across the drawing room floor to pour tea for Mrs Johnstone-Carruthers and she smiled, which caused her guest to look at her in the strangest way for had she not just remarked that the news from the Peninsula was no better.

'Mrs Johnstone-Carruthers,' interrupted Charlotte, 'have you discovered this modiste in Arbroath? She is *naturellement*, a French émigrée.'

Fashion was a topic guaranteed to keep the conversation flying across the room from dowager to debutante.

'Liddy,' hissed Charlotte, 'you are not hearing a word your guests are saying. Did you not see the look of surprise on Mrs Johnstone-Carruthers' face when you smiled at the idea of bad news? Why did you smile, dearest, for I know you were not attending? In truth, since Papa is returned I find myself smiling at odd moments, too.'

Liddy, however, was not smiling at the thought of her papa. The active part of her powerful mind was firmly fixed on her 'other' life.

Since her father's return, she had tried virtuously to be 'daughter of the house'. She had fallen in with all her father's suggestions, and had dutifully arranged several gatherings to reintroduce her papa to the society he had quite easily dismissed from his mind. Thanks to the position of her new bedchamber she was now able to slip out and to return unseen, and Liddy had reflected upon her decision to call a halt to their activities, but realized that by blowing life into the once defunct lady smugglers, she had kindled a fire which would not easily be put out. The men were in deadly earnest and had made it clear that, with or without Euan Pate, they intended to continue their lucrative business. Since this was so, Liddy had decided that it was better to have some control over their activities and, God help her, she felt some responsibility for her smugglers. She would stay with the band she had created until such time as she could hit upon a viable reason for them to disperse. No brilliant idea had yet occurred and since she had organized another most successful trip to France, she was even farther from the straight and narrow precepts in which she had been reared. How long would their luck last? Rumour of their existence must have reached the authorities since almost everyone in the area was involved in one way or another. The tidewaiters would be on the lookout for them, and perhaps the military.

Her senior guest chastised her at the same moment as she heard Charlotte's frantic whisper.

'Miss Carpenter. My dear, I do believe you have scarcely heard a word.'

Thus, both rudely and gently brought back to the present reality, Liddy flushed angrily and apologized.

'Do you know,' Mrs Johnstone-Carruthers went on coyly, 'I have found that there is only one reason for a young woman to be distracted. Perhaps we will soon be reading an interesting announcement, my Lord?'

His Lordship raised his glass and surveyed his guest as if she were something nasty discovered under a stone. 'An announcement, Ma'am,' he said putting down the glass. 'Why, yes, although I had not thought to formally announce my family's removal to town.'

'Not immediately, I hope, my Lord,' broke in Mrs Wallace in an attempt to cover the awkward moment. 'We are all delighted to have you with us again.'

Liddy smiled at her. 'Papa expects to be in London for the next season, Mrs Wallace. There are matters here that require his attention in the meantime.'

'How can you say so, my dear,' smiled Lord Balgowan. He turned to Mrs Wallace. 'My daughter is so worthy an executant that I could almost wish she were a boy and able to inherit.'

Liddy turned away to hide the quick tears. Her father was pretending to tease but she could feel the anger behind his words; anger that his son was dead and he left with a parcel of useless women.

'Miss Carpenter,' said the Honourable Jamie who was sitting on a window seat near Charlotte, 'has all our admiration, sir, but we would not wish her to be anything other than her lovely self.'

Liddy started in surprise and quite forgot to smile her thanks. He was more like his brother than she had supposed. He shone better when out of the light of the sun that was Lord Pittenmuir.

She did look to see if Charlotte had appreciated the interchange but that young lady was hanging on the words of Mister Wallace. 'Silly child,' thought her sister. 'She hurts Jamie and young John both by her actions.'

She fretted through the rest of the tea party and was glad when the last carriage rolled away. She went to her room ostensibly to rest before dressing for dinner, but she did not rest. She paced up and down, thinking. To go to London would perhaps be the easy way out. She must talk to Papa about hiring John and the rest could take their own chances. This decision lasted until she opened a new bar of soap. Old Charlie had brought it to her, believing it was a gift for a ladylove.

'Were the sweetest smelling I could find. I hope she thanks you.'

No, she could not abandon Charlie.

She wore the blue dress her father had brought her and asked Madame to take special trouble with her hair. She would never be so beautiful as Charlotte and might possess too masculine a brain, but she would contrive to please her papa.

'This room is not right for you,' scolded Madame as she fussed over her young mistress. 'Dare I suggest your late mama's rooms till these tedious decorators be finished.'

'I do well enough here, thank you, Madame.'

'If Miss Carpenter wishes always to wash in lukewarm water.'

Cold water is a small price to pay for privacy, Liddy commented to herself.

Dinner was not too distressing. General Fairweather had been invited and so Liddy was not thrown too much into her father's company. She seemed never to please him and it was obvious that he found small doses of the company of his youngest daughters barely palatable, but thankfully appeared to be quite *bouleversé* over Charlotte.

'And how does Miss Fairweather, sir?' asked Liddy politely.

'Naughty puss insisted on returning to town. I had hoped she'd spend a month or two here, but now that Pittenmuir is returned . . .' He shrugged and smiled complacently.

'Are we to expect an announcement?' asked Lord Balgowan.

'Not yet. Didn't even know she had a tendre for him till that party of his. What he thinks is anyone's guess and from what I hear every matchmaking mama in London has her guns trained on him.'

Liddy rose abruptly and led her sister from the room leaving the gentlemen to their port.

'Such clever questions Papa asked the general,' said Charlotte into the silence. 'In fact I was amazed he could bear to discuss the war.'

'Perhaps he was being diplomatic since the general has no other conversation except his man-hungry granddaughter.'

'Liddy,' interposed Rattles gently. 'Perhaps His Lordship asked about the war because of Harry. Had my son died in action I should want to know all about the progress of the conflict.'

Liddy stood up and walked across to the fireplace where a small fire burned. She shivered. Keir and Leonora Fairweather. Surely not. Surely he could see how shallow she was, or perhaps all he saw was Miss Fairweather – too much of her – if that last dress she had been wearing was typical of her wardrobe. 'These days of rain have quite taken away our summer.'

Miss Rattray frowned and then smiled. 'I had forgotten until you mentioned the weather, Liddy. The general did have a second topic – smugglers.'

'Yes, Liddy, what do you think,' asked Charlotte. 'Are there smugglers?'

'Had you paid attention to my lessons, dear Charlotte, you

would know that there have always been smugglers on this coast. To engage in smuggling was almost acceptable.'

'That was history, Rattles, this is now and vastly exciting. I shall scour the estuary for sightings and shall inform the tidewaiters.'

'Tidewaiters, Charlotte?' Lord Balgowan and General Fairweather had come in. 'Smugglers are not romantic, Miss Charlotte, but cut-throat scum to be exterminated,' went on the General seating himself by the fire. 'As if we had not enough to concern us with Napoleon.'

'Come, General,' said Lord Balgowan. 'Have we not agreed that our defences in this area are such that the upstart will not dare invade?'

'There are miles of unprotected coast where an army could land and us not the whit the wiser till we woke up looking down the muzzle of a French bayonet.'

'Say you not so, General,' begged Charlotte clasping her hands to her throat.

'Do not fret, Charlotte. You may watch for French militiamen instead of smugglers and warn us all.'

The general and her father looked at Miss Carpenter. It was obvious that both found Liddy's humour unfeminine. 'Your sister's fears do her credit, Miss. Indeed am I to suppose you are ready to fight on the beach?' thundered His Lordship.

'Possibly a useful attitude to adopt in the circumstances. If you will forgive me, Papa, General, I will retire.'

She curtseyed and was gone. With militant heart she climbed to her room. No use to try to co-exist with Papa. Neither found anything to admire in the other.

Her windows told her that the night was dark and wild; fit to match her mood. She would not wait tonight. She would dress and go now while this mood was upon her. With strangely steady hands she unlocked the door that led to the outside and retrieved her breeches. One day I shall cut my hair, she thought as she pulled a brush through Madame's creation. She hung her gown in the fitted wardrobe and took out a nightdress intending to hide it so that anyone visiting her chamber would assume that she was elsewhere in the house.

The latch on the door was raised. 'Miss Carpenter?'

'One moment, Madame,' said Liddy calmly as she stuffed Harry's clothes under the bed. Then she opened the door.

'Why, Miss Lydia, you are wearing nothing but your shift and will catch your death. His Lordship was concerned and bade me help you. Here, slip into this charming dressing gown.' She offered Liddy a dashing confection embroidered all over in forget-me-nots. 'Such feminine fripperies suit you, miss. Indeed they become you. One does not have to look like Miss Charlotte to wear pretty things.'

'Were my gowns embroidered like this, Madame, I should look like a maypole.'

'The gentlemen love femininity. Your papa would approve of this gown. Here, let me brush your hair.'

'Pray don't, Madame. I have a headache.'

'As you wish, but if I may advise, Miss Liddy, gentlemen have no time for ladies who are constantly unwell. I will summon a physician before you remove to town since you must be well enough to enjoy your season. Dances and picnics and routs every day. What fun.'

Realizing that the abigail had her best interests at heart Liddy softened. 'I promise to be well, Madame, but now I will sleep.'

Liddy listened until the sound of her footfalls had quite died away and then leapt from the bed. She pulled on the breeches and shirt over her shift, and sat down to tie her cravat, a tongue biting exercise that was becoming easier. She tied her hair back ruthlessly – no sign of the headache now. The coat slipped on easily and then, in stockinged feet, she slipped out of the tower and locked the door behind her. She fled down the staircase, found her chapeau bras, her greatcoat, and her boots and then Euan Pate slipped outside.

Keeping close to the walls she hurried to the stables. The house was ablaze but there were no lights in the stables. Tom must have retired as soon as the General's coach was ordered. Thankfully, Lord Balgowan's groom and coachmen were housed in the big house, the stable accommodation being too poor for them. No need to take risks. The groom was conscientious and checked his animals at night. Only the horses moved and sighed in the darkness and soon Amber was ready. Once they reached the grass verge Liddy coaxed her into a canter.

There was little visibility and she found the castle more by luck than navigation.

A shadow slipped out of the gloom. 'That you, Pate?'

Liddy breathed deeply to steady her wildly beating heart. 'Aye. What brings you early, Charlie?'

'I want to ask a favour of you. Got the son of an old chum with me, down on his luck, but a good sailor and an excellent shot, should the need ever arise. I can vouch for the boy. We've had the devil's luck so far but how long can it last?'

'I pray you're wrong, Charlie, and as to hiring, that's for the vote.' Liddy hoped the others would reject the new recruit. One more man on the wrong side of the law was not a good idea.

When the others arrived Liddy got her first look at the would-be smuggler, a rough-looking, unshaven fellow of more than average height. He would have appeared to better advantage had he looked the world in the eye, as any friend of Charlie should have been able to do. She did not like him at all.

'Give 'un a chance, yer worship,' he coaxed in a most unpleasant guttural voice. He was down on his luck and Liddy wanted to be Christian but oh, how she despised people who said 'yer worship' in just that toadying way.

Charlie argued for the value of his friend and none objected – bar Tam.

'One man more means less for us.'

'The weather be changing like Charlie says,' said one, 'and like we'll need good sailors.'

'And he knows his way around a pistol.'

Tam stood up. He was a burly man, feared by the others, and he swaggered around Scott who sat on a barrel, looking at the ground as if this were naught to do with him. 'Guns. It's hand to hand we mun' think on. How good are ye with yer fists, mate?'

His answer exploded off the barrel, taking him by surprise and he fell to the ground, his assailant on top of him. For a moment or two they rolled around like two large cats, but then Tam, with a prodigious heave, threw off his attacker and scrambled to his feet. Before Scott could follow, Tam sought to punish him by aiming a kick straight at the downed man's face. A sixth sense must have warned him, for he managed to twist so that the blow, aimed for his eyes, glanced across his cheek. Blood was pouring from his face as he pulled himself up and launched himself into the fray. Liddy felt sick and tried not to look away since John and all the others were forming an excited ring around the antagonists.

The fight ended as quickly as it had begun. Massive damaging punches were thrown – no Marquis of Queensberry rules either and still less science – and each man giving as good as he got, until suddenly, Scott darted away, picked up a stick and brought it down as hard as he could on Tam's head. Tam crumpled in a heap.

'My, but you're a grand dirty fighter, lad,' yelled Charlie. 'He's in, lads. Anyone who beats Tam in a fair fight is worth hiring.'

For the first time in her smuggling career, Liddy held out her mug for a tot of brandy. The men welcomed their new comrade. Brandy went round, and round again. Even Tam, when he came to, appeared to harbour no ill will but shook hands with Scott and threw his great arms around his shoulders as if they were brothers.

'No doubt he would have ended the contest in just such a way,' thought Liddy in disgust.

She would have been displeased to know that Scott was trying to get his good eye to focus on her. He had been surprised at the extreme youth of the smugglers' leader and had racked his brains to uncover who Mr Pate was. Apart from Jamie there were no sprigs of nobility in this area and the lad was of gentle blood. He reminded Keir of someone.

He sat quietly and listened to Pate outlining their next trip. He realized that he was under scrutiny from young John, so he schooled his face to show nothing as the boy rose and approached.

'More brandy . . . Ian?'

Keir scowled as he rejected the offer, his voice even gruffer and less refined than before. The boy hesitated for a second, looking down at him, and Keir thanked God for the dim light. Then he turned away but he was, Keir knew, suspicious and frightened. Keir could smell the fear, but why was the boy afraid? He has seen me but once and he was in distress. He cannot know me. To dispel any lingering doubts he spat vigorously on the floor. Not the action of a gentleman.

A hush had fallen over the gathering. Keir looked around and saw that all were looking at Pate who appeared somewhat disconcerted. Now what had been said that he missed?

'There's no need.' It was John who spoke.

'Especially now you have a new recruit, Tam,' laughed Pate.

'Come on, you can't have it both ways – and besides, it would be damned inconvenient for me to be from home this week.'

Keir listened eagerly. He knew that voice, damned if he did not. A puzzle but he would find the thread and unravel the conundrum. It was obvious that Pate never sailed with his men and this did not sit well. Mayhap he had a delicate stomach, or required parental permission to be from home. He believed the lad was not afraid. There was something about the set of that young chin. He wished he could see the eyes in the shadows. Eyes told so much.

'We are agreed then. The *Shuska* leaves tomorrow at first tide. Her papers are in order. She is bound for Denmark but will, however, make a slight detour. Upon your return – and I look for you in six days – look for a light among the Balmossie trees. There's a well-known burial mound there. Head straight for it and you will find the sweetest landing place. The tidesmen would give much to know of it. A track leads direct from the beach to the trees and thence here.'

'I thought this to become unsafe,' argued Tam.

There was hesitation so slight it passed almost unnoticed. 'I am told His Lordship gives no orders for restoration and this is easily the best place.'

'Who be staying as land smugglers?' broke in Charlie thus avoiding more awkward questions.

The land smugglers, that is 'the ladies' who would meet the *Shuska* with ponies, were decided upon and the meeting broke up. For differing reasons Euan Pate and Ian Scott wished to have words with John but he had melted away before either could apprehend him.

Liddy waited until she was alone and then doused the lamp and slipped out of the castle. Her nerves tonight were stretched to breaking point and she wished herself done with subterfuge. To console herself she owned that at two o'clock on a rainy morning, even the most intrepid spirit might feel low.

Amber was where she had left her, calmly grazing, and her warm whinny cheered her mistress. A twig cracked and Liddy's heart seemed to stop beating, and then, as if to make up, began to beat faster than ever. The pony was unconcerned though and Liddy whispered, 'All is well, old lady,' to reassure herself.

The moon was too shy to show herself and the night was thus very dark. Were one of a nervous disposition one might imagine menace hidden behind every bush. Liddy forced herself to keep to a trot as it would be easy to stumble on such a night. How silent it was. Madame was forever bemoaning the silence of the countryside but Liddy, who had never lived anywhere else, knew that the night was usually loud with calls. Tonight even the birds seemed asleep. Just then the imperturbable Amber put forward her ears at a flutter of white seen on a gorse bush and shied violently. Liddy gave a most unmasculine sob of pure fright, and pony and mistress stood trembling, peering into the darkness. Amber was ashamed of herself and recovered almost immediately and, anxious to make amends, set off again.

Never had Liddy been so glad to see the bulk of her home rearing up before her. All was quiet; no lights gleamed through the gloom and so Liddy rode direct to the stable door. She was not completely lost to caution, however, and quietly opened the door and closed it again behind her. Some straw served to rub Amber down, and after giving her some oats, Liddy left the stable and went to put away the saddle in the tackroom.

She had just put her hand to the latch to let herself out of the room, when a sibilant whisper startled her almost clean out of her wits. The whisper had not been for her, but who else was in the grounds at this hour? She dared not open the door. She put her ear to a crack and listened. There it was again . . . Dare she risk opening the door to both see and hear? The moon refused to shine bright enough to enable Liddy to discern much even when she'd persuaded herself to slowly inch the door open.

'Calmly, Liddy.' She risked another look. Nothing. She listened, every nerve quivering. Someone was just outside. She could hear breathing. Petrified, she held her breath. Was it a housebreaker? A homeless gypsy? Cautiously she crept backwards and thanked old Tom for being so tidy a worker and there was nought to catch her unawares. The man reached the door. Liddy flattened herself against the wall and, to her shame, closed her eyes.

There came a muffled laugh. 'It's only a door left unlocked.' The unmistakable sound of a key being turned and Miss Carpenter was locked inside the tackroom.

For a moment she remained quiet. This had been no ordinary housebreaker, and had she not recognized that voice? There were few fluent speakers of the French tongue around Balgowan. It must be Etienne. One problem solved. Now to escape. Rouse old Tom and risk explanations or set her faith in Rattles discovering that she had not returned. There was a loft and there must be a window. Liddy crept to the door and listened but heard nothing but the gentle shuffling of the horses. Etienne had assuredly returned to the house. The stair. Where was it? Somewhere beyond the door. Liddy edged her way across the floor, wishing she had a lantern, wishing she was having a bad dream from which she would wake soon. She was so physically exhausted that she felt her mind was not working too well. At last she felt the rough wood of the ladder that led to the loft. In breeches it was easy to scramble up to that forbidden but magical place where she had played with Harry and Keir, all those years ago.

The windows, grimy and festooned with cobwebs, would have revolted the least conscientious of housewives but, after some application of pressure, one opened. Liddy poked her head through. How far away the ground looked and the distance was all distorted in the dark. A rope, she must find a rope and lower herself down. The servants would soon be stirring and Madame would find her gone and would alert Papa. It was not to be borne. She must lower herself out and . . . drop.

'Don't Liddy,' came a loved voice. 'I have the key.'

Rattles, oh faithful Rattles.

Fifteen minutes later she was sitting up in bed with her hands warming themselves on a mug of hot chocolate.

'Now I will tell you all, Liddy, and then we will both sleep. I have waited for you each time you have been out and tonight I saw you return and went to the schoolroom to warm some milk, but you did not come. I went to your former apartment and it was empty. Then I went to the kitchen to see if you had returned the stable key and . . . who do you think I saw?'

'Etienne.'

'Ah, he surprised you, did he? But Liddy, why was Monsieur outside at this hour and if it was simply that he heard a noise and went to investigate—'

'Why did he wait to pull on all his clothes?'

'Exactly. All is not well,' said Miss Rattray and moved to catch the mug before it fell to the floor. Lydia was fast asleep.

Eight

Miss Lydia Carpenter woke very late on the day after her adventure in the stables. She stretched like a healthy young cat, and then sat up very quickly as the memories of the previous evening rushed in upon her.

She had been too exhausted to assimilate the whole, but her mind was now clear. Only Papa and Etienne spoke French. To whom, therefore, had Etienne been speaking? Nonsensical to think Lord Balgowan had been sneaking into his own home.

Also, her new smuggling recruit disturbed her; she knew not why. He was uncouth, but so were the others. She disliked grown men who shuffled their feet and mentally pulled their forelocks, but this was hardly kind since she had no right to judge what his life was like that it had made him so subservient. Also, that insufferable stoop . . . She remembered another tall man who carried himself proudly, whose blue eyes did not refuse to look at one. She laughed. To think an oafish smuggler should make her think of Keir. But, the boy Keir had grown into the intolerable Lord Pittenmuir who liked empty-headed women like Leonora Fairweather.

Fifteen minutes later, charmingly if somewhat unfashionably attired in a pale blue round-necked gown of soft wool, she descended to the kitchens where she found Mrs Harper surrounded by enticing smells, and steam.

'I'm sorry, Miss Liddy, but jam don't wait. Gin I boil these plums a minute too long, it'll be that thick we'll have to cut it with a knife.'

'Smells wonderful,' said Liddy fetching down a teapot to the kettle that was always on the boil.

'You may taste the first of my jam,' began Mrs Harper and then added in scandalized tones, 'Miss Lydia, you are throwing tea in that pot as if it grew wild in the garden.'

Since Miss Carpenter had smuggled the tea herself she felt she could be as profligate as she chose, but obligingly she returned one teaspoon to the caddy. As a reward she was given the first spoonful of the delicious jam and immediately she saw herself, Harry, and Keir picking the fruits, eating as many as they put in their pails, their skin burned brown with the sun so that Keir's eyes looked like two deep, blue pools. Another memory tugged but she pushed it away.

'Mrs Harper, did you hear anything last night?' she asked idly. 'I came down for hot milk and fancied I heard someone outside.'

'Funny you should ask, Miss Liddy. Wasn't last night, but a few nights ago I was sure I heard something, some muffled talk. I musta been dreaming for the words didn't make no sense.'

Liddy nibbled her bread for a moment. 'If you did not understand, Mrs Harper, perhaps the language was not English.'

The housekeeper turned away from her boiling jam. 'That's it o'course. Miss Lydia, you have fair relieved my mind. You see, my granny went like that, hearing voices and answering them, too.'

'You are far from your dotage. Now look to your preserves and I shall find my sister.'

Charlotte was in the music room. She jumped to her feet. 'Dearest. I have been so worried. Let us send for a physician.'

For a moment Liddy was at a loss and then she remembered her non-existent headache. 'Silly, I am quite recovered.'

'But you are pale and tired still.'

'Caused merely by lack of fresh air. Since Papa's return we seem to have done nothing but entertain. Do let us walk in the gardens.'

Charlotte agreed and soon the young ladies were strolling beside beds that were no longer at their best.

'Papa says we will remove to town, Liddy, as soon as his business here is ended. Will it not be fun to be presented and to attend parties and balls?'

Readily Liddy assented and allowed her sister to rattle on about breakfast parties and tea dances and new gowns, but her own mind was flying. What business kept her father in Balgowan? He had ridden but once round the estate and had put no improvements in train. And to talk of debuts and parties! The expense did not bear thinking of and it was unfair of him to promise Charlotte what he could not afford.

'Liddy, I declare you have not heard a word.' Charlotte had stopped in the path and was regarding her sister in some annoyance.

Liddy was spared answering by the arrival of their father who dismounted from a splendid hunter upon seeing his two elder daughters.

'Behold the two fairest flowers in my gardens.'

'There are no flowers at this season, sir,' said the practical Lydia.

'Dearest Papa, how very French you are,' said Charlotte and won a kiss.

'Do you not ride, girls?'

'Apart from your own horses, sir, there is only one suitable horse in the stables,' explained Liddy.

'Hmm . . .' said His Lordship frowning. 'There is much at fault in your management of the stables, Lydia. The fabric of the buildings: doors, windows, bolts . . . they are all insecure.'

How unfair. A sob rose up from the very depths of her soul and she suppressed it. She had tried so hard, scrimping here and saving there.

'Repairs have been needed for some time, sir—'

She was not allowed to finish. 'Enough. Young ladies should have other matters to discuss. For example – Almacks. Is that not a more convenable topic, Charlotte? I vow you know nothing of rotting woodwork.'

Liddy felt both hurt and angry. Her papa had invited her opinion and when she ventured to give it had hushed her.

Charlotte, usually so gentle, leapt to her defence. 'That is unkind of you, Papa. You know that my sister has worked endlessly to preserve the estate. How can you scold her?'

'Forgive me, Liddy,' coaxed her papa at his most endearing. 'You must know that I harbour unbearable feelings of guilt when I think of how you have struggled to hold these worthless acres together just because I, your father, who should have taken the burden from your shoulders, could not bear to remain here after the death of my beloved son. I have returned, girls, but such monies as I have that this iniquitous tax system does not wrest from me, I wish to spend on my girls, not on Balgowan. You cannot inherit, Liddy, and so we will go, lock the doors behind us, and leave the place to rot.'

Charlotte was weeping. 'We understand, Papa, do we not, Liddy? To remain here with memories of dearest Harry must be nigh unbearable.'

Liddy tried, but one part of her clear logical mind reminded her that Lord Balgowan had left his Scottish seat years before his son was killed.

Charlotte smiled through her tears. 'It will be lovely to be all together again, Papa, will it not, Liddy? Shall we live in town all year? I have heard that people of our sort live there only part of the year.'

'No more questions, my love. I have business that forces me to remain in Scotland, but then, dear daughters, we shall decide where we choose to live. Liddy –' he held her shoulders and gently kissed her forehead – 'I will be gone for a day or two and so, once more I leave all in your capable hands. Soon you will live as the daughters of Balgowan should.'

He left the girls to their stroll while he repaired to the stable.

'I wish he would stay here for ever, Liddy. It is more fun with Papa in residence, is it not?'

Liddy answered innocuously. She fought her tears but had to turn away from her sister as they walked the path.

'You are unhappy, dearest. You prefer to remain here, sister? Is that it?'

Liddy smiled, a real, warm smile. 'What a kind and loving heart you have. It's merely that I assumed we would return here as others do. But I see that Papa hates it and I . . . I could not live happily anywhere else.'

Charlotte slipped her arm through her sister's. 'Silly, when you are the belle of the ball you will forget Balgowan.'

Liddy knew that when Charlotte graced a room there could be only one belle but she knew Charlotte was trying to cheer her. 'Shall we be gay to dissipation, Charlotte? Will royal princes vie for our favour?'

'How disagreeable that would be. They are all of them appallingly fat.'

Liddy giggled at the picture and she and Charlotte were happy again.

They returned to the house in time to meet Rattles who had just dismissed the babes to their nursemaid. Charlotte returned to the music room, whilst Liddy and Miss Rattray decided to brew themselves some tea in the nursery and were soon seated together on the old sofa.

'You look worried, my dear. Tell me how I can help.'

Liddy looked into the warm brown eyes of her former governess and she was twelve years old again and able to share her burden with the one person who had never deserted her.

'Last night, those Frenchmen, did you recognize the voices?'

'I did not really hear them, only the murmur of voices, and then seeing Etienne fully dressed so late . . . I cannot swear. What do you fear?'

'You must know, Rattles, that the war in Europe is at a crucial stage; invasion is a real threat. Would a spy find anything to interest Napoleon's generals in this little community of a few farmers, a few fishermen?'

Rattles said nothing but her former pupil knew that her considerable intellect would be put to the problem. 'If our navy keeps the south coast safe then, no doubt, Napoleon would look for an easier landing place. This coast is a goldmine of sheltered anchorages. He might also wish to know the strengths of the garrisons; there are Royal Marines at Arbroath and Dundee. A spy would earn his pay, Liddy.'

They looked at one another aghast and each was afraid of the truth in what they were thinking.

'I should say nothing to His Lordship of your concerns, Liddy.' Miss Rattray spoke in measured tones but Liddy did not pretend to misunderstand.

'Papa is to be from home – a matter of business. We must keep watch, two women, like the amazons of old.'

'You might consult Lord Pittenmuir,' ventured Rattles.

Three years ago, two even, she would have hurried to share her burden with him. 'He is from home,' was all she said.

'Master Jamie might have word of his return. He *is* Lord Lieutenant, Liddy,' she added tentatively.

Liddy did not flare up. 'Naturally, should we suspect that a French spy is operating within His Lordship's jurisdiction we are in honour bound to apprise His Lordship.'

'Exactly. It is our duty.'

Miss Rattray accompanied Liddy back to her room to change into her riding habit, a severely masculine garment that suited her tall slenderness admirably.

'What are the fashions now for riding in the London parks, Rattles? This is old but I like to wear it.' Mention of London brought another worry to mind. 'Rattles, do you accompany us to London? I feel sure that Papa does not intend to remain there long.'

'His Lordship will, no doubt, remain until he has seen you and dear Charlotte creditably situated.'

Her usually undemonstrative former pupil bestowed a warm hug upon her. 'You have relieved my mind for, although Charlotte will take, I am such a longshanks that I will soon repose upon the dustiest shelf in London, and a relieved Papa can send me back to Balgowan. Shall you return with me, dear friend?'

She expected no answer; there were the babes to consider. Instead Liddy took herself off to the stable where Tom saddled Amber, grumbling all the time that there was no groom to ride with her.

'I am but calling at Pittenmuir, Tom. I need no escort on such a mission.'

''Taint fittin', Miss Liddy. You ought to have a maid at least, or even John . . . If that lad wants to be kept on he'd best be more regular. His Lordship was here looking at locks an' all, meaning to put things in order, I reckon.'

Liddy cantered off to the Pittenmuir home slowly enough to observe how trim were the hedges and neat the cottages. The tone was of wealth and sound management.

The Honourable Jamie was at home and expressed himself delighted to have a visit from at least one of the Carpenters.

'M'brother's in town, Liddy, and I have no notion when he will return, but his secretary is arrived and must have knowledge of him. Do come in and we will tackle him together.'

Liddy had never before refined too much on the customs prevailing in society, but at the mention of Major Fordyce she realized that it was not done for a gently reared young woman to be calling on two bachelors. 'Perhaps if I take a stroll in the gardens, Jamie, the major might join me there.' It was the best compromise in the circumstances.

She had not long to walk along well-tended paths. Major Fordyce hurried out to meet her. 'If your business with His Lordship is urgent, Miss, I have an address where he can be reached but only, forgive me, if the matter is vital.'

Liddy looked at him carefully, assessing both the major and the situation. 'Pray do not laugh, Major, but I very much fear that a French spy may be operating in this area.'

Major Fordyce did not laugh; he more near choked.

'Good gracious, Miss Carpenter,' he said when he had heard the whole, 'I will apprise His Lordship of your suspicions upon the instant. You are right to tell the Lord Lieutenant.'

'Pity the Lord Lieutenant spends so little time in the county, Major. You will tell him how devastated we are to tear him from the capital's attractions.'

Liddy was furious with herself. She had allowed her heart once more to rule her head, and more importantly, her tongue. Hardly the secretary's fault that his master put his pleasure before his duty. 'Please to forgive me, Major. I have no right to censure His Lordship. We used to be friends.'

Miss Carpenter rode home, her heart troubled. If the spy existed, was he close to her family; so close in fact as to be one of them? If so, what had she done to her family's future by alerting Pittenmuir?

'If the spy is apprehended before he has done any damage, there can be no harm done.' She wept a little for her lost dreams of a Stewart revival. The Jacobite story was past. Invasion by a foreign power was now a frightening reality and not to be supported in any way. She would watch Etienne . . . and everyone else very carefully.

The difficulty was the necessity of being in two places at the one time but Rattles was an admirable ally and promised to keep Monsieur Etienne in sight at all times. She did not foresee that the very Gallic Frenchman would read a completely different interpretation into her interest and she was compelled to slap him soundly by way of repelling his advances. Her erstwhile pupil's hilarity in no way mended her bruised feelings.

While her smugglers were on the high seas Liddy was free to devote herself to her father. 'You spoke of being from home on business, Papa. I had thought you meant to leave us immediately upon that announcement.'

'Matters too weighty for the intelligence of a young lady, my dear Liddy,' said His Lordship somewhat ponderously, 'cause me to remain here somewhat longer than I had anticipated.'

Since Liddy knew that he would be drawn no further, she

abandoned her attempts to uncover his concerns by fair means and resolved to discover them by foul, if necessary. Her perambulations had taken her to the library where she hoped to refresh her memory regarding her French relations. None of them had she met but, before the deaths of her Jacobite Grandpère and her French mama, they had been spoken of often, and with affection. It would really be too bad if the wrong ones had perished in the Terror leaving Lord Balgowan, as Harry's heir, next in line for property not confiscated. The family bible had not been updated; even Harry's too early death was not recorded.

Lord Balgowan joined the ladies in the drawing room very shortly after dinner and to Liddy's surprise, was still there when the tea tray was brought in. He played chess with Miss Rattray, saying that of all the ladies her intellect most matched his own. Liddy, however, knew that Rattles had allowed him to win and determined to scold her later.

Were they to stay abroad all night? Charlotte excused herself and an hour later Rattles too bid them goodnight. Still Liddy sat, vowing to grow roots if need be.

Such a sacrifice was found to be unnecessary, Lord Balgowan announcing – at one o'clock in the morning – that he could scarce keep his eyes open and wondering that his dear child should not have sought her rest long since.

'So late? Already?' Liddy feigned surprise. 'I can only blame your most scholarly interpretation of events in Europe, Sir, and can only thank you for an enlightening evening.'

Did His Lordship preen himself a little at her empty, affected words of praise? Liddy heard herself speak so to the man who was her father and felt bitterly sad for the days and the feelings that were gone. She kissed him dutifully and, candle in hand, walked before him into the hall.

'I cannot like your remaining so far from your sister, Liddy,' he said as she turned towards the door that led to her isolated quarters. I have quite forgot why a move seemed expedient.'

Liddy's heart beat faster. She could not return to the central wing. 'Decorators, Papa. I am to change my furnishings.'

'If you are still of like mind, order it done. Should anyone break into your tower, I would not hear and I cannot but worry.'

Liddy warmed to the note of sincerity in his voice and she

kissed his cheek. 'I am in no danger, Papa. Indeed, my tower could withstand a siege.'

'I trust it will not have to. To bed.'

Dutifully Liddy retired but not to sleep. Wrapped in her cloak she crept down to the door. Cautiously she drew back the bolts. Outside all was dark and still. For some time she stood listening, half fearing that Lord Balgowan or Etienne, the groom, were waiting for her. Nothing moved and a very cold and cramped young girl eventually succumbed to fatigue and returned to her room.

Nine

On the morning of his first excursion as a smuggler, Lord Pittenmuir found himself awake at an early hour. There were several contributing factors, but the main one being the difficulty of stretching out his full length on Charlie's bed. He would say nothing, of course, since his rest had still to be superior to that enjoyed by his host. They must come to a more sensible arrangement.

He found Charlie curled up in the chair by the fire. 'Awake, lad?' he asked. 'I'll soon have some tea on the boil.' He peered at his noble guest and laughed. 'You look a right mess. I challenge your own brother to know you.'

Keir smiled ruefully and inspected his face in the cracked and spotted shaving glass. Even allowing for the glass's distortion, he was unrecognizable. His left eye was closed and that side of his face bruised and swollen.

'As well I'm not vain, Charlie, but there was one there who might have recognized me.'

'John Reid?' Charlie laughed. 'You're never seeing him as a French spy.'

'No, but perhaps the dupe of one.'

They finished their breakfast in contemplative silence. The wind had abated and there was a steady rain falling.

'Grand day for our enterprise,' said Charlie as if he could read Keir's thoughts.

Keir stood up. 'I'll walk a little in the village. 'It would suit me to meet young John and see if his suspicions are quiet.'

'Don't be away long. Betsy, Tam's wife, is sewing a dress for you and she's none too pleased by the length of you. Don't keep her waiting.'

His Lordship was amused. ''Struth, you terrify me. One of her own dresses? Does she deliver a punch like her husband?' he asked as he opened the door. 'I swear she will find me meek as a lamb.'

Outside he could see that Auchmithie was scarce more than a collection of fishermen's cottages strung along the top of some magnificent cliffs. The shed where Charlie had stabled the horse was behind the inn and this was Keir's first stop.

The horse was not in the shed but grazing on the cliffs with several others. Tam was there, and John and two of the men.

'These be land smugglers this trip,' Tam greeted him, 'and they could certainly use this nag of yours. Grand strong beast.'

'He is as fast as needs be.' Keir avoided looking at John whom he could sense was staring at him just as he had done the night before. He decided to challenge the boy. 'Yer pa not teach you not to stare, lad?' he asked in as uncultured a voice as possible.

The boy started and blushed to the roots of his red hair. 'Sorry. It's just that you be an awful big fellow. I only ever met one man as long as you and there was summat about your eyes reminded me of him.'

'Who'd he mind you on, lad, great stick of a man as he be?' asked Tam.

John looked squarely at Keir. 'Someone as was kind to me once – a gentleman.'

Tam gave a great burst of laughter and threw his massive arms round Keir's shoulders. 'This here bonnie fighter's no gentleman, lad. Now come on, my Betsy'll be waiting to sew your dress and you're not near big enough to stand up to her.'

They turned away together and walked up the main street, Keir aware that John stood looking after them.

Keir's thoughts were busy. I pray I have this business attended to before my eye heals. That lad is no fool, but I think he has a kindness for the real me, and would not willingly expose me.

Luckily, since Betsy was a singularly quarrelsome woman, they arrived at the house just as she was approaching from the other end of the village.

'Well, ye great gowk,' she addressed Keir, Lord Pittenmuir. 'If you're not a long drink of water. Charlie best feed you up some.'

Greatly chastened, but mindful that he was unable to explain that he had lost weight in the service of the realm, Keir followed Betsy into the cottage and meekly did as he was bid. He could not help contrasting the manner in which Betsy pulled and pushed his new dress across his shoulders – after telling him brusquely to 'step out of them breeches. I ain't got all day' – with the care and solicitude used by the various tailors who enjoyed his patronage.

This experience will do your character a deal of good, Pittenmuir, he told himself and began to laugh.

'Tickly, are we?' asked Betsy. 'Stand still till I'm done. There you are, sweetheart,' she said at last giving him a playful and intimate nip.

'No one will take me for a woman.'

'Don't let no one close enough to look,' said Tam. 'We'll give you a scarf for your head but keep yourself bent over. I have seen some tall women in my time but you ought to be in a rarey show.'

Keir could only be glad that all seemed harmony between them.

It was still there a few days later when they set sail again for France. His Lordship had found dodging among the bushes on his own estate yet another illuminating experience. The *Shuska* had anchored in a bay not a mile as the crow flies from his principal seat. He stood on the beach for a moment and reflected that if he could have but craned his neck up and over the cliff, no doubt he could have peered in the windows of his own library and seen his brother comfortably settled with a book and unsmuggled brandy.

'Stop dawdling and lend a hand here,' whispered Charlie fiercely. 'We sail with this tide an' everyone pulls his weight.'

'Sorry,' he muttered in a sulky tone and did as he was bid. John was there but of Pate there was no sign.

'Where's his nibs then, Tam?' Keir remembered that Tam had been one of the smugglers complaining over their leader's absence from the actual smuggling and he felt that if he showed willing to side with Tam he might more easily find out as much as possible about that mysterious young man. He had tried but could remember no reference to any Pate anywhere in this surrounding area.

'Sitting in his fine house, eating his dinner.'

'Related to Pittenmuir or Balgowan?'

Tam looked at him speculatively for a moment. 'You'm awful interested in the boy. Why?'

'No reason 'cept liking to know who I deal with.'

94

'He ain't a Galloway. I know Master Jamie to see in the street like. There ain't no boys at Balgowan. What does it matter? He's got a rare head on his shoulders; we've never had no trouble and it better stay that way,' added Tam threateningly.

He moved away and Keir cursed himself for his heavy handedness. He could afford to alienate no one and especially not Tam.

For several hours there was time to think of nothing but sailing the little ship out to sea and avoiding His Majesty's Navy and the local excise men. It was an exhilarating experience, man against the elements, and His Lordship would almost have enjoyed it, had he not had so much to think about. Captain Visieux kept him very busy, but he did try to keep an eye on several members of the crew. Smuggling was a perfect cover for spying and although, in all honesty, he had to admit that none seemed right for it, one could never tell.

He was exhausted when he was finally sent below to find a hammock into which he fell gratefully. He was not destined to sleep long for a squall blew up and it was all hands on deck.

He almost lost his footing as the ship dipped strongly into a trough. He managed to grab a rope and was thankful a moment later when the railing beside him, broken by the weight of a loose box, disappeared into the yawning mouth of the angry sea. He had not time to pause for, just as he was about to look around to decide the safest way to manoeuvre, young John was swept off his feet and slid down the deck past him, too scared even to scream. Keir grabbed wildly and caught the boy's shirt.

'Try to gain your feet, lad,' he begged but the boy slipped and slid, completely at the mercy of the elements.

The ship rolled and John slid back. The rope round his hand burned Keir's flesh, but he ignored the pain as he tried to obtain a better hold. Again, the ship rolled and John slid, his shirt tearing almost in two

'Help,' he screamed, 'please', as his feet went right over the side and only that tiny piece of material held him.

Still holding the tearing shirt, Keir struggled to his feet. He would have to risk letting go of the boy and grabbing him again as he rolled for the next time the ship rolled, his weight would tear the cloth and he would be over the side.

'Trust me, John,' he whispered more to himself than to the

youngster. He braced himself and as the ship rolled and John slid towards him he loosened his hold, hating the look of terror the boy threw at him. Then, as the lad slid past towards the broken rail he bent and grabbed his breeches. John's precipitate flight to certain doom was halted and he turned and scrambled like a crab, grabbed his rescuer's legs and tried to regain his balance.

At last he found his balance and stood up clinging to Keir. The arm taking John's had been smashed by a musket bullet at Vimiero and screamed in silent agony. I can't last much longer, was Keir's thought as John clawed his way to his feet and managed to grab a safe length of railing. Together they inched their way along to where Charlie and some others fought with the bucking sails.

'Part of the railing's gone amidships. The boy was near over the side.'

'Lend a hand here, Ian, or are you both weak as kittens?'

John answered bravely, if a tad breathlessly. 'We be fine, Charlie. Takes more than a wee storm to stop Auchmithie sailors.'

The storm blew for fifteen hours and when at last the wind admitted defeat and allowed the ship to rest awhile, Keir Galloway acknowledged that never since the Peninsula had he experienced such total exhaustion. Some of the men slept where they had slumped on the deck once the captain had given the all clear.

Too much damage, both to the vessel herself and to the crew, had been done for the *Shuska* to continue. Keir was proud to be thought of as one of those more able to do without rest in order to start repairs. John and Charlie, youngest and oldest of the crew, were also among the work party. Did John deliberately manoeuvre to work beside him? He could feel the boy's eyes on him and several times it seemed as if he were about to speak. At last he made up his mind.

'Don't look at me and say nothing for there's others close,' whispered John fiercely. 'I have remembered who you mind me on. It was when you spoke. Why? Why? It can't be that you need money. I don't want to know and I'll keep your secret so long as you don't cause trouble for . . . someone,' finished the boy and he turned away but not before Keir had seen tears sparkling in his eyes.

He looked round but the men were asleep or too busy to eavesdrop. John knew him. Of course he would recognize one who had so recently come to his assistance. He cursed himself for letting his guard down in the heat of the rescue. John would not betray him for someone else's sake. Who? Charlie? Did the youngster think he had gulled Charlie into believing he was a bona fide smuggler? Unlikely. Then it had to be young Pate. Who was he?

'What were you and John having such a solemn jaw about?'

Tam seemed relaxed but Keir felt his alertness. Some truth is better than none. 'He were talking about how my long legs remind him of some gentry mort. Thinks he's seen me afore but I was explaining I been in the army – in the Peninsula – till I took a ball and got sent home.'

Tam nodded sagely. 'You got the look of a soldier about you; certainly never was a sailor.' He stood up and Keir pulled himself up beside him. 'You'd ha starved to death for sure.' Tam laughed and delivered another of his mighty but affectionate punches. 'Yer not bad, not good neither, but you know nout about runnin a ship. Howsomever, if yer army, that explains it.'

He turned again as he was about to go below. 'Where did ye say ye learned to sail?'

'I dunno that I did, but Charlie learned me when I was a lad.'

With that, Tam's suspicions, if such there had been, seemed to have been lulled and the remainder of the voyage passed with no animosity between them. John spoke little and never to Keir whom he avoided as much as possible, but now and again Keir would feel the young eyes on him.

As a law-abiding citizen and a magistrate besides, Lord Pittenmuir was somewhat overwhelmed by the efficiency of the smuggling fraternity. The range of merchandise all set to make its new home in Scotland amazed him and mentally he congratulated the organizational skills of young Pate. As to his other little business, he found that the storm had played to his advantage; the *Shuska* needed more professional repairs to her masts than the crew had been able to effect. To the smugglers' annoyance it seemed that they might lie at anchor for as much as forty-eight hours. Keir listened to the sound of hammers for a while and then found Charlie.

'You're on your own, lad,' said Charlie when he had explained. 'I won't be able to hold up if Visieux sails before you return.'

'Understood. Cover for me if you can.'

He waited for nightfall when the crew, bored with their enforced inactivity, were making inroads into their share of brandy. A simple matter to slip overboard into a rowing boat. Keep them singing, he prayed as he rowed for the shore. He pulled the boat up onto the shingle a few miles down from their anchorage and then struck out in the direction of a little village that had been visible from the *Shuska*. There was sure to be a tavern there; as good a place as any to begin looking for a spy.

There was, and apart from the overwhelming odour of garlic, it could have been The Eagle's Nest in Arbroath, or any fisherman's drinking place in any part of the world. It was a wooden shack, no more. There were two half-open dirt windows, a smoking fire on one wall, several heavy tables and benches, a scarred serving counter, and sailors of every size and shape. Most of these added to the unhealthy atmosphere by smoking pipes filled with malodorous tobaccos.

Lord Pittenmuir ordered rum and sat down beside the fire to watch and listen. He had hardly expected that within a few minutes he would be approached by the very man he hoped to find, but, to his surprise, he was. A thickset man in the outfit typical of the Breton sailor left the group with whom he had been drinking and moved to sit beside Keir.

'Fine after the storm.'

'Does he think me smuggler, spy, or sailor?' thought Keir.

'Aye, delayed us by hours.'

That was obviously the right answer for the man relaxed and smiled, showing a mouthful of blackened teeth.

'But the journey was successful.'

Keir thought quickly. Could he take the place of the spy who was expected? He had no false information to stall with. 'It might or again it might not, if you get my meaning.'

'I am authorized to pay well for anything that will help the glorious cause.'

The glorious cause? Napoleon's cause. What would they want to know? 'No doubt if there be a map of sweet hidden anchorages . . .' he began slowly, feeling his way.

'We had been led to expect news of the placements of troops on the east coast of a certain small nation,' said the man looking doubtfully at Keir and beginning to rise to his feet.

'*Ca va sans dire*,' said Keir scornfully, 'but, I am a poor man and, *sans doute*, safe and secluded harbours will also fetch a premium.'

The door opened and a gust of wind caused the fire to belch forth more smoke. 'Damn and blast,' swore Lord Pittenmuir looking at the door as he recognized a belligerent John Reid.

'You were saying, friend?' His new acquaintance was showing impatience.

Keir watched for a moment as John moved to the counter and ordered rum.

'You know the boy?' The contact made to move again.

'Cabin boy on my ship,' said Keir rising to his feet. 'He is no threat to any but himself. I will take him back with me ere the Captain misses him.'

A hard hand on his sore arm pulled him down again. 'First our business, *mon ami*, the boy can wait.'

Keir looked into the cold eyes and shivered in spite of himself. 'I will need paper and some charcoal from the fire. Show me your credentials.'

'Such sweet music,' he added as his companion held up a heavy little bag and shook it gently.

With the charcoal he proceeded to draw a beautifully detailed map of that part of the Scottish coast that stretched between Dundee and Montrose. Miss Rattray would have been delighted with his skill and imagination, but even she would not have recognized the safe anchorages he delineated. Any soldiers foolish enough to disembark there would walk either into a battalion of His Majesty's marines or a swamp. He added the main military camps, with their strengths, since these were well known and no doubt Napoleon was already in possession of this worthless information. He had just transferred the bag to his breeches pocket when he sensed, rather than saw, John hurtling himself across the room towards him. Pity, but there was no help for it. He turned and met the boy's scowling face with a punch that had all his strength behind it. John collapsed against him.

'These stupid Scotchmen cannot drink,' said Lord Pittenmuir calmly and threw the boy over his shoulder and carried him out of the inn.

He was, of course, incapable of carrying him all the way to the *Shuska* and he put him down on the sand near the harbour entrance. He laughed grimly as he massaged his own throbbing shoulder. A bullet there was his supposed reason for selling out and when he thought of the punishment he had taken in the past few days, he almost wished for the comparative peace of a military campaign.

John groaned and stirred. 'You have a hard head, lad. I flatter myself that that punch should have rendered you unconscious for longer.'

John looked at him and then, as recollection returned, he tried to rise. 'Rotten spy. That is why you came, to sell secrets to the frogs.'

'Guard your mouth,' advised Keir fastening a hand of iron over the boy's mouth. 'If you promise to stay quiet I will release you.'

The boy glared at him out of hurt angry eyes but he recognized the implied threat for he nodded acquiescence and allowed himself to be helped up. Then he shrugged off Keir's hand as if he could not bear his touch.

'John, something evil is abroad at Auchmithie, but I swear I am not part of it. Now, lest our French friends are suspicious, I want you to lean on me until we are out of sight. I have a rowing boat hidden and when we are on our way I will tell you as much as you need to know.'

'How did you get ashore, by the way?' he asked when they reached the boat.

'Swam o'course' John answered through his teeth. 'All's soaked under my breeches. I put them on my head. That's why it took so long – swimming like a damned duck.'

'I am grateful that it did delay you. You make a formidable opponent, young man.'

He looked over at the bulk of the *Shuska* from where came sounds of revelry. How to get himself and the boy aboard? 'If Visieux spots us we're for the cat, you understand that?' Even in the dark he saw the colour drain from the boy's face. 'Charlie keeps watch but we must be silent as the grave. Trust me, lad. I am no spy.'

With which inaccuracy Lord Pittenmuir began to row. With heartfelt relief he saw Charlie's lined face peering at them over the side. If he was surprised to see John he said nothing.

'Get below, lad, and you take the next watch,' he ordered Keir just as the hatch opened revealing the captain.

'Changin' the watch, Cap'n.'

'I thought I felt the bump of a boat?'

'Naught of concern, sir. Some . . . ahh . . . ladies, if you get my drift, but all boarders were repelled.'

'*Bien.*' Visieux looked at the sky. 'We sail with the dawn. Arrange everything.'

For a few moments after he had disappeared down the hatchway the three conspirators looked at one another in silence.

'Get below, boy, and rest. I'll deal with you later.'

''Tis a brave lad, Charlie. He thought me a spy for France.'

'Rules is rules. Can't have the crew sloping off when the fancy moves them.'

'I hit him, and besides, he had to drink some indifferent rum. Methinks he is punished enough.'

Charlie laughed with him. 'I got work to do. Two hours, lad,' he added forcibly, 'and then you snatch some rest afore we sail.'

Lord Pittenmuir vanished and Ian Scott remained on watch and, thanks to the soft heart of old Charlie, was asleep when the *Shuska* turned her face towards Scotland.

He surfaced to a biting wind that threw salt spray angrily against his face.

'If this wind stays with us,' yelled Tam who had also come on deck, 'we'll see home afore dark.'

'Any sign of revenuers?'

'Not for hours yet, if they be expecting us, but we could run afoul of the navy. Can hardly pretend to be innocent fishermen this close to Froggy's coast.'

The wind stayed with them and Captain Visieux piled on sail to take advantage of the weather. The little ship, fully laden as she was, still skipped merrily ahead of the wind. There was a change in the atmosphere aboard the ship. These next were crucial hours. Could they sail up the coast unchallenged? Visieux prayed aloud that the navy was involved keeping a watchful eye on French boats. Their own best hope was to stay far enough out to avoid detection and then to run in under cover of darkness.

And then the wind dropped.

'Fog's come in, too,' Charlie pointed out. 'Good and bad in that. The navy can't see us, but we can't see them neither.'

They sat becalmed for seven and a half hours.

'Young Monsieur Pate will be *un peu* concerned, do you not

agree, Charlie?' asked Visieux. 'He had arranged a light for us, but voilà, we are not in the right place at the right time.'

'*Un peu* concerned,' whispered John angrily. 'He will be out of his mind with worry.'

Keir looked keenly at him. Why should the lad worry so much?

'If we be boarded,' said Charlie, 'we can say truly that we are registered in Bergen. This becalming and the fog give us an excuse to head for a Scottish port; we need provisions and Scotland is closer than Norway.'

'Will they not suspect since we are quite far off course?' asked Ian Scott.

'We drifted, laddie,' said Tam with a grim laugh.

'I have heard the navy stations a man on board to watch such ships as they load provisions,' said Scott again.

'Aye, 'tis true, and more than once I've been forced to sail for Bergen to keep up pretence, but that is something to worry over should the need arise.'

Gradually the fog lifted and they were relieved not to see a ship standing near them.

'Let the wind only rise and we can make harbour under cover of darkness,' prayed Charlie.

Tam looked at the ocean. 'All that water and us thirsty as Arabs.'

The cry they were waiting for came eventually from John who was on look-out. 'Ship ahoy.'

'Eternal damnation to her captain,' was Visieux's pious ejaculation. 'She is British.'

Conscious of a hold crammed full of goods on which no tax had been paid, the smugglers watched nervously as the sloop skimmed across the waves. Were the sails stirring? Indeed there was sighing in the rigging or did they merely see what they longed to see?

The ship was closer.

'Had that sail flapped?

'Run up the Norwegian flag,' ordered the captain, 'and remember we are on our way to Bergen and become lost in the fog.'

'She's bearing down fast, lad. Think fast what role to play,' Charlie whispered.

Then the miracle.

'By God, she's turning,' yelled Tam. 'She's leaving us.'

And so indeed she was. When the sloop was so close that she could have put a shot across the *Shuska*'s deck, she turned against the wind and avoided them.

'It's the damned French she is seeking – not law-abiding gentlemen,' laughed the French captain.

They experienced no more delays until they were as Charlie said, 'close enough to home to smell smoked fish', and they lay off shore to wait until nightfall.

'Why the delay, Charlie?' asked Keir. 'I doubt the excise men expect a smuggling vessel to unload under their very noses.'

'Pate changes the landing place each time. We needs must wait for dark to see the signal.'

'Where did you unload last time?'

'A cave on Pittenmuir land. There are hundreds of them.'

Keir smiled to himself but said nothing for there were others around. So he helped the gentlemen, did he?

'Do you know, Tam,' he said after an hour or two of waiting. 'I believe you are right. I smell smokies and each one dripping with butter. I could eat a dozen and thank you for a second helping.'

'Aye, and the thirst they'd raise would need a gallon of ale. Beautiful.'

'I'm for a sirloin big as a horse,' put in John.

But still they sat while the captain watched the skyline.

'There it is,' he said at last.

'I see no signal,' said Keir.

'Look, lad, there, a wee light.'

Keir followed the direction of Charlie's pointing finger. 'It can't be. Hunger has made me disorientated. The Abbey ruins lie there.'

'Aye, the lad has hung a light in the south transept.'

'Good God. How? The transept is a death trap. A spider would have difficulty climbing that wall, let alone a delicate youth. I applaud his courage.'

'There be more to him than first appears; I have always thought that.'

They became too busy for chatter for it was no easy task to anchor even a small vessel under the cliff face. There appeared to

103

be no beach and tide and wind both conspired to heave them against the cliff should Visieux allow them.

'He be a grand skipper for all he's a frog,' was the crew's accolade as the *Shuska* slipped sweetly into the mouth of a cave.

Ten

Liddy had been watching the weather, but with the strong winds and the driving rain, she realized that it must be worse at sea, and she worried for the safe passage of her smugglers.

She began to look for them six days after they sailed as she had arranged with Captain Visieux. Knowing that it was time Euan Pate was resurrected, she found an excuse to visit the kitchens and assured herself that the stable key still hung beside the door. When the house was still later that night, she crept downstairs and groped her way across the flagstoned floor to the wall. The key was gone.

'That's impossible. I have but lost my way.' But no matter how she felt with her hands along the walls, no heavy iron key surrendered into her keeping.

A most unladylike expression found its way to her lips. If the key was missing someone else had to be using it. A second smothered oath followed the first and, feeling somewhat better, Miss Carpenter found her way to the door. It was unlocked and so it followed that whoever had gone out through the door felt no compunction at all over being discovered absent from the house. Liddy followed, but then returned for it was possible that if she did not exit through her tower, upon her return she might well find the doors bolted against her.

Hating the necessity of wasting time, she sped to her room and left the house through the tower door. The key to the stable block was in the lock. No lights showed and the only sound she heard with her ear pressed against the door was the breathing of the horses. Trying not to feel that at any moment a heavy blow might descend on her unprotected head, she pushed the door open and looked on. Her horses and her papa's carriage horses were there, but of the fine pair that pulled her father's phaeton, there was no sign.

'Two horses, two riders,' muttered Liddy. 'Who and where?'

A quandary indeed. She had to rendezvous with her land smugglers to tell them where and when to meet the *Shuska* since there looked to be a delay, but if she rode she might find her father waiting when she returned.

She would walk. She slipped Amber a sugar lump and left as quietly as she had entered.

Outside she listened to the night sounds but there was nothing untoward. She heard night birds, the squeal of a small rodent. Like a shadow she melted into the rhododendrons and hurried as quickly as was safe to the castle.

She caught a glimmer of light through the darkness. Liddy turned back and slipped into an outbuilding. The packing cases that had been there since she and her brother had played here as children were still tumbled against the walls. She pulled one aside to reveal an opening in the wall and backed into it, pulling the packing case back to hide the opening. Only once had she entered the castle this way for it was so narrow. She had been eleven years old and furiously angry with the boys for leaving her. They knew her dislike of moving backwards in dirt and darkness, so she had done exactly that and waited calmly for them while they searched for her, fearful that she had sustained an injury. But this was real and there was no loving brother to dust her off and scold her.

At last she reached the end of the tunnel and back into the remains of the ancient kitchens. Just as she was about to light her lamp, a smothered sound reached her ear. She darted into what was left of the pantry and crouched behind a fallen stone. Another sound followed the first.

'A rat, methinks.' The voice was familiar, but too low for recognition. A second voice replied to it – still unrecognizable. They moved away and she heard them leave the kitchen. Still she waited lest it be a ruse. At last she stepped out and cautiously hurried across the room.

Where had they gone? Her men would be here soon. She was almost at the great hall and there was a sliver of light up ahead. I pray they do not hear the chattering of my teeth, she whispered to herself, greatly fearing that she was not of the stuff of heroines.

She peered through the chink and saw three men gathered in the window that faced the sea. Their backs were to her and she could hear only low murmuring. One man was above average height and slender, the others of average height and one with a good breadth of shoulder. Oh, to see their faces. She leaned closer to the crack in the door, but suddenly it groaned loudly as it opened almost precipitating her into the room. She had a quick glimpse of three faces before she turned and fled. She had a good head start but they were close behind her and one, she feared, had as good a knowledge of the castle as she had herself. She had no light and was forced to slow down and feel her way and for once there was no distaste, for her whole spirit was disordered. Silence, black and cloying, sheltered her and a sob escaped her. She brushed her eyes angrily and doing so scraped her knuckles on the stone.

There was no sound of pursuit. She stopped and sucked her knuckles. She must go on . . . She was at the entrance, now. Pray God, they did not await her. She could hear rain and a strong wind forced her almost double as she left her tunnel, but she was alone and she pushed on through broom that tore at her clothes before almost falling under the hooves of a pony.

'Some welcome, Mr Pate,' said a voice as she was unceremoniously hauled to her feet. 'You do look like all 'em ghosts is achasing you.'

Gratefully Liddy looked up into the face of one of her smugglers, Pete Smith, who had stayed on land for this trip.

'Worse. The castle is occupied by revenuers,' she improvised boldly.

Without a word the troop of ponies was turned and led back down the bridle path. Eventually they took refuge in a cave.

'Did hear marines be swarmin' all over Arbroath but folk say they be looking for spies, not honest smugglers.'

Liddy's heart lurched uncomfortably. 'Say you not so. Yet, if they be looking for a spy, they will have no time to concern themselves with our enterprise . . .'

'We should be safe using Maiden's Cove, Mr Pate. How do ye get messages to a ship at sea? Be you a bird, lad?'

Liddy laughed. 'Leave me to earn my share of the profits, Pete,' she said, delighted to have found at least one way to stop mutterings about unfairness. Striving to look as brave as she sounded, she stood up, straightened the rather old-fashioned lace at her throat, and left the cave.

The wind was even stronger and the rain lashed down in a fury. Despite her own discomfort she found her thoughts winging to her men somewhere at sea: young John and old Charlie and . . . Why ever should an image of that ruffian, Scott, come into her head?

So deep in thought was she that she almost stumbled into the courtyard of her home without a thought as to who might observe her, but her instincts surfaced and she edged along in the shadow of the wall that circled the stable. All was quiet; she looked up at the house but no chink of light showed so she risked running across and trying the stable door.

Locked. How wise she had been not to take Amber. She reached for the key to the tower and felt a rush of almost unbearable terror as it evaded her searching fingers. It yielded itself up, however, from the capacious depths and shakily she inserted it and opened the door. The relief. She forced her aching body up the stairs.

There was a light in her room. The door opened and Rattles stood there, candle in hand. 'Dear child, you are soaked to the skin.'

Liddy, to her embarrassment, burst into tears and threw herself into the outstretched arms of her governess.

Later, tucked up in bed with Rattles's splendid new Paisley shawl about her shoulders and sipping hot milk generously laced with brandy, she felt better.

'Conceive of my horror, Rattles, when I recognized the voice of one I had been taught to revere; it was his face I knew too when I all but pitched into the room.'

'But consider, child – nothing you have said makes him a spy in French pay.'

'They spoke in French and why should Papa need to steal from his own home in the middle of the night to entertain his friends in a ruin unless it is nefarious? Rattles, you must know that a run of cards could not finance our new lifestyle.'

'You are overwrought,' said Rattles, taking the cup and pushing her down among the pillows. 'Sleep. I will make all straight here – for there is a considerable pool on the floor – and then I will retire. We will talk tomorrow.'

'I must be abroad at my usual hour. There must be no thread of suspicion. Besides I must be in Arbroath tomorrow.'

A very tired Lydia was roused at nine and begged to be allowed to sleep. Then the recollections of the preceding night surfaced and she stumbled from her bed. To her relief, her papa, said Etienne, was yet in his chamber.

Liddy looked at the Frenchman. Average height, slight. He was one of them – and the third. It could not be Papa's groom for he was of no great height and the third man had been exceptionally tall. Did she know anyone of such a height?

She banished a memory of Keir Galloway smiling down at Leonora Fairweather.

He is from home, Liddy, or so says his brother. It could not be. Why, he is Lord Lieutenant of the county. Blast, if it is he, I have just alerted his secretary to give him warning. She thought of her tangled affairs and longed for her petticoats. I am tired of them all: smugglers, spies, Papa, Keir.

She took herself off to the schoolroom where she found Rattles engaged as usual in the education of her little sisters. They were excited to have their lessons interrupted and were even more surprised and delighted when Liddy invited Miss Rattray and her pupils to accompany her on a tour of the ancient ruined Abbey, an enterprise to which Miss Rattray agreed.

'So educational.'

Poor Miss Rattray. The thoughts in the Honourable Lydia's mind were far from being of an educational nature.

Eleven

While her smugglers were at sea Liddy had visited the abbey four times. She went first with her sisters and their governess and astounded that lady by the wealth of her accumulated knowledge.

'Liddy, you are almost become a bluestocking,' said Charlotte. 'Is this what you studied on Papa's shelves?'

'And a great deal more besides,' laughed Liddy wickedly. Dear Charlotte sounded quite shocked at her sister's polymathy.

'I think your sisters have had enough learning and would enjoy a gentle stroll in the grounds,' counselled Miss Rattray who had detected in the eldest Miss Carpenter an astonishing ability to climb upon broken walls in an effort to impart erudition to her sisters. 'I have no doubt, Liddy, that progressive educationalists would agree that to discover the past by scaling ruined walls is sounder than merely listening to learned discourse or even reading. Had you not been born into that class of society that precludes its members from earning their own bread, I might say that you have the seeds of a teacher in you.'

Thus they avoided discussing the real reason for this sudden interest in the ruined abbey. Miss Carpenter smiled, hid a yawn behind her glove, and made notes of such ruined walls, transepts, and galleries as aroused her notice. Their papa awaited them upon their return and Liddy was glad that the natural exuberance of the younger girls masked any awkwardness she might have felt. Either Lord Balgowan was a consummate actor or had no reason to suspect his daughter's presence in the castle in the middle of the night.

Tonight he elected to keep town hours, which meant that dinner would be late. That told Liddy that her papa had no business outside the house, which was all to the good since she did not want him to discover her horse gone from the stable when she returned, as she must, to the abbey.

Dinner seemed interminable. Mrs Harper was going from strength to strength and each meal was a *tour de force*.

Liddy threw down the gauntlet. 'I cannot believe that such excess as this is good for one, either physically or morally.'

Charlotte looked at her in horror. His Lordship exploded. 'I pray you do not intend to utter such ill-considered remarks if you find yourself in the society of your peers. I begin to think you quite incapable of gracing the station in life to which you were bred.' His Lordship looked at a course that offered such delicacies as filets of sole with a simple butter sauce, ducklings with a hunters' sauce, flanked by a dish of spinach with a simple hot olive oil and diced egg yokes, and roared, 'Lydia, go to your room.'

Miss Carpenter, who could not remember the last time she had received such a punishment, hardly knew how to keep her countenance. She swept, with regal splendour, from the dining room, and trusting Rattles to keep invaders at bay, fled to her room.

'Now, I have forgotten the key.'

Contriving to conceal her agitation as best she could, Liddy passed trembling hands across her brow, and turned and went to the kitchens. Mrs Harper and Bessie were there, alone.

'Behold me in deep disgrace,' confessed Liddy, 'but I must have a cup of your delicious coffee to bear me company.'

'Course, Miss Liddy. That Etienne was telling us that you got on His Lordship's bad side. Here, let me.'

'Nay, I'll not disturb you. A mug from the cupboard here.'

Boldly Liddy walked to the corner cupboard and glanced along the corridor at the wall where the key should be. It was not there. Don't panic, she told herself. Someone is from home, but who?

'Mrs Harper? Etienne is in the dining room; does Madame not dine here? Mrs Harper laughed. 'Lord love you, Miss Lydia, she's much too grand for us. That Sam takes his mutton with us, but he's off to the Eagle's Nest, since His Lordship don't want him. Now, miss, your coff—'

But Miss Liddy, who had so badly wanted coffee, had turned with a swift goodnight and almost run from the room. There was no understanding Miss Liddy these days.

Her mind at rest, Liddy had no need of the reviving properties of coffee. From the groom she had nought to fear. His favourite barmaid would keep him busy until long after she was home – she hoped.

So experienced had she become that it took scarce a moment to attire herself as Euan Pate. Her fingers trembled as she fastened the heavy belt round her slim waist – tonight she was to do something extremely dangerous. First she had to leave the house and saddle Amber while every member of the household was awake. There was no choice. Amber whinnied a welcome but, apart from horses, the stable stood empty. She saddled the horse and bound her hooves with pieces of dustsheet.

She looked up, but although Balgowan house blazed with lights no one stood at a window looking out. She urged Amber to a canter and escaped. The wind had dropped and the rain that had plagued farmers and fishermen for days had also abated. Since there was a moon, she urged Amber into a gallop and for a few minutes neither horse nor rider thought of anything but the pleasure of unrestricted movement.

Nearer Arbroath, however, it was different. She dared not fall foul of the soldiers who patrolled the streets. Better to dismount, undo the sacking round Amber's hooves, and lead the horse. No, that in itself were suspicious. Boldly she rode through the narrow streets that wound round near the new harbour and up into the town. Once the watch hailed her.

'Got a lass somewhere?'

'That'd be telling,' laughed Liddy in the deeper tones of Pate and was allowed to pass.

She reached the abbey and tethered Amber among some bushes and then, her heart again firmly in her mouth, she climbed the wall built to keep out intruders. Her goal was directly ahead, the huge ruined wall of the south transept with its gaping window. The height had looked frightening enough in broad daylight, but now, with only the little light allowed when the clouds uncovered a fitful moon, it was terrifying.

Nonsense, Liddy; you have climbed higher cliffs with Keir and Harry and were encumbered by petticoats. At last you have the opportunity to climb with all the advantages of a boy. She found the lamp she had hidden there that morning, still safely in place. What had seemed a simple plan when she had voiced it to Visieux now assumed heroic proportions. She was to light a lamp in the window and the little beacon would tell the smugglers that it was

112

unsafe to land at Arbroath and so to go to the safer cove. If Visieux already lay off Arbroath she would need to scale the wall only once but if he should still be at sea . . . She would think of nothing but the climb. It could not possibly be more than fifty feet, a mere nothing compared to the Auchmithie cliffs.

With the lamp fastened to her back she embarked on her voyage up the wall. More than once she cursed the skill of the medieval masons who had fashioned it, for there was scarce a finger or toe hold anywhere. She dared not look up and to look down would be fatal. At last her seeking fingers discovered a ledge to which she could cling so that for a moment the inter-minable strain was taken from her shoulders. Now she dared look and could have cried with vexation. She had barely come her own length from the ground and had been sure she was almost at the window.

Her resting place showed her that the next part would be easier for the richness of detail with which the craftsmen had adorned the building was in great evidence here and afforded hand and footholds. She reached the first row of windows and was able to haul herself up and rest and here she found reason to bless her height; by standing on the window ledge she reached easily a wide carved ledge above that had been invisible from the ground. Euan Pate did not find climbing on to that ledge as simple as the child Liddy would have done, but at last she was there, the lamp still in one piece and only the same height again to climb.

Why did I not bring a rope, for God knows how I am to come down again? If I fall I will be dashed to pieces on such stones as these worthy townspeople have been unable to haul away for building projects and besides, I can never go into company again, for my hands are quite ruined.

Filling her despairing soul with these and suchlike philoso-phies, Liddy climbed on. Twice she slipped, once she experienced vertigo but she fought it and clung on, thoughts of the safety of faithful John keeping her from withdrawing. She soon found herself at the base of the great round window and raised herself to sit in the embrasure. She was so relieved to have reached her goal that the lamp almost slid to the ground in her relief. She cautiously pulled it up close to her, and waited . . .

The *Shuska* would appear and she would light the lamp and descend. From then on, she vowed, the Honourable Lydia

Carpenter would climb not a whit higher than her bed. She gazed out to sea, trying to pretend that she was not sitting for anyone to see in the window of a ruined church. The sea was empty; not even a fishing boat alleviated her boredom.

I am falling asleep. If I do I will die. What can I think on? Laughing blue eyes. They were none too merry the last time she saw them. We are changed, Keir. Why did I have to climb so high to see that your eyes did smile when you looked at Miss Fairweather? The general is hoping for such a splendid match. You do not dally in her company in town, do you? No, Lydia. Enough. Think on your smugglers.

But the face that intruded on her thoughts was that of the new man. Had he blue eyes? He was of his height or at least he would be if he but carried himself with pride. Oh . . . I care not. Five minutes and I leave.

The *Shuska* did not appear. Liddy slid and scrambled back to the ground leaving the lamp wedged tight in a nook and resolved to scan the sea from a less dangerous vantage point. She was so weary that she could scarce ride back home and almost rode straight into the stable yard before she recollected the time and the clothes she wore. All was dark and not a sound disturbed the silence. Liddy dismounted and led Amber to the door. It was locked.

'Forgive me, Amber,' she whispered as she pulled off the saddle and unbridled her. She dumped the tack at the tower door and led Amber to an orchard where she again removed the cloths from her hooves and left her to graze. Then she hurried back, picked up her discarded saddle and carried them up to her tower.

Thanks to Rattles a fire yet glowed. Liddy sat down and stretched her poor hands to the heat. She knew no more till a hand on her shoulder shook her awake.

'Rattles,' she gasped. 'You frightened me to death.'

'Consider the state of your nerves had Madame discovered you, you foolish child.'

Liddy said no more but allowed Rattles to pull her out of the clothes and bundle her into a warm bed gown.

'I will get rid of these,' and she pointed to the saddle which sat staring at them from the middle of the room, 'and then do something about your hands. No, do not explain. Frankly, I am almost at the point where I prefer not to know.'

Several hours later a much-refreshed Liddy watched Madame remove her breakfast tray and lay back to await Rattles. She had not long to wait.

'I have lied to Tom who thinks that he left Amber out. You must make up to him somehow. Where will this end? It has gone too far. How do you explain the condition of your hands this afternoon?'

Liddy looked at her blankly and then realization dawned. 'We are to take tea with Mrs Wallace. Anne has returned from Edinburgh.' She thought quickly. 'I will wear my gloves, roses y'know.'

Was there a most unladylike sniff? 'I can only hope no gardener asks a question for you scarce know a petal from a leaf.'

Liddy supposed rightly that Mrs Wallace would be too well bred to question any idiosyncrasy in her guests and Anne so delighted at being the centre of attention for the first time among the young ladies of the area that she would scarce have noticed had Liddy arrived in sackcloth and ashes. It was the longest afternoon of Liddy's life, but at last she was able to bid her hostess goodbye, and return home to lie down upon her bed until dinner. She was asleep immediately.

Sir Thomas Downing was invited for dinner. His conversation was only ever of horses and fond though she was of the species, Liddy found Thomas a dead bore. She dressed, however, in one of her new gowns, a jonquil crêpe with coffee-coloured ribbons. Her toilette was complete when Charlotte danced into the room in a froth of blue silk embroidered all over with forget-me-nots.

'Charlotte,' exclaimed Liddy – who had smuggled the gown from France – 'are you run mad? I thought you meant to reserve that dress for the day Pittenmuir returns or we remove to London. To waste it on Tommy Downing, really.'

'Pooh, Liddy,' teased Charlotte. 'Have I not too many new gowns?' She laughed gaily. 'I expected you to scold but, dearest, we are to entertain a second gentleman. This lovely gown is not to be wasted on Sir Thomas. Guess.'

All colour drained from Liddy's face and her heart began to behave in the most ridiculous way. Major Fordyce had contacted him and he was returned. She could say nothing.

'Captain Ogilvie-Fenton, Liddy. He is come to visit his great aunt, Lady Staples, you know, and is bored to tears, Papa says.'

She looked closely at her sister and saw the colour ebb and flow in her cheeks. 'Liddy, whom did you think I meant?'

Liddy brushed the question aside. 'Is the captain worthy of the debut of such a gown.'

'Indeed it is the most beautiful dress in the world and it called, *wear me* and I could withstand its entreaties no longer.'

Liddy laughed and said no more.

Sir Thomas had no more conversation than before but Captain Ogilvie-Fenton, while assuring the ladies that there was no need for worry, was *au courant* with the latest rumours.

'French spies,' breathed Charlotte, 'but why here?'

'I misdoubt me that it's nought but nonsense,' broke in Lord Balgowan. 'There have been rumours for years. French invasions indeed.'

The gallant captain was not so easily dismissed. 'Napoleon is keen on annexation. Britain has been a thorn in his side for years and he knows he cannot succeed through the Channel, so illustrious is our navy.'

Liddy sat, in something approaching horror, and listened. For a moment she had believed the captain to be the third man in the castle, but listening to the heated argument, she was forced to believe that either each man was completely honourable or one was playing a deep game. Her papa had been in the castle; he had been speaking French. Why? Was he aiding and abetting another who was the spy?

At last she rose. 'Gentlemen, we will leave you to your port.'

Her mind racing, she led her sister to the drawing room. Pray they would not linger long for she had a four-mile gallop to the abbey. Perhaps they would be at outs with one another and the captain would leave early but no, barely half an hour later, all three strolled into the room, ready for cards or music or whatever the ladies had planned.

'I say, old girl, you ain't looking quite the thing,' remarked Captain Ogilvie-Fenton to Liddy.

Liddy smiled up at him. 'I don't know why it is, but all political chat gives me the headache.'

'Talk of ought but the price of sheep gives you the headache, Lydia,' her father said. 'How you will manage to support a fashionable lifestyle I know not, for everything puts you to sleep.'

Since Liddy could not admit that lack of sleep caused her

occasional yawn, she bore this public scold with fortitude and soon the gentlemen, feeling the atmosphere somewhat strained, bid their host and his daughters goodnight. Lord Balgowan did not return to the drawing room and to avoid conversation with her sister, Liddy too fled.

In her room she almost tore off the lovely dress. She flew to the window and looked out. Could she not hang a lamp there for her smugglers? No, to do so would destroy her anonymity. There was a clatter of hooves in the courtyard and she looked down in time to see her father wheel his horse round and gallop off in the direction of the castle.

A fishing boat was heading steadily for Arbroath, but the horizon was empty. Should she follow her father or go to the abbey? Could she do both? The stables and the house were still lit. She could not walk boldly down in her brother's clothes. Would they ever go to bed? Pray, do not have your groom wait for you, Papa. She turned down her lamp and sat by the window, helpless with frustration. The stable lamp went out and a candle glowed briefly in the apartment above. Go to sleep, Tom. Obligingly he blew out his candle. Light spilled across the courtyard, proving that the kitchen staff were still cleaning.

A few minutes later she stood listening outside the tower door. She had to cross the courtyard without being seen by Mrs Harper. In no time at all, Amber was saddled and she was heading out of the yard.

The cry she had been dreading rang out, 'Where be you agoing with that mare?' It was Sam, for once at his post and not at the tavern.

Liddy vaulted into the saddle. 'Out of my way, man. Miss Carpenter has authorised my use of her pony. Discuss it with her.'

Sam was so surprised that he fell back and Liddy galloped off, her heart thumping in her ribcage.

I fear I am not made for a life of crime. How will I return? Worry later, Liddy, she argued with herself and allowed Amber to gallop. No time to follow Lord Balgowan. She must reach the Abbey. She did not climb the wall this time but straddled an outer wall with a good view of the sea. An hour later a naval vessel loomed on the horizon and then a small private vessel, but never the *Shuska*.

Liddy waited long past the time agreed with Visieux and then headed home. Instead of striking out across country she went back along the coast. She supposed that the identity of the small boat she had observed had concerned her for she was almost unsurprised to find it anchored in one of the many hidden coves. Should she investigate? She dismounted and crept forward. A crew member looked to be on guard.Whoever had come in must be concealed in one of the caves. She suddenly ducked down as she heard some scrabbling from the rocks below.

'You will explain that it was the weather delayed me, Yves.'

'Much better, m'Lord, if you explain yourself. I am bidden to bring you with me since you are a week late for your meeting and yet someone else kept it for you. Who was that, sir?'

The voices retreated down the beach as the men, one willing, the other perhaps unwilling, went to the boat and Liddy lay in the sand and watched it go. She rode back to the house ready to be discovered, and unwilling to do ought to prevent it. Wearily she dismounted in full view of the dark windows of the house and led Amber to her stall. The stable was open and a welcoming lamp shone in the dark, but of Tom or Sam there was no sign. Almost in a stupor she locked up and returned to the house. In the same half dream state she undressed, remembering to hide her clothes, and fell into bed.

Full remembrance of the evening returned the next morning together with her morning tea. She begged Madame to send Miss Rattray to her if that lady were not too involved with the babes and when she appeared a few minutes later poured out the whole story.

'And why did Sam not wait up?'

'How adept I am become at prevarication, Liddy. I invented a young man, in penurious circumstances, though of excellent birth, who is allowed use of Amber.'

'Rattles, what of Papa?'

Miss Rattray's heart bled at the despair in the young voice but she had never mollycoddled her charges. 'A message was received last night. His Lordship is to be from home for upwards of seven days.'

'He did say he had business intended, but Rattles, he said nought of being coerced, for so I think it was, into boarding that

118

boat. I must assume he is gone to France, for they spoke French and all was so . . . clandestine. I have thought and thought and if someone met someone whom Papa was supposed to meet and that was in France, then it could well have been one of my smugglers. It is all so improbable . . . isn't it?' She did not expect an answer.

'I will see Sam. Perhaps he knows something.'

But Sam professed to know nothing of his master's business. 'And I am sorry as I yelled at your friend, Miss Lydia, but I left all right and tight for him.'

'He was grateful, Sam, but Papa's horse . . . ?'

'The messenger did bring him, Miss, saying as His Lordship did not require him.'

'Did you know the messenger?'

'Can't say I did, Miss Lydia, but then I knows only them as I sees in The Eagle's Nest.'

Liddy thanked him and returned to the house. The messenger was not French then for Sam had supposed him local. She took a deep breath. She must lay the whole situation before Pittenmuir when he was returned and this thought, which had filled her with tremulous joy a week before, now made her almost faint with horror.

For a girl who saw ruin staring her in the face Miss Carpenter managed to go through the day with remarkable composure. She chatted with her sisters and fielded questions about the sudden departure of their papa with commendable virtuosity. All the time, under her calm appearance, her brain was seething.

By the time she again cantered out on her way to the abbey she was in a fever of anticipation. Tonight the *Shuska* must show for the storm had abated and, although the weather was unkind, it would by no means hinder such good seamen. She dreaded the climb, but knew there was no other way. Whether they looked for spies or smugglers the militia were out in force and she must not fall foul of them.

There was some activity out to sea and twice she was sure she saw her ship and at last, when she had all but decided to ride home, she recognized the particular lights for which she searched. No time to lose. With a sickening feeling in her stomach, which she attempted to banish by assuring herself that this indeed was the last time, she began her ascent.

Spurred on by recollection that this time she was in earnest, she struggled on, found a finger hold, then a toe hold and a ledge to cling to, but did not look down. She climbed higher and higher, her breath coming in noisy gasps. Then came the moment she had dreaded; she knew that to save her life she could go no farther. She stretched her bruised hand upwards, fumbled with the flint and the lamp was lit. 'I can do no more. Pray God he reads it.'

A feeling of euphoria stole over her; I have succeeded. She looked down and could not see the ground. Shaken, she clung to her window and her euphoria deserted her. Either she had to climb down or remain, either until she fell or the watch discovered her. She bit her lip and began to descend. Liddy closed her eyes . . . she had to jump. She landed on the boulder-strewn grass and lay for a moment dazed. Every bone felt broken but no, she was able to rise and, sobbing softly, she hobbled over to the encircling wall. She somehow managed to mount Amber, and keeping to the back streets, headed for the cove.

Captain Visieux did not in fact find the waters so calm as he had been led to believe, but he was a sailor and although several very choice, very French expressions passed his lips, only one of his crew understood and appreciated them. One and all applauded his seamanship and long before Pate came exhaustedly into the cove, they were busily unloading the ship into the hands of the land waiters who had been waiting anxiously.

Liddy was so tired and in such pain from her cut hands and innumerable bruises that she almost fell at their feet and saw John push himself forward to catch her.

'Pray do not concern yourself. I am not hurt,' gasped the young man.

'But you be bleeding,' said John.

'It's nought but scratches,' laughed Keir as he lifted the boy's hands to examine them and was startled when the youngster pulled them away, blushing furiously. What a delicate lad to be sure, thought Keir, for the hands had been as soft as those of a young girl. John was still standing guard over the lad, like a dog over his favourite bone. Hero worship, thought Keir, and why not if so fragile a boy with his girlish hands is yet capable of shinning up a ruined wall. He returned to his labours, and when they were done, Pate and his horse had disappeared.

The ruffian Scott's touch had set Liddy's body atingling in a new and utterly incomprehensible way but she had snatched her hands away that he might not see the remains of her manicure. After that she hardly knew what she said or did but was conscious that she had been rash in riding in upon the group.

'Tomorrow night, in the hall at Balgowan Castle,' said Tam. 'We do get our shares then. Best to disperse and get home for his young Lordship says the militia be on the look-out. Get back to Auchmithie, Ian, with old Charlie and, as you walk, remember you are a lassie.'

Keir, who had completely forgotten that he was once again wearing Tam's wife's second best frock, laughed and they parted amicably. He and Charlie were alone on the beach.

'What's wrong?' he asked.

'Nothing, lad. Just I have seen that lad's horse afore and strap me if I can remember where.'

'It was so dark and they were all of them so busy; none could recognize Amber,' Liddy told herself repeatedly as, once back at Balgowan House, she drifted off to sleep.

Sleep was slow in coming for her mind was full of that strange feeling she had experienced when Scott, firmly but somehow, oh so gently, had held her hands.

Twelve

Miss Carpenter and my Lord Pittenmuir each woke thinking of hands; he thought of delicate hands with pink-tipped nails cruelly bruised and battered.

'I must look at that abbey wall,' he said to himself, 'for if my memory serves me right, it should have been impossible to climb . . . and in the dark too.'

Tonight he would have a much closer look at Master Pate, for there was something oddly familiar about the boy.

Miss Liddy woke and blushed to remember how she had coloured when Scott had taken her hand. She told herself that embarrassment was merely because she feared he might know the hands for those of a woman and vowed not to allow him near her this evening. Would she even manage to meet them, for a night's rest had not improved her physical well-being? She had never felt worse in her life. Every bone and muscle protested whenever she moved. How lovely just to lie here, allow Madame and Rattles to wait upon her, and never think of spies or smugglers again.

She fell to musing about the lifestyle of a social butterfly. Indeed what bliss it would be to worry only about gowns or the success of a ball. I should be bored to death in a minute. But would that not be better than going to jail as a smuggler or being ostracized because one was the daughter of a . . . Her mind refused to say the word.

She sat up groaning and talked to herself briskly. One you brought upon yourself, Liddy, and the other is not of your doing and so we will refine no more upon either and attend to the business on hand. She had crawled out of bed and hobbled to her dressing table when a knock on the door heralded the arrival of Madame. She took the hairbrush with which Liddy had been attempting to restore some semblance of style to her disordered locks and brushed as she told her, 'Major Fordyce is come and wishes to speak with you, Miss Lydia. I told him you were not below stairs yet, but he says you would be wishful for him to wait.'

It had come then. Keir was returned and she must tell him about her father. How could she, and yet, how could she not? Harry had died for this little island.

'I do wish to see the major, Madame. Be so good as to tell him that I will be with him directly and then come back and finish my hair, if you please.'

Madame was delighted that Miss Lydia should show enough interest in a man to suffer having her hair done. Liddy, perfectly aware of the thoughts going through her abigail's head, hurried to pull on a dress lest Madame see her bruises.

'Miss Lydia, really. You cannot see a gentleman in such an old gown,' was that woman's disappointed comment when she returned.

Liddy smiled as Madame accepted defeat almost gracefully. She suffered Madame to do her best with her hair but angrily brushed aside her suggestion of a little rouge. Rouge? Liddy looked measuringly at herself in the glass and admitted to looking a trifle hagged. Her usually pale complexion had no colour at all and there were deep shadows under her eyes. That ruffian, Scott, no doubt appreciated painted hussies. Abruptly she dismissed Madame.

'Go to Charlotte, Madame. She is more worthy of your skills.'

Going downstairs was, for Liddy, perfect agony. Her legs seemed to have set themselves overnight and absolutely refused to obey requests to go downstairs normally. Major Fordyce noticed her pallor. He said nothing but bowed politely.

'He is come then?' Liddy enquired, immediately. No social chitter-chatter about this young woman.

'I am in receipt of a message from His Lordship, Miss Carpenter. He expects to be with us tomorrow and will call upon you as soon as may be convenient for you. I regret that Lord Balgowan has been called away. Lord Pittenmuir would wish that they might have time for—' He stopped unable to continue.

'For what?' asked Liddy coldly. 'A chat over old times. Lord Pittenmuir has not seen my father since before my brother's death. Even at that time there was but a polite letter of condolence, writ, if I remember rightly, by yourself.'

She stood up and perforce the major had to do likewise. 'Miss Carpenter,' he began. 'His Lordship—'

'Pray do not distress yourself, Major. His Lordship made a jest with Miss Fairweather: he found it impossible to tear himself away from the beauties of Portugal.'

'But Miss Carpenter—,' he tried again.

'Yes,' she said but it was not a welcoming sound.

He shook his head and could not meet her direct gaze.

Etienne came in answer to her ring. 'Show Major Fordyce out. I give you good day, Major.' How glad she was that he had reminded her of Pittenmuir's superficiality. It would be easier to deal with him tomorrow.

She decided to spend some time in the library going over the accounts that she had not touched since her father's return. It took but a few minutes to realize that, despite his fine words, Lord Balgowan had done nothing to remove any strain on the estate. Indeed, it looked as if they were in an even more precarious position.

'Liddy, what is this story of Madame's?' It was Charlotte. 'Papa gone. Why should he make such a decision in the middle of the night?'

Liddy thought quickly. Were their father to be arrested for treason, Charlotte would not be long in ignorance of the fact, but there was no need to tell her before it was absolutely necessary. Hopefully, something could be arranged with Lord Pittenmuir, though she would hate asking a favour of him. Papa might even be allowed to live abroad and they could live quietly somewhere.

'Silly puss,' she chided, catching Charlotte's hands and pulling her down on to the sofa. 'You must know that gentlemen are forever deciding at odd hours that they must do this or that. It is an infantile ploy to make themselves feel important, and an attempt to convince we poor women that they are important. Any woman would arrange to pack trunks, have a good night's sleep against the trials of the journey, but a man?'

Charlotte still looked doubtful. 'But he said nothing at all.'

'We talked of his removal at dinner not three nights ago. Come, Charlotte, you must know that Papa thinks very little of our intellectual capability. He considers women incapable of rational thought. He pictures us quite in awe of our important father who is called away in the middle of the night, when all we

124

think is that he would have done better to wait till morning and breakfast.'

Charlotte laughed but she was still troubled. 'Why did he send his horse back? I know you will say because he did not need it, but it is strange. Should his friends not rather have met him here?'

'Naturally they should, but the minds of men do not work sensibly, although it is they who think themselves subtle. In a week or so Papa will return and expect us to be agog with pride in his importance.'

'He had no clothes with him.'

'Charlotte,' said Liddy in the voice one uses to explain things to a very young child, 'we do not know that. We know very little of Papa, where he lives, his friends, anything. He might keep trunks in a dozen houses for all we know. Please, dearest, no more worries, for that will give you wrinkles and – Lord Pittenmuir returns tomorrow.'

This delightful news, as Liddy had known full well, caused Charlotte to smile. No doubt she was dreaming of captivating His Lordship. Poor Charlotte. Yes, Lord Pittenmuir could be considered well looking – even handsome – and he was an eligible bachelor, but he was not for Charlotte. He is not right for such a gentle girl, she thought. She would always be in awe of him and that would bore him to death and he would be unkind to her. No, he would not be unkind but he would be miserable and . . . oh enough. Why do I even think of him?'

'Mayhap he will hold a party where I may wear my dress,' Charlotte said, hopefully.

'Never say so, Charlotte, for remember that Sir Thomas must also be a guest and has seen it already. Now go off, foolish child, and leave me to my books.'

Liddy's heart was heavy as Charlotte danced from the room. There would be no parties for the daughter of a disgraced man, no matter how pretty. Charlotte's life could not be ruined, so Liddy spent several hours trying to devise ways of persuading Lord Pittenmuir not to bring the full weight of the law down upon Balgowan House – at least until Charlotte was established.

'I had nurtured hopes of Jamie for her, but I cannot blame him for his brother's ill manners. She did seem to look on him with favour before Pittenmuir smiled and turned her silly head. We must look elsewhere.' Not once did it occur to Miss Carpenter to weep any tears for her own life that looked set to be ruined.

She prepared for her meeting with the smugglers with a stoicism bordering on the fatalistic. Tonight would be her last chance to see them; she must disband the group for who knew what Lord Pittenmuir would demand on the morrow? Midnight found her in the great hall of the castle with several bright lamps around her. She had had enough of the dark and the hall was so vast that still she sat in shadow. The night was dark and though she strained her eyes gazing out of the great windows she saw nothing of the smugglers coming until she heard hooves in the courtyard.

Not lost to caution she waited lest they be revenuers before she opened the doors. As a gesture this was unnecessary but Miss Carpenter wished them to see that she was quite recovered. She trusted none saw her wince as she greeted them. First she had to hear the tale of their adventures and their battle with the sea.

'Here's John, who was near drownded,' shouted Tam as she closed her eyes in horror at the thought and opened them again quickly for fear they see her squeamishness.

'I was not,' said John. 'I but lost my balance and Scott there held me till I could get a foothold.'

She glanced at the tall man who sat silently in a corner, but his eyes shied away. So he does not want to be a hero, thought Liddy. How surprising to find such delicacy of feeling in such a one.

'I have visited the abbey today, lad,' said Charlie. 'That was a daft thing you did climbing up that wall.'

Liddy shrugged nonchalantly. 'I was used to climb walls with my—' She stopped in confusion for John was looking at her in horror and she could also feel Scott's eyes upon her. 'Anyone could have done it,' she amended, 'and besides,' she finished honestly, 'I could think of no other way.'

'It was bravely done, lad,' said old Charlie, 'and you were right to steer us away from Arbroath. Even Auchmithie is alive with marines and rumours abound.'

'They talk of spies. What would Napoleon want with this bit of coastline? He'd not get far though. We were forever sighting the bloody navy.' It was Tam who spoke.

Liddy could see John blush with embarrassment at Tam's language and so suggested that they celebrate their safe return.

She waited until they were enjoying their second measure and said, 'Think you this should be our last trip, lads. We cannot hope to continue so lucky.'

There was an immediate babble and Liddy sat while arguments raged back and forth, but it appeared only John agreed with her.

'While we're prepared to take the risks, my fine young buck,' sneered Scott, 'we'll thank you to sit safe and watch for us.'

'We have made a deal of money,' said Liddy. 'You, Tam, seem set to become respectable.'

Tam, whose wife had begun selling provisions from the front room of their cottage and talked of expansion, looked chagrined. 'You have eyes everywhere, young fella. Aye, I'm of a mind to give up the sea . . .'

Scott stood up with no stoop and less cringing. In height he dominated every man and there was something indefinable about him. 'I have not,' he said. 'Come, men, while the navy looks for spies they will not trouble us. A few more trips like this and we all retire. I have a fancy to become inn-keeper,' and he pranced around filling all the mugs while the men laughed and agreed that he would make a prodigious generous host.'

'Damn, the man is a nuisance and so I will tell Charlie,' vowed Liddy as angrily she held her mug away from the over-generous barman.

'No stomach for a real man's drink, pretty boy?' goaded the oafish lout and Liddy wished she might run him through for his impertinence She did not see him look at her hands and then up at her face.

Even the news that Lord Pittenmuir was returned failed to frighten the smugglers. 'We are a match for any prancing Lord,' scoffed Tam, 'are we not, friend?' Drunkenly he threw his arms round Scott who agreed with him enthusiastically.

It was time for Liddy to go. John agreed with her. Alone among the smugglers he was not drinking. Mind you, she had not actually seen Scott share the liquor he was so liberally pouring for the others. 'Get you home afore they're drunk,' hissed John.

'Before? Surely they are.'

'Not them. They're sober but on their way. I mislike the way Scott eyes you.'

'He cannot guess.'

'Have a care, Miss Lydia,' whispered the troubled John. 'Slip out now. I will work in the gardens tomorrow and tell you how all works out.'

'But I go to see Pittenmuir tomorrow.'

'Oh, God,' groaned John. 'Go home.'

What could have occasioned such a start as that in John? What did he know of Keir? As far as she knew the boy had never seen His Lordship. She rode home, stabled Amber, and went to bed thinking of what to say to Pittenmuir.

In the morning, to Madame's surprise and delight, she actually asked Madame to fix her hair. Madame took courage in both hands. 'A little rouge, Miss Carpenter?'

Liddy laughed. 'Why not indeed? We frail women must use all the weapons in our armoury.' She noted the formal use of her title and unbent a little. The woman, after all, had done nothing to deserve her disapprobation.

'Your gown, Miss Carpenter?'

'What would you suggest, Madame? A new gown?'

Madame considered. 'No, not a new gown. I suggest that lovely dark green wool with the velvet epaulettes à la militaire.'

'Fie, Madame,' teased Liddy although the gown in question was a particular favourite. 'That gown must be quite five seasons old.'

'A woman of style always knows what suits her, Miss Lydia.' Madame too moved half-way.' If you will forgive the familiarity, miss, our dear Miss Charlotte has beauty and is so young and pretty that everything suits her, but you, Miss Carpenter, you have style.'

Liddy thanked her gravely and sent her off knowing full well that the abigail would likely go to the ballroom from which windows she could easily watch the front drive. She could pretend to be dusting should anyone discover her. Even the dustiest of unused ballrooms cannot be dusted for ever and fate took Madame above stairs to the nurseries. It was, therefore, Etienne who stepped ponderously above stairs to answer the loud knocking on the front door and who admitted, not at eleven, but at nearer to three o'clock, Keir, Lord Pittenmuir. Miss Carpenter, who had expected a morning caller and so had risen too early, was testy and greeted His Lordship coldly. She did not give him her hand and had the pleasure of seeing him look a trifle discomfited and not at all his usual elegant self.

'Please do sit down, my Lord,' she said formally indicating a sofa as far away from herself as it was possible for him to sit and still converse with her.

'Liddy, why are you so angry?' he asked, ignoring the proffered chair and instead sitting down beside her.

Liddy chose not to understand. 'You have come, I am sure, about my allegation that a spy might be operating in this area.'

'A spy for the French is operating in this area, Miss Carpenter. We have it on the highest authority.'

Liddy rose and unconsciously clasped her hands to her bosom. She was oblivious of everything but concern for her father and did not see the startled look on Pittenmuir's face as he glimpsed her poor battered fingers.

'How long have you known, Keir?' It was the old Liddy who spoke.

Lord Pittenmuir had risen when his hostess did and now walked to the window and looked out. He could not believe it, but of course it was Liddy, foolish, brave and totally exasperating Liddy. Dear God, she might have been killed. He tried to keep the anger, occasioned by fear for her, from his face. He would like to wring her neck – and he would, if he could but bring an end to this business. Had she recognized him? Thank God he had kept his face from her and then there was the beard, ruthlessly scraped off that very morning.

'Naturally as Lord Lieutenant of Forfarshire, I am apprised of everything that is toward,' he said in his most patronizing tone – as different from the tones of Ian Scott as he could make them – and felt instinctively that he had successfully annoyed her. No doubt she had the same plan for his neck as he had for hers.

'And how much do you know or may one not ask the Lord Lieutenant such a question?' How pompous he was become. She turned so that he might not see her face.

'You may ask what you like, Miss Carpenter, but I would point out to you that a loyal subject of His Majesty should rather be telling me what she knows.'

'I know the identity of the spy,' she said quietly and had the satisfaction of seeing the supercilious look wiped from his face.

'Then no doubt, Madame, you will be kind enough to tell me.'

'There is a price.'

'There always is,' answered Keir wearily, conscious of a feeling of disappointment quite as sharp as the blow that had felled him at Vimiero. 'How much?' Obviously it would be for financial gain – she was hardly running a smuggling enterprise for fun but, spying . . . he could scarce believe it, not of the Liddy he had grown up with and loved. Dear God, he had loved her all his life.

She was not looking at him but down at her hands. 'A pardon, signed by Perceval.'

'Good heavens,' he began angrily.

She held up her hands to silence him. 'And complete anonymity.'

'You ask too much. I had thought money was your God.'

'Money?' She looked down at her gown, so foolishly chosen since it suited her tall elegance. 'Had you spent any time in the county, my Lord, you would know, as all our neighbours do, that this gown is five years old.'

He grabbed her by the upper arms and pulled her round as he had done time and again in childhood. 'What stupid lengths would you go to in order to replenish your wardrobe, Liddy, or to what depths would you sink?'

'How dare you, sir.' Had he not had tight hold of her arms she would have slapped him as she had done time without number in the long ago days.

He saw the intent in her furious eyes. 'Shall I release you Liddy, you little cat? Will you slap me? To do so is frowned on in society, you know.'

'What care I for society? Wishy-washy. Miss Fairweather and the like are too fatigued to show spirit.'

He looked at her and had to hide a smile. If he laughed she surely would box his ears. Liddy, Liddy. How he wanted to shake her. He would tease her instead.

'Fatigued? Miss Fairweather? No, indeed, Miss Carpenter.' He smiled reminiscently. 'What a woman. She can dance all night and still be as fresh as a mountain daisy for breakfast parties.' He walked away from her to control his laughter and then turned as if struck by a kind thought. 'Why, Liddy, I have it. Shall I beseech Leonora to give you lessons in assuming ennuie. In society a lady pretends to be bored by her courtiers. No matter how angry he made her she would never resort to violence – it's just too immature.'

Liddy blushed furiously and Keir, Lord Pittenmuir, fought with his growing desire to kiss her lips, to force her to confide in him, to tell him all. But did he want to hear her say that she loved another so much that she would become smuggler for him, traitor for him even?

She drooped suddenly like a flower that can no longer withstand the force of the gale and he released her. 'Take my offer or leave it,' she said quietly. She turned away from him to hide the tears. 'I will find some other way if you do not agree to help me.'

Anger so fierce swelled up in him, and he wanted to shake her. Who was her lover that she tried so hard to protect him? Compassion swamped her anger. How young she looked and so defenceless, standing there looking at her broken fingernails but, as if conscious of the warring emotions in his breast, Liddy pulled herself up and raised her head proudly.

'Well, my Lord?' she asked, looking into his eyes. 'Do we have an agreement?'

Should he tell her he knew her for a smuggler? Would she beg? No, more like tell him to prove it.

'Do I understand that you want me to ask pardon for a traitor? Why should I, Liddy?'

'For Harry's sake,' she said quietly.

God, this became more and more a quagmire. What is it that I cannot see? 'For Harry's sake?' he asked. 'You know the identity of a spy and I must ask pardon for him for Harry . . . ?' No, dear God, she cannot mean what I fear she means. 'I must inform the Prime Minister.'

'Naturally.'

'This will take time and much damage could be done in the meantime.'

'I have a strong reason to hope that there will be no further transfer of information from my source,' said Liddy who wondered how she could forcibly manhandle her own father if she were compelled, as well she might, to do so. How could she tell him that something she had overheard made her suspect that another agent was active – possibly one of her smugglers? Lord Balgowan had not kept his appointment; that was because inclement weather had forced him to remain in Scotland. Someone, however, had kept his rendezvous and the *Shuska* had been in France at the time. This was no coincidence, was it? Her head was reeling and she had an almost overwhelming desire to burst into tears.

Lord Pittenmuir watched her and mastered the desire to put his arms around her and tell her that all would be well. Had Harry's death changed her? No matter what he had said in the heat of anger he knew that she had never been swayed by thoughts of monetary gain. Be ruthless, he advised himself. What do I know of her? I knew a child and the child has become this woman and her I . . . do not know at all.

'I will leave you to reflect on your situation, Miss Carpenter. Please remember that we are discussing treason. Pray allow me to remind you that every second you waste with your absurd scruples helps the career of the man whose lust for personal glory led, at least indirectly, to the death of your brother.'

He was not allowed to finish. To his astonishment, the docile chastened girl in front of him turned into a veritable virago and boxed his ears. 'How dare you mention him, you . . . you . . . false friend. Get out,' she screamed and so that he would not have the satisfaction of seeing her tears, she fled from the room.

Lord Pittenmuir nursed his jaw and then laughed. That was Liddy, the shrew, who slapped him, but why 'false friend'? He would have to ask John. The memories of several painful weeks in Portugal were quite hazy, but surely he was guilty of nothing that could make Liddy call him that.

Thirteen

'Why do I weep?' Angrily, Liddy taxed herself with the vexing question, but since no satisfactory answer vouchsafed itself, she gave herself up to an exhausting but extremely satisfying bout of tears. It seemed that she wept for everything and that all the fears and frustrations of the years since her mama's death were now at last being washed out of her system.

'If you could but weep, Liddy.' How many times had those with her best interests at heart spoken so to her, but resolutely Liddy had stiffened her backbone and refused to succumb? Why, if she were to indulge in a flood of tears, who would comfort the babes, or soothe Charlotte, or order provisions, or speak to old Tom about his fears that he might lose not only his employment but his home, or . . . ? The list was endless but now that hateful, supercilious, pompous, patronizing oaf had opened the floodgates and Liddy Carpenter wept. Not for long. Somehow, finding choice adjectives with which to adorn the arrogance, the condescension, the pretension of that man dried the tears and lit the torch of battle. All was not yet lost.

She just had to persuade her papa not to continue, to uncover and hand over to the authorities any other spy in the vicinity, and to disband, against their wishes, her merry band. Furious with herself for having crushed her almost favourite gown, she rose from the bed and shook out its folds just as a timid knock on the door heralded the arrival of Charlotte closely followed by Miss Rattray.

'Liddy, dearest, what has Lord Pittenmuir said to cast you into mopes? I had hoped he was come on a pleasant errand. Does he not plan to entertain while he is here?' asked a hopeful Charlotte.

'I know not, Charlotte, and had I my way I would never again willingly set eyes on His Lordship. Pray ask me no more until I am composed.' Knowing that this was not enough for her sister, she added somewhat mendaciously, 'We spoke of Harry.'

133

Since the sensitive Charlotte could do nothing but hold her sister's hands in hers, Miss Rattray said, 'It has taken three years, Liddy, but it is all to the good. Did we not say, Charlotte my love, that it was not good for Liddy to bottle up her grief? Now, if you will leave us, my dear, I will try to soothe your sister.'

'Shall I prepare a tisane for you, dearest?' asked Charlotte, unwilling to yield her place, but when this kind offer was rejected she agreed to pick flowers with which to cheer her sister and her rather austere chamber.

'I am in no need of soothing, Rattles,' said Liddy as soon as the door had closed behind her sister.

'What occurred, Liddy? It was not Harry, I vow.'

As usual in moments of distress, Liddy walked around the room, eventually stopping by the window so that she might look out to sea. Today its nature, even more restless than her own, failed to comfort her and she returned to Miss Rattray's side.

'Dear friend,' she said, taking the older woman's hand, 'you can have no idea how earnestly I wish that you had left us when Papa first failed to pay your totally inadequate salary.'

'You are blue-devilled,' exclaimed Rattles. 'What can Lord Pittenmuir have said to so overset you?'

Liddy laughed, a harsh unpleasant sound.

'Rattles, you know that several weeks ago I encountered some men in the castle and, for reasons I need not divulge, I assumed them spies. All my childish Jacobite sympathies melted in the heat of the hideous reality before me. I rushed to inform Lord Pittenmuir – in his guise as Lord Lieutenant, you understand – and today His Lordship, looking sadly dissipated I might add, managed to tear himself away from the delights of town, and came to demand the identity of my spy.'

Again she stood up and paced about the room but Rattles said nothing, knowing that she would continue when she was ready.

'Since first I spoke to Major Fordyce I have uncovered the spy. Oh, Rattles, it was possible to measure the contempt in his voice when he spoke to me, but I disconcerted him and slapped him too which was immeasurably satisfying.'

This satisfaction had not lasted for she fell to weeping again and Miss Rattray, who had understood not a word of the last disjointed part of the monologue, soothed her quietly and waited for her to be calm.

'Liddy, my dearest child, a most disquieting feeling is growing in me.'

She looked down at the sobbing girl and was angry. 'I should enjoy giving Keir a piece of my mind. How dare he upset you like this when you have no-one but a useless old governess to protect you.'

Liddy raised her head. 'Useless, never say it. What would the babes, Charlotte, Harry, and I have done without your care all these years?'

'I loved your mama, my dear, and grew to love all her children. Now no more maudlin talk.'

'Very well.' Liddy blew her nose fiercely on one of Harry's old handkerchiefs. 'Rattles, you know the spy, admit it.'

Mutely Rattles nodded as Liddy continued. 'I asked His Lordship to obtain a pardon for him in return for a promise that he would remain abroad. Had you but heard the disdain in his voice . . .'

Miss Rattray was becoming sadly bogged down under the weight of pronouns. 'He, your spy, is abroad, Liddy?'

'I believe him gone, somewhat unwillingly, to France.'

Rattles waited quietly while Liddy told her all about the conversation she had overheard.

'And you think that one of your men is also a spy?'

'That seems obvious. Someone met the French contact. It is possible that a second boat reached France last week but, Rattles, in time of war how many boats sail between adversaries?'

'True, my dear, but remember that you are not the only smugglers to ply between Britain and France.'

'It is difficult to explain, and makes no sense, but I have a strong feeling and then there is a new member of our band, a friend of old Charlie who was used to teach Harry and me to sail. There is something about him, almost a feeling that I know him, but I could not, could I?'

'If he is a friend of Charlie, you might have met him years ago.'

Liddy again rose and began her pacing. 'Perhaps . . . and Rattles, he held my hands when I came into the cove and . . .' She looked directly at Miss Rattray. 'There was such a strange feeling passed as if . . . I must get out. Walk with me in the gardens, down to the beach or to the castle.'

They took their shawls since it was a blustery day and Rattles changed into stout walking shoes; although she had no intention of walking to the beach, a good three miles away, she knew she would have to walk far. So it proved. The grounds at Balgowan House could not hold Liddy. She led the governess out and up the hill to the ruins but did not stop and continued walking, Miss Rattray almost running by her side.

'Liddy, I can go no farther. Indeed, I have a stitch.'

Immediately Liddy was all contrition. 'Such a boor I am. Why do you tolerate me? Sit here on this boulder, dear friend.' She spread her shawl over the large rock and Miss Rattray sat down thankfully.

Miss Rattray could see that Liddy was still full of nervous energy. 'You walk to the top of the hill, Liddy, and we will talk on your return.'

Obediently Liddy went off and when she reached the top she stopped and looked down. She could see the sea, the castle and between, the two Balgowan homes; one ancient and a ruin, the other new and homely, but both close to her heart. Two small red dots, her sisters, were running around the gardens in a frenzy, and there was Charlotte in the rose garden.

'I will protect them, even if I have to crawl on bended knees to Pittenmuir.'

There was someone else in the garden and she had to see him.

'Quickly, Rattles, let us return. John is in the gardens and I must talk with him.'

'Then do you go on. I have no desire to fly downhill, my hair streaming behind like a Valkyrie.'

Liddy looked at her in amazement. 'Do I really walk so quickly; it is all fault of my long legs. Indeed, we will stroll home like ladies of leisure enjoying this early autumnal air.'

If they did so, poor Rattles was still exhausted upon their return, but made no complaint and went off thankfully to enjoy a reviving cup of tea, caring not whether or no it was smuggled.

John was busy among the vegetables. He looked up at Liddy's approach. 'I have spoken with Lord Pittenmuir,' she spoke gently but firmly and was surprised to see not embarrassment but relief on the boy's face. 'Why your concern, John? Did you fear I might tell him of our activities so that he would stop our enterprise?'

John was shocked and hurt. 'Miss Lydia, I know you wouldn't

do nothing like that. I was afeared as how His Lordship might ask you about the smuggling, thinking as how you might have heard of it.'

As he finished speaking he flushed darkly and failed to meet her eyes. Liddy was puzzled. He was lying, but why?

'His Lordship was here on another matter, John. Mayhap he is one of those archaic gentlemen who perceive the activities of smugglers as an unsuitable subject of conversation for gently bred young ladies but he certainly made no mention of it.'

'The vote was to go on, Miss Lydia.'

'I suppose that ghastly new fellow was at the bottom of it?' said Liddy but John, who heartily agreed with her, appeared to find it well nigh impossible to phrase an answer.

'I mislike the thought, John, but I suspect I have met him somewhere, but surely 'tis not possible. Although when I was a girl, I had the most marvellous fun with my brother and . . . and a friend. We used to sail our boat into all the coves from Auchmithie to Dundee. I met so many fisherfolk then.'

'Ahh, that's nice, Miss Lydia,' said John while he did his best to uproot a row of cabbages carefully planted by Tom for the coming winter.

'Weed round them, John, not over them,' advised Liddy. 'Why do you suppose the others listen to him, Tam for instance?'

John straightened up. 'He made it sound like fun, Miss Lydia, like we had enjoyed ourselves. Even when we was talking about me near falling overboard, he made us laugh, me an'all. Yet, when it were happening I were scared to death.'

'A very dangerous man,' said Liddy thoughtfully, a strange suspicion growing in her mind. 'Look, Tom is coming. I must speak to him. Finish here and meet me in the succession house.'

But when she had chatted with the old man, Liddy did not go immediately to look for the boy. Her mind was in a whirl. Scott reminded her of someone, but of whom? If only she had been able to look closely at his face. Had he deliberately kept out of her line of vision and if he had, why?

When Liddy caught up with John, she asked him about that most suspicious of men. 'Quickly, ere I return to the house. One question only. Did Scott ever leave the ship?'

'Might ha' done, Miss Liddy.' John , whose life had twice been saved by His Lordship, took refuge in prevarication.

'I knew it,' said Liddy, and deeply satisfied, returned to the house.

There she sat like an angel and allowed Madame to brush and curl her hair. She permitted a little rouge on her pale cheeks. In truth, she scarce knew what was happening and cared less. She knew her spy. Now, to catch him and hand him on a platter to the hateful and hated Lord Lieutenant.

Her heart was light and she could now see a clear way ahead. She could not only stop her father's disloyal activities, but also catch and hand over a second spy so Keir would be forced to accede to her terms. Liddy was well aware of the penalty for spying but, she argued, if a spy were uncovered and exposed he became useless to his masters. She also knew only too well how she and the girls would be ostracized if their father's activities became known. How unfair was the polite world to punish Charlotte and the babes for their father's sins. No, Keir had been fond of them once, so he could be made to ensure that no censure fell on the girls. Lord Balgowan's continued absence would raise no comment as he had never been fond of Scotland, anyway.

At dinner she was able to stall Charlotte who was not satisfied with her report of the interview with their illustrious neighbour. 'I told you that I know not whether His Lordship means to entertain. He is here on government business. It appears that there is a spy for the French working in this area.'

As she had expected, this made interesting dinner table conversation. The little girls were half-frightened, half-excited and Rattles enjoyed filling their ears and, she hoped, their minds, with facts. Since the family rarely met anyone other than their few members of staff, the local minister and a few county families, they had a very small list of suspects and Liddy was soon able to make them forget their fears by assuring them that only Rattles and Mr Wallace, the minister, were possessed of enough intelligence to make good spies. Visions of this unholy alliance caused even Charlotte to choke with laughter and Liddy was able to turn her own mind to the perplexing problem of how to catch a spy.

The view from her bedchamber inspired her, but not with a spy-catching recipe. A lovely summer had given way to a beautiful autumn and the world outside was painted in delightful shades of yellow and brown. There were no half measures with Forfarshire autumn days. They were either foggy and dreich (she loved that lovely Scottish word that describes so well the wet and cold, damp and darkness of such a Scottish day) or they were quite simply glorious, as these past days had been. The sky, clear and blue, looked down on trees whose uplifted arms sent showers of leaves – yellow, golden, and red, rustling to the fields where the tilled brown earth formed a perfect backdrop. Liddy loved the undulation of the earth as it waved its way down to the sea. It made every day different and how the sun was shining or the wind was blowing subtly changed the canvas spread out before her. Only the trees remained the same, standing stark and still against the skyline.

The night gave her no repose. Liddy tossed and turned at a loss as to how to hand over Scott the spy to Keir. What did he look like, really, this man who was prepared to betray his country? When she tried to tell herself that she should have no remorse, he was the worst kind of criminal, her words rang hollow, for was not so her own papa?

She was up before Mrs Harper and with a warm cloak over her dress, went off for a brisk walk, through the gardens and up to the castle. It was still dark but the air promised that the day would be fine. For a while she sat on a broken wall and looked out to sea. At last her mind was made up and she hurried back to the house. Rattles was still in her room, brushing her hair back into its usual tidy knot.

'Rattles, dear, will you please help me kidnap a spy?'

Fourteen

Relief and incomparable sadness rode home with Lord Pittenmuir. In the drawing room at Balgowan House he had really faced the fact that he had loved Lydia Carpenter all his life and had been waiting for the end of this dreadful war to ask her to become his wife. Her disguise was good; it had never occurred to him that she and Euan Pate were one and the same, but what had possessed her to engage in such an enterprise?

Keir Galloway had inherited his title together with several prosperous estates as a very young man. His life had been wrapped in luxury and wealth. He'd never had to consider the price of anything he desired. He had a very real perception of absolute poverty and was a kind and considerate landlord, but the genteel poverty that had dogged Lydia Carpenter all her life was a complete stranger to him. For one of his own class to engage in anything underhand struck him as unalloyed greed. There had to be some other reason for Liddy to be a smuggler.

Could Harry have left some debts that she wished to pay without informing their father? He let his mind dwell on his first and dearest friend. No, it could not be Harry. Liddy had always been extremely modest in her dress. Why, at his last party she had worn a dress he had seen several times before. He laughed a little as he remembered her masterly set-down of Miss Fairweather. That gave him an idea. He would host another, more elegant party. Liddy's enterprise was most successful; according to Tam, dress lengths and even a gown of surpassing loveliness had been smuggled. If Liddy came to the party in such a gown he would know that she had sold her principles for trumpery silk and lace. At least he would know what to do about her request that he obtain a pardon for her friend. How she must love him to take such appalling risks.

No point in such thoughts, Keir, he chided himself as he rode home. You made no effort to fix your interest with her, taking it for granted that, because you had understood one another so well as children, there would be no need of explanation. Now all you may do for her is to ensure that she comes to no harm through her enterprise.

His brother was waiting for him as he dismounted, and Keir had the feeling that he had been watching for his return. 'Acquit me of trying my luck with the beautiful Charlotte,' he said as Jamie hurried down the steps towards him.

'Joke me no more jokes, Keir. I am determined that you will fob me off with half truths no longer.'

Keir handed the reins to the waiting groom with a smile of thanks before turning to his brother. 'Very well, Jamie,' he said. His tone was dangerously soft; the smile even more devastating. 'But pray do not rake me down on my own doorstep – the library is surely a more suitable place.' He put his arm around his brother's shoulders to take the sting from the rebuke and Jamie had the grace to blush.

'Try some of this sherry,' Keir offered when they were settled in the library. 'I could not acquire a taste for port but there are some deuced fine sherries to be found in the Peninsula.'

'Damn it, Keir, you are doing it again. You are too much in the habit of thinking yourself responsible for me. Look at me, sir, I have been grown up for quite some time.'

'You are in the right of it, Jamie, but I do not think you a child. It is only that the secrets are not my own.' He sat down and idly played with the delicate glass held in his long, slim fingers.

Jamie walked across the room and looked down at his brother. 'You are working for the government.' It was statement, not question.

In a few terse sentences, Lord Pittenmuir apprised his brother of most of the story of the last few months. He told him, of course, that he was on the track of a French spy but did not tell him of the involvement of the Honourable Lydia Carpenter in a smugglers' ring.

'I am charged to meet my smuggling friends again soon – do not look so displeased, Jamie, they are a rattling good bunch of fellows.'

Jamie smiled and looked very like his brother. 'My displeasure is only at not being made a part of so exciting an undertaking. It was always the same, you, Harry and Liddy off on such adventures while I stood at the nursery windows begging to be allowed to go, too.'

'Was I such an unkind brother?'

'You were the best of brothers. I was too young.'

'I cannot allow you a large part of this adventure either, Jamie. You are my heir, but now that you know, I will be able to use you to keep my two identities apart. Ian Scott must now grow his beard while my Lord Pittenmuir presents a smooth cheek to the beautiful ladies of—'

'What beautiful ladies,' interrupted the Honourable Jamie. 'Antidotes every one – except Charlotte.'

If this remark were a fly thrown to land a fish, the fish refused to rise. 'Really, it would be better if I do not go abroad for a week or two. You will let it be known that I am indisposed, some trifling residue of my injuries. Only you, Henry, and my valet of course, will be allowed to see me. There is a lad, John Reid, he knows.'

'The boy you brought here?'

'The same.' Keir stopped suddenly as if struck by some thought. 'That's it. He knows all. No wonder he was ready to tackle me, the valiant young tiger. We must do something for him when this is all over, Jamie. You would like him, heart of oak and such loyalty. Poor lad, when I think of what we have put him through.'

Jamie rose from the sofa on which he had been lounging and in a few strides was upon his brother. The years rolled back and they were boys again and, as when they had been children, the older, stronger one vanquished the younger.

'Apologize for upending my dignity and I will allow you up from the floor,' challenged Keir.

'Never,' panted Jamie. 'I have scarce understood a word you have said and I swear you do it deliberately.'

Keir stood up and helped his brother to his feet. 'Forgive me. It is not my secret, but I hope to reveal all in a day or two.'

'The boy John?' asked Jamie.

'Knows who I am and since he works here and for the Carpenters, you may use him to carry messages to Charlie should you need me.'

'I thought you were to remain here, Keir.'

'Only until such time as I am disreputable enough to return to Auchmithie.'

In much better harmony, the brothers went above stairs to dress for dinner at which Major Fordyce joined them. They none of them wished to allow worries over spies and smugglers to interfere with their enjoyment of the excellent meal prepared so lovingly by the genius in the kitchen. Broiled chickens with mushrooms followed a dressed lobster and a casserole of winter vegetables disguised by a wine sauce. A compote of pears and apples, with a trifle for Jamie who had a sweet tooth, completed this meal which was washed down by several bottles of a very fine white wine imported from France by the late Lord Pittenmuir at the turn of the century. When the covers had been removed and the servants had withdrawn, three contented young men sat long over the table discussing the recent events, Lord Pittenmuir having decided to take his heir almost fully into his confidence.

'I still feel, Keir, that Miss Carpenter must be prevailed upon to reveal the identity of this man,' suggested the major. 'A defenceless young girl is no match for one who must, by all reckoning, be quite without conscience.'

'Good Lord, Henry, if you have found a way to make a woman do something she does not want to do, without resorting to violence, I do must humbly congratulate you.'

Lord Pittenmuir said no more but occupied himself for some time by making little armies of nuts march along the snow-white cloth. Neither his brother nor his secretary made the mistake of assuming that his keen mind was not wholly involved with the problem presented by Miss Carpenter.

'Henry, be so good as to send out invitations for . . . a country dance, yes, a country dance and dinner before for . . . how was it used to be done, Jamie?'

'Those from a distance.'

'Yes, of course, and ask the Carpenters. Some time since we have entertained His Lordship.'

He saw the younger man's face and knew he thought him of the lovely Charlotte and he frowned. The daughter of a convicted traitor could never marry with the Pittenmuir heir.

Jamie was enthusiastic; he threw himself into the preparations. Musicians must be sent for from Edinburgh, flowers, guest rooms, the public rooms to be prepared; the list was endless.

'Let me compile the list for you, Henry. No need for you to trouble with such trivialities.'

'Come up with me, Henry,' suggested Keir as soon as Jamie had gone. 'If I am to pretend indisposition, I had best start as soon as possible.'

'Surely you have no more need of the smugglers, Keir, since you have a lead to your spy.' He stopped, almost in horror. 'Where on earth had you that dressing gown?'

His Lordship had shrugged himself into a resplendent garment of red brocaded silk which in truth suited his saturnine darkness extremely well but was so much at variance with His Lordship's usual conservative attire that his friend was slightly stunned.

Lord Pittenmuir laughed. 'Jealous, Henry? It was a gift from Jamie to brighten my convalescence and has only just returned from chasing me all over the Peninsula. I feel that if I try very hard, I may grow to like it.'

Major Fordyce shook his head in disbelief. 'Why a formal party with your mind so full of your spies?'

Idly Keir stirred the coals with the long brass poker that formed part of a set of andirons in the fireplace. 'My neighbours and my senior tenants would be rightfully distressed if I ignored them during my stay. Was it you, or more likely my little brother, who flew the flag?'

Henry laughed. 'Your standard? I am not near so conscious of your dignity, my Lord.'

'I rather wish that our sainted mama had not put such awe of me – or rather of the title – into Jamie. It would have suited me better to lie low.'

They spent what was left of the evening playing chess, being disturbed only twice by Jamie with his lists and suggestions. His Lordship's valet quite happily carried up His Lordship's breakfast next morning and was in no way perturbed when informed that His Lordship did not wish to be shaved.

His supine Lordship saw his manservant look with eloquent eyebrows at the empty plates left by his master on his bedside table and knew that he would ask nothing but wait for an explanation which might or might not come. His Lordship smiled. 'I do not wish to be badgered, Tregarth, and I must be off again as soon as may be.'

Tregarth's voice was expressionless. 'I assume, sir, that I am to return home.'

'Don't take that martyred tone with me,' sighed His Lordship. 'Indeed it would serve you well if I sent you packing back to London but we really must give the posting inns of this small island a chance to recover from your last visit. Besides,' and here he smiled warmly at his servant, 'how can I pretend to be ill if you are racketing about in London?'

Contentedly Tregarth picked up the tray. 'It's the travelling, m'Lord, more than the inadequacies of the inns. I do like firm ground under my feet.'

Lord Pittenmuir prepared for a few days of enforced inactivity. Less than forty-eight hours later, however, John presented himself at the servants' entrance to Pittenmuir Castle, asking to be admitted to His Lordship's presence. Since he refused to move and was too big to throw out, the footman hurried off to summon His Lordship's superior butler who could be depended upon to rid the house of far worse threats than one fisherlad.

'I regret that His Lordship is unwell and is seeing no one,' said Freshwater, his tone assuring John that His Lordship would be highly unlikely to see such a one as John Reid even if he were enjoying the best of health.

'He'll see me,' said John, not insolently but calmly. 'Please tell him I carry a message from Euan Pate.'

'I will communicate with His Lordship's private secretary and he will decide whether or not to mention your visit.'

A few minutes later, to the chagrin of several devoted retainers among the staff who would have done anything to be allowed to wait upon His Lordship, Major Fordyce escorted John to His Lordship's bedchamber. Lord Pittenmuir, a sombre blue dressing gown thrown over his shirt and breeches, greeted John with a smile. It was not returned.

He is wondering if I know, thought Keir, but he merely said, 'You have a message for me, John.'

'Not just for you. Euan wants a meeting. You must know that . . . he . . . he wants to stop.'

'I presume my identity is still our secret?'

'I told you I would say nowt. He sent me to go to Charlie and fetch you.'

'Sit down, John. Come along, man, don't be so stiff-rumped. I

145

will not explain what I was up to in that inn for it is none of your business, but you *can* trust me.'

The boy sat down grudgingly. 'You are to come to the castle tonight so . . . Euan . . . can try talking some sense into you. Why do you want to go on? You can't need money.'

'It suits me to play smuggler at the moment, but I would like to know why your Mr Pate wants out. Has he amassed sufficient funds?'

For a second it looked as if John might be completely honest and then, with a catch in his voice, he said, 'You would not understand; I wish you could. He should never have got involved, but never mind.'

He stood up abruptly. 'Your servants'll be talking – me being up here like this.'

'Great heavens,' said Lord Pittenmuir who had never concerned himself with the conversations of his staff. 'You may tell . . . Mr Pate that I will keep the rendezvous but that I do not promise to lend him my support. Are you wishful to cease free trading, lad? We could find regular work and quarters for you here.'

John was as dignified in his homespun tweeds as was His Lordship in his fine lawn shirt and exquisitely fashioned breeches. 'I thank you, m'Lord. But I believe Lord Balgowan will be taking on extra men as he puts the estate in order.'

'Please yourself, lad,' said His Lordship nonchalantly. 'The offer stays open. Mayhap we will talk again when this sorry affair is resolved.' He turned his back on a very puzzled John who was shown from the room by Major Fordyce. No sooner had the door closed behind them than Keir hastened to examine his face in a pier glass that hung above a charming rosewood table on which reposed his silver brushes.

'Damn it! Of course she will know me.'

The bruises which he had acquired in his forced fight with the smuggler, Tam, had all but faded and although he had not shaved now for almost seventy-two hours, the face that stared moodily back at him from the glass would have been recognizable to many not near so well-acquainted with him as his childhood friend, the Honourable Lydia Carpenter.

'Hell and damnation take you, Liddy. Could you not have waited two more days?'

His secretary returned to find him ruthlessly brushing his usually carefully ordered locks into deliberate wildness.

'Blast! It will not serve, Henry. How foolish I was to shave. She should have been forced to confide in you.'

'She would not do so and it is wasted effort to consider it,' said Major Fordyce calmly. 'Reflect, the meeting is set for late at night in an ill-lit ruin. Doubtless you might turn up in Weston's best and she would not know you.'

'Schultz, please.'

Major Fordyce shrugged, pleased to see his employer in better humour. 'As you wish, m'Lord, but reflect, Keir, another twenty-four hours, a homespun suit and some strategically placed dirt . . .'

'And Miss Carpenter will be unable to recognize one who was as close to her as a brother and whom she saw in her own house not above two days ago. You fill me with enthusiasm.'

Major Fordyce, however, was in the right of it. Miss Carpenter did not know her old friend – at first. Lord Pittenmuir, in his smuggler's guise, kept his appointment in the hall at Balgowan Castle. He was slightly uneasy to find that no one else was there. Never in his wildest imaginings would he have thought that Liddy was capable of trickery. At first he thought that she had been delayed – he could understand that it might be difficult to leave the house. He settled down to wait, fully expecting to see some others in the band. Darkness and silence settled around him.

'Surely I have not mistaken the time. I will remain in this . . .' He stopped, frowning. He had heard a sound. All the suspicions he had suppressed surfaced and an instinct for danger made him look round for a weapon. For a meeting with the girl, Liddy, he had carried nothing. He listened keenly. If there was to be an attack he wanted to be ready. He edged back so that the wall was behind him and slowly inched along away from the window embrasures. No point in offering a clear target. What seemed to be a sensible move was in fact the wrong tactic. Lord Pittenmuir crept along and thus offered his defenceless back to a tunnel entrance that he had completely forgotten. Liddy steeled herself, grateful that her victim had walked into her trap, and clubbed him. He dropped like a nut from a tree.

'Oh, God, I have killed him, Rattles.'

Miss Rattray knelt quickly beside the inert form and listened to his heart. 'Faint, but he is alive. Come now, Liddy. We have come this far and we must not falter now.'

'Yes, yes, you are the right of it, Rattles. The rope, quickly.'

Rattles produced two lengths of whipcord and trying to force down the nausea that had threatened to overwhelm her since she had felt the crunch of the club against Scott's skull, Liddy quickly bound the unconscious man's wrists and ankles.

'Now we must strive to haul him into the tunnel and then to the alcove.'

It was extremely difficult to pull the inert body backwards into the tunnel and Liddy was terribly conscious of the smuggler's head banging on the hard stone floor. She was exhausted and in tears by the time she had her prey secreted in one of the hidden cavities; Miss Rattray was almost as bad.

Lord Pittenmuir stirred some moments later and attempted to open his eyes. He was aware of a swimming head that ached and throbbed, and nausea almost as strong as that experienced by Miss Carpenter, and then of bonds against which he tried to struggle.

'Please lie still, Mr Scott,' said a low gentle voice that he had no difficulty in recognizing. 'Indeed I have no desire . . . had no desire to hurt you and I regret the blow that felled you.'

'She does not recognize me,' was Keir's incredulous thought and in the voice of the smuggler he snarled, 'Could not take me from the front, could you?'

'Of course I could not and I do assure you that it was only the utmost necessity that forced me to this pass. Please let me give you a little brandy.'

'How very good of you,' he said coldly in his own voice.

She knelt down beside him, a slim figure in her shirt and breeches, and bent to lift his head. Even in the dark he could see the colour drain from her face. 'Dear God . . . it cannot be so . . . why, Rattles, it is . . .'

Miss Rattray approached and set the lamp down. 'Of all the foolish starts, Lord Pittenmuir. Indeed you have brought this whole business on yourself. Take this brandy and we will contrive to make you more comfortable.'

Lord Pittenmuir was so stung by the complete injustice of this remark that he was about to give vent to his fury but a mug of brandy was held to his lips and he could do no less than swallow it. When this was accomplished the ladies helped their unfortunate victim struggle to his feet. The ground fairly rocked beneath him but he compelled it to remain still and fixed Miss Carpenter with as angry a glare as he could muster.

'If you would be so kind as to tell me why you kidnapped me?'

'I thought you were a French spy and I was planning to turn you over to . . . well . . . you.'

Lord Pittenmuir had no difficulty in cutting his way through this ungrammatical maze and so he answered 'Why, you wretch, is it not you who has been bosom beaux with spies? Who is your lover? One of your friends among the smugglers I have no doubt.'

Liddy was furious and would dearly have loved to strike his angry face but its pallor, caused by her blow, gave her pause and she took refuge in counter-recrimination.

'Unmask me a suitable candidate, my Lord; would you suggest Tam or John or mayhap old Tom?'

'Of all that's wonderful. Is he in it too? I would never have believed it of him but mind I never knew him half so well as I thought I knew you and here you are, unprincipled, completely lost to all sense of propriety.'

Seeing that the squabble was about to degenerate, as all their childhood quarrels had, into blows and then tears, Rattles effectively stopped it.

'Children, children,' was all she needed to say.

Miss Carpenter swallowed her tears and Lord Pittenmuir his ire.

'The Arbroath smugglers will continue until such time as I choose that they should stop. In the meantime I will escort you and Miss Rattray home.' He turned upon his first governess. 'What possessed you to encourage her in this folly?'

If Miss Rattray felt that His Lordship was more in need of escort than either herself or Miss Carpenter, she had sense enough to say nothing. Miss Carpenter too seemed to have no further wish to speak but turned meekly and went back along the passage until, followed by the others, she emerged in the grounds of Balgowan House.

'I will do myself the honour of calling upon you later, Madame,' bowed Lord Pittenmuir, and then he was gone.

Fifteen

S leep did not visit Miss Carpenter that night and she found herself hoping devoutly that Lord Pittenmuir was awake also. In her mind, she went over and over the meeting between them and this time her ripostes were educated and cultured and not at all as they had been in the darkness of the passageway. She regretted, naturally, the dastardly felling of His Lordship; even now she shuddered and felt sick as she recalled how he had fallen at her feet like a pole-axed steer, and she felt again the awful crunch of wood on human skull.

She also regretted not having had the presence of mind to ask His Lordship why she should believe that he was not a spy for France; there was only his word for it, and he *had* indeed left the ship and *could* therefore have been the man who had met the French spy instead of Lord Balgowan. She would not be browbeaten in their next meeting. Lord Pittenmuir would find himself challenged by one who was a match for him. She tossed and turned but could find no cool, comfortable place. How dared he attack poor Rattles, as if Miss Rattray enjoyed creeping through slimy tunnels in the middle of the night, or aiding and abetting in the capture of a spy. Again she punched the hapless pillow.

At last she must have dozed off for she arose much later in the morning with a headache to match the one she had given Lord Pittenmuir and with suspiciously swollen eyes.

'Pray return to your bed, Liddy, before your sisters see you. The whole story of last night is writ large upon your face. Put cold compresses on your eyelids if you wish His Lordship to feel that you do not care a fig for anything.'

Liddy looked at her former teacher. How old was Rattles? She had been with them now for at least fifteen years and she always looked the same, but today she seemed old, and that was Liddy's fault. Becoming a smuggler had seemed so simple but now she regretted it. Far better to have lost their home than to have subjected poor dear Rattles to all this. If only it could all be undone. I must make the best of the situation as it exists, she thought to herself, and somehow try to undo some of the harm I have done. From now on, nothing must disturb Miss Rattray's peace.

Liddy sat on a sofa and gently pulled Rattles down beside her. 'Dear old friend, it is you who should be resting. I have caused you enough worry for a lifetime, Rattles, and it is over. I will see Lord Pittenmuir today if he is not spying for the French, no doubt he will be willing to help me unravel the mess I have made. I will confess Papa's guilt as I must, but there will be an end to smuggling and spying.'

'Do try not to provoke him, Liddy. You are wont to treat him as if he were indeed still the little boy with whom you played. My experience of the more intimate feelings of gentlemen is some-what limited, but I believe they like to think themselves the stronger and wiser of the sexes. It can do little harm to humour them.'

Liddy gave a shout of laughter so like her old self that Miss Rattray was relieved in her mind and went off to the old school room to supervise the younger girls. Left to herself Liddy wondered how to avoid Charlotte for she felt that conversation with her vulnerable young sister would be difficult, if not im-possible, to sustain. No solace was to be found in the account books in the library. Heretofore she had been able to congra-tulate herself on a job well done. Now, it was all for nothing; the estate would pass out of their hands and a cousin they did not even know would perhaps sit in this selfsame chair trying to make one guinea do the work of ten.

There was a discreet knock at the door. 'My Lord Pittenmuir has called, Miss Carpenter. Miss Charlotte is with him in the yellow drawing room.'

'Thank you, Etienne,' said Liddy calmly as if her whole being were not in tumult. No way to avoid Charlotte now. 'Be so good as to bring coffee to us and perhaps His Lordship would like to try father's Spanish sherry.'

Etienne bowed and withdrew and, for the first time in her life, Lydia Carpenter found herself gazing into a mirror in an attempt to titivate her appearance.

'Why bother, Liddy? He has already seen Charlotte . . . and besides, even were you possessed of twice Charlotte's beauty it would serve you nothing in this case.'

Lord Pittenmuir and the Honourable Charlotte were laughing together over some amusing advertisement in the local paper. If His Lordship was furious with Liddy, he was not allowing his wrath to spill over into his dealings with her sisters. Charlotte sprang up from the chair in which she was sitting and turned impulsively to her sister.

'Liddy, here is Lord Pittenmuir come to invite us to a country dance, and there is such a droll advertisement for a dancing master in the paper and His Lordship says we must positively hire him before the rest of the county.'

Liddy smiled at her sister and gave her hand to His Lordship who had, of course, risen to meet her.

'Miss Charlotte informs me that His Lordship is from home, Miss Carpenter. I had thought to pay my respects to him,' His Lordship said coolly, quite as if he had not been in violent confrontation with his hostess a few hours earlier.

'How kind of you to call, m'Lord,' said Liddy. 'Unfortunately you have missed Papa by no more than a few hours,' lied she without a qualm.

Scarcely waiting for an invitation, an unpardonable breach of etiquette, His Lordship made himself comfortable on a sofa. Liddy smothered her first desire which was to laugh at his audacity and set her mind to contriving a reason for sending Charlotte out of the room. Short of saying, 'Please leave,' she could think of nothing and was compelled to sit smiling sweetly, pouring coffee, and pretending an interest in a dance which she could not for a moment believe was ever intended to take place.

'It is an age since there was a country dance, a private one that is, Liddy.' Charlotte was ecstatic. 'I remember the last one, don't you? You went with Harry, so handsome in his regimentals, and you had the prettiest green gown. Do you not remember it too, my Lord?'

'I do indeed, Charlotte, and I am sure the dresses you ladies will wear at this party will be equally memorable. Indeed I find myself anxious to see and admire them.'

Liddy cast him a glance that could best be described as explosive. How dare he? He must know that their gowns were like to have been smuggled, but yet she would disconcert him for only Charlotte should have a new gown. So pleased was she with this thought that she smiled at His Lordship so sweetly that his suspicions were aroused immediately.

'Miss Charlotte,' he began, but if he was about to get rid of her young sister Liddy was never to discover for at that moment a knock on the door heralded the arrival of Miss Rattray who begged His Lordship's indulgence but she had to see Miss Charlotte for a moment. Being a well-brought-up young lady Charlotte had perforce to excuse herself, no matter what rebellious fires were smouldering in her bosom.

Liddy stood up. Lord Pittenmuir did also and she was forced to look up into his face. Damn him. Why must he always put her at a disadvantage?

'Come, Madame, all cards upon the table. Tell me all you know about this spy including, do I have to add, his identity and I will endeavour to do what I can to mitigate the punishment.'

Liddy looked at him coolly. Now that they were face to face, she no longer felt afraid, but rather alert. One might even say the Honourable Lydia was excited. 'No,' she said.

His Lordship took a deep breath. He had not expected such defiance. 'Miss Carpenter, I am striving to remember that you are . . . that we were . . .'

Miss Lydia held up an imperative hand. 'Lord Pittenmuir, can you prove to me that you are not a spy in the service of the French? You travelled to France in the guise of smuggler and I know you left the *Shuska* and met someone in an inn – I would hazard a guess that it was not a chance meeting. Perhaps your friends in Whitehall should be apprised of your activities.'

This time it was he who interrupted. 'The Prime Minister is already well aware of my every move. The only piece of information he does not have is the identity of the spy who has been operating from this area. You are the holder of that information. Need I remind you that – but for my love of Harry – I would have handed any other person over to the authorities long since.'

She was about to exclaim grandly that she wanted no favours when she remembered that that was exactly what she did want.

'The smuggling enterprise, m'Lord?'

He took a turn about the room. 'Is a perfect cover for 'em, Liddy.'

She tried not to notice his use of her name as he went on. 'It is vital to the safety of the nation that this spy is apprehended. You cannot mean to shield him; no matter how much you love him, Liddy . . . you cannot . . .'

'No, I cannot shield him but I cannot explain, not yet. I will give you his name but he must be allowed . . . to go free to make a life abroad . . . something?'

She stopped, no longer in control of her voice. She could not look at him, but if she had all might have been well as, just for a moment all that was in his heart was in his eyes. 'Can you prove to me that you are not using my men to camouflage a spying mission of your own? It would indeed be perfect cover for a spy.' she said when she was once more in command.

'And has been so, if I make no mistake. Is he among your smugglers?'

It was her turn to stride around the room. If she gave away the name of the spy no bargaining power was left to her. 'I will tell you nothing until you promise concessions. Oh Keir, please, it is not for me but I can say no more for now.'

'And if I have you arrested?'

All colour fled from her face. 'You cannot mean it. What would you gain from my family's disgrace?'

'Personally? Nothing. I speak as Lord Lieutenant of this county and it is my duty to do what I must to uphold the safety of the realm.'

'So do I, too, wish to bolster national security.'

'This argument is become singularly unprofitable. Will you tell me his name?'

As he spoke he turned and grasped her arms. He pulled her towards him so roughly that she could feel the strength of his fingers through the fabric of her gown. For a second he looked deep into her eyes and she longed just to relax into his arms but then, as quickly as if she were red hot he let her go and she stumbled and almost fell. 'Damn it, Liddy, I will protect the blackguard for you if you but give me his name.'

'My father,' she whispered and sank back into a chair.'

Relief flooded His Lordship. And then he was swept over by a feeling of intense empathy for his dear Liddy. He looked down at her; how vulnerable and fragile she looked in her grief. Should he take her in his arms and kiss away all her trouble? Would she welcome his kisses or was there too much unhappiness and misunderstanding between them?

As if she could read his mind she stood up to evade him and once more she was herself, totally resilient, capable. 'For the sake of the children and for Charlotte I need your help. I promise that father represents no more danger to the country. When he returns I will undertake to persuade him to retire quietly from society. It would be kind in you to arrange that Charlotte . . . I wish her to make her debut into society, my Lord.' She knew this was a ridiculous request but she held her head up proudly as though there was nothing untoward in her bargaining.

'You have strange priorities, Liddy. A few dances for Charlotte – an eccentric price for her father's freedom.'

'How very like a man,' said Liddy disdainfully. 'It is Charlotte's future we are debating. Without what you term "a few dances" she has no chance of making a proper alliance.'

'Nonsense. No man who loved her will hold her father's tr . . . folly against her.'

'And how is she to meet this veritable paragon? Would you suggest yourself, your brother, the Minister's earnest and pimply boy?'

She was right of course.

'Convention makes slaves of us all. I recognize the dilemma.' He did not add that he could see too that difficulties lay ahead for Miss Lydia but as she chose to disregard them he had no right to say anything.

'I will do what I can to avoid scandal. It is all I can do for Harry. In the meantime, you will encourage your smugglers to continue their free trading.' He could tell by the tense lines of her body that she was about to spring to the defence of her crew and he raised a hand to quell the interruption. 'They sail under the protection of the Royal Navy, until such time as the Crown has no further use for them, whereupon they will disband and . . . disappear.'

'Thank you,' she murmured as graciously as she could.

He continued as if he had heard nothing. 'Naturally they must not know of this arrangement. There will be no further need, *ça va sans dire*, for such bravado as scaling walls in the dead of night.'

She forgot everything and, like the twelve-year-old minx she had once been, she sprang at him. 'Bravado,' she gasped. 'How dare you.'

She was tall and strong but he was much taller and stronger. His deceptively gentle looking hands gripped her wrists like iron clasps and her gasp this time was from pain. He held her for a long moment staring down into her angry eyes. 'Do not try me too far, Liddy,' he said coldly and throwing her from him as if she had been a featherweight, he strode from the room calling for his horse.

Liddy sank to the ground and leaned her head against the sofa. Her whole being was in turmoil. She examined her wrists where the marks of his hands stood out against the white skin. She could not help herself as she raised those bruised wrists to her lips and kissed them gently and then, beset by too many feelings and longings she did not fully understand, she burst into tears.

Miss Carpenter would have felt even worse if she had known that after his first fury had abated, Keir Galloway, Lord Pittenmuir, feeling as he had many times before in his childhood, had started to laugh.

Sixteen

Much to Miss Carpenter's surprise, invitations to a country dance were delivered to Balgowan House. Under separate cover, a cryptic note from Lord Pittenmuir suggested that the Arbroath smugglers had best make another voyage before the weather deteriorated too badly.

Miss Carpenter sent for John. He was shown into the library and naturally his visit occasioned no comment since Liddy was used to interviewing him about work she wished him to undertake.

She did not hesitate. 'John, you have always known who Ian Scott really is. Why did you not tell me?'

John flushed, hung his head, and then looked at her straight. 'I could not, Miss Liddy. I owe him too much.' And he explained how Keir had helped him when he had cut his leg with the axe.

Liddy's look softened. 'You like him, then?'

John shifted on his chair with embarrassment. 'Well, aye, Miss Liddy. He were so good to me. Even so, I watched him careful. I would never let harm come to you, Miss. It hurt, to think him a smuggler, maybe to pay for his . . . well, whatever the young lords get up to in London town. I could accept that, Miss, but then he jumped ship to meet the Frenchie and I did not know how to act or what to do. Maybe he had saved my life but . . .' His voice tailed off.

One of her suspicions was confirmed. His Lordship *had* gone ashore while the *Shuska* was in France.

'His Lordship is working for the Prime Minister, John. He is trying to uncover a spy who has been operating from this area. Indeed he thought it was one of us.'

A smile of pure joy illuminated John's pleasant country face. 'He be not a traitor then? Oh, Miss, a spy must be the wickedest sort of a man, selling his own . . .' Again his voice stopped.

157

Liddy fought to control herself. She essayed a slight smile. 'His Lordship is using us as cover for his activities; our enterprise has become almost patriotic, but I would ask you to let none know anything of this. I will get a message to Captain Visieux and you alert Charlie to bring the others to the castle three nights from now. I think it may perhaps be our last voyage.' Under her breath she added that this time one Euan Pate would also be aboard.

Charlotte was full of joy at the possibility of an evening's dancing. 'Liddy, is it possible there might be money enough to hire this dancing fellow?'

Liddy was spared having to answer this when Etienne announced Mrs Johnstone-Carruthers and Amanda. They, too, had received the elegant gilt-edged invitations.

'Dear Charlotte, and you too, dear Miss Carpenter, so exciting. Mama read this advertisement in the newspaper and has managed to engage the services of a dancing master to teach us the latest country dances.'

'The silly chit is trying to ask you and Charlotte to form part of a set in order to learn, Miss Carpenter. Silly to teach one girl the positions of two, four, or eight. We will ask Pittenmuir and his brother to join us, the young people from the manse, and possibly a few others. It is to be *the* event of the season, my dear, and we must not be found lacking. Invitations have gone as far as Perth and even Edinburgh.'

Liddy found herself wondering how that privileged information had found its way to Mrs Johnstone-Carruthers, but she smiled and seemed suitably impressed, saying that of course they would be delighted to join in the lessons, although she herself expected to be from home on business for a few days sometime before the party.

All the while she watched and waited for her father's return or some kind of message from him. She found herself reduced to asking Etienne if he had word of his master, but it seemed that the butler was as ignorant as she was herself.

'If I may be so bold, Miss Carpenter, I would venture that it is better not to worry. His Lordship is often from home with no word and then, one morning, there he is in his bed and ringing for his chocolate.'

He bowed and walked from the room leaving Liddy prey to

doubt. Was Etienne merely what he seemed or did he know far more than he was telling? As always when her head was too full of questions she decided to go riding. How wonderful to able to don Harry's clothes but no, it was not worth the risk. There was a troop of militia working in the area. She might not evade them so easily this time.

Tom saddled Amber for her, muttering all the time of how in his young day, no daughter of Balgowan would have ridden outside the family's grounds without a groom in attendance, but Liddy let him mutter. Soon she was galloping as fast as Amber could manage along the old road that led from the castle to the beach. She pulled up in the trees of the Danish burial ground. No need to risk Amber's legs in a twisted root system.

She dismounted to lead Amber through the ancient trees and stopped as they reached the clear brow of the hill. Below them stretched an expanse of fields – a good gallop to the sea at this time of year when all the fields were harvested. But the cropless fields were not empty. Snaking lines of red-coated dragoons marched inexorably through them, heading for the castle.

They cannot be looking for me, was Liddy's first thought.

'I should hazard a guess that they are looking for signs of our activities,' said a voice behind her, and there, mounted on a tall black horse, was Lord Pittenmuir. He did not look at her but kept his eyes on the approaching soldiers and so she did the same.

'Shall we play local laird and go down to ask these mindless oafs what they mean by ploughing up our fields?'

He did not wait for her reply but jumped effortlessly from the saddle and gave her his hands to use as a mounting block. 'I but defer to your skirts; in your breeches I know you would vault into the saddle with ease.'

She flushed at the mention of breeches but said caustically, 'And so I could too in my skirts.'

He laughed and encouraged his horse to move ahead of her down the hill.

The sergeant in charge of the military detachment halted his men when he saw them approach. There was no doubting His Lordship's power and even in an ancient riding habit and mounted on an inferior pony, Liddy's state was obvious; the soldier removed his hat in deference.

'What are you looking for in fields of stubble, Sergeant?' asked

His Lordship in his most superior tone. 'Must be someone scarce the size of a mouse if you expect to uncover him here.'

'Begging your pardon m'Lord, m'Lady. We have been informed as how a smuggling ring is operating in this area and we are searching for what them free traders call bolt-holes which is places what they stash their booty in.'

'You're scarce likely to uncover a bolt-hole in the middle of an empty field,' said Liddy dryly.

'Them smugglers is dashed clever, Miss. My superiors have ordered me to comb this entire area. They are said to be able to disappear into thin air.'

Liddy laughed. 'Say you not so, sir.'

His Lordship patted her hand in the most patronizing manner. 'When you return to base, Sergeant, you might ask your commanding officer, Colonel Hepworth is it not, to do me the honour of calling upon me to assure me that there will be no further damage done to my fields in the course of this exercise. I am Pittenmuir.'

'The Lord Lieutenant?' gasped the poor soldier.

Keir nodded. 'No doubt you will agree that these scum – riff-raff – would scarce presume to hide out on my land.'

The poor sergeant was looking more and more ill at ease. 'Of course, m'Lord. The colonel will assuredly agree too.'

'Ah, but the smuggling mentality is extremely devious, Sergeant,' said Liddy with a provocative look at His Lordship. 'Do you see that clump of trees yonder? That is an ancient burial ground. The locals think it haunted by the spirits of dead warriors. They too disappear into thin air. Then there is the old castle at Balgowan. It too would be an ideal place; haunted of course, but that would scarce worry you or your men.'

The sergeant hastened to agree but Liddy was satisfied by the obvious frightened glances passed from one man to the next.

'With your permission, m'Lord, m'Lady, we will carry on. I myself will see to it that my men do no harm to the fields and I will have the castle and the clump of trees watched at night too.'

'And you will give Colonel Hepworth my message.'

The sergeant saluted by way of reply and Liddy and Keir restrained their horses and watched the men make their slow way to the tall straight trees that stood so dark and forbidding against the skyline.

When the last man was out of earshot Keir turned furiously to Liddy. 'I could box your ears. Of all the stupid, senseless, harebrained things to do – to send them to the very meeting place of the people for whom they are searching.'

'When you are quite finished.' Liddy looked back at him defiantly, both of them for a moment twelve years old again and furiously angry one with the other. 'Think, Keir. We know there will be no one near the castle or the burial ground for three days. The militia will investigate and we must ensure that they find ghosts. I have arranged to meet the men in the great hall in three days time, but you and I must meet there tonight – perhaps with help from John – and scare the soldiers.'

'Frighten soldiers? Have you lost what little is left of your wits?'

She chose to ignore that slur. 'Soldiers? Did you not look at them? Boys, frightened unsophisticated boys. Our *soldiers* are lying dead in Europe,' she pointed out coldly. 'These are plough boys pretending to be soldiers.'

He said nothing, but thought for a while and when he spoke it was with the generosity she remembered he had displayed in boyhood. 'Very well, Liddy, you may be in the right of it. You always were more adventurous than I. So be it; I will play ghost again with you. It will be like old times.' He laughed in delight and she joined in wholeheartedly, but quickly he sobered. 'In the meantime, is your father gone to France, Liddy? Please tell me. You have asked for my help but I can do nothing while I am struggling with a sack tied over my head.'

She looked into his eyes, blue and clear and, above all, honest. How could she ever have thought him a spy but, there was Harry's death. Why had he not come when Harry had fallen? 'Keir?' She had used his name. 'When Harry died . . . you never . . . there was no letter, just a note of sympathy from your secretary. From infancy, Harry was your dearest friend . . .' She stopped, she could say no more.

He was thunderstruck and fought with his emotions: his grief at the loss of his dearest friend, his inability to do that man honour by mourning him with his family, his worry over Liddy. She had thought him unfeeling . . .

'What fools men are. I was injured, Liddy, badly. I thought we . . . I wished to spare you added pain. When I recovered sufficiently to return home the Prime Minister asked me to undertake a little matter for him in Portugal. It was for Harry . . . a blow against the French.'

She looked at his face and knew for the first time that he too had suffered; not only physically but mentally. He too had loved Harry and her attitude had added to his hurt. With a heart grown suddenly light she told him all she knew of her father's activities. 'And so I shall accompany you on this voyage to try to find him,' she finished. Her ill-chosen words had spoiled the moment.

'Will you ever grow up? Is it not enough that the daughter of Balgowan has sported around here like a wanton, climbing walls in the dead of night and swilling rum with a bunch of cut-throats, that now she wants to go to sea with them?'

'Don't be so patronizing and I have never *swilled* anything in my life. Besides it wasn't rum, but a rather fine claret. And let me assure you, Lord Lieutenant, that there are no villains among my men, just maybe those with a slight disregard for the laws of the land, but some of those laws are unjust and the men are very poor.'

He looked at her, exasperation writ clearly on his handsome face. 'This is neither the time nor the place for a discussion on social injustice. You will not sail with the *Shuska* and that is final.'

Almost violently Liddy thrust her heels into Amber's undeserving sides and the pony leapt forward. 'Sorry, Amber my darling,' she bent over and whispered into her ears. 'I meant it for him.'

There was no possibility of escape. His great horse thundered up beside her and a strong hand on the reins stopped Amber's flight. 'Tonight, Liddy, in the great hall. Wear your breeches.'

And he was gone.

To ignore his demands would have been a delightful but pointless luxury. As soon as it was dark Miss Carpenter began to make her way to the castle.

'Lord Pittenmuir has encouraged you in this mad start, Liddy?' Miss Rattray had gasped upon Liddy's asking for help in avoiding her sisters. 'You two are to frighten away an entire troop of militiamen?'

'Oh, no, Rattles. No doubt we shall have help from John ,' said Liddy with large innocent eyes and a naughty smile.

'That indeed comforts me,' Miss Rattray said dryly but as always, lent her aid.

Liddy used the tunnel that ran from the gardens to the castle and emerged among the dilapidated outbuildings inside what remained of the main boundary wall. She looked around, not nervously but carefully, and, satisfied that she was alone, ran across to a tumbledown hovel and quickly disappeared inside. Less than five minutes later she was alone in the great hall.

It was bathed in moonlight. Light poured through the shells of the huge windows and spilled wantonly across the stone floor. Liddy stood for a minute or two watching the moonbeams play among the cobwebs and dust and then stepped back into the shadows to wait.

She had forgotten that he knew the castle almost as well as she did herself. Her heart leapt into her mouth where it was stopped by the firm grasp of a gloved hand.

'Good evening, Madame,' he whispered maliciously into her ear. 'What if I were indeed a brigand?'

He released her as he spoke and she rubbed her hand furiously across her reddened cheek.

'Does John join us?' she asked in as steady a voice as she could muster.

'He and Charlie have gone to the copse. Methinks if Charlie sees too much of you he will assuredly recognize you and is like to be shocked.'

She ignored this. 'If we are to get to work we had as well start now.'

Taking it for granted that he would follow, she left the hall and hurried through the ruins to what had once been the kitchens. 'I left some gunpowder here,' she said with no thought of shocking him. 'You take half and make trails along some tunnels – not enough to destroy them, a hail of stones rattling around should suffice. I will do the same on the other side.'

'Take care, Liddy. This is dangerous material.'

She looked at him provocatively. 'Afraid, m'Lord?' she asked as she picked up a bag and made for her tunnel. Such bravado, Liddy, she scolded herself, when all the time your own knees are knocking in the most craven manner.

Despite the darkness and the discomfort of bending almost double in the cramped space, Liddy managed to lay a very thin trail of gunpowder along the passageways. She assumed that, with his greater knowledge of explosives, His Lordship would also have placed his powder strategically.

She had scarce finished when she heard a murmur of voices. Unable to turn round she was compelled to crawl backwards to the mouth of her bolt-hole. Lord Pittenmuir was waiting for her and to her chagrin her first thought was that she wished she might have presented a more attractive aspect. His Lordship seemed oblivious of her undignified exit.

'A troop has arrived. We shall let them settle before the fun starts. How are your screeches?'

'As splendid as ever.'

He smiled at her, a smile she allowed to warm her heart and set butterflies fluttering in her stomach.

Unaware of their presence, the commander positioned his men. Quiet and darkness settled round them.

'Remember what you and Harry tried?'

He nodded and crawled as quietly as possible into her tunnel. Liddy listened for a few minutes and crept to the kitchens. An owl hooted outside to be answered a few minutes later by another. Liddy moved to a window that had once overlooked the courtyard. From that height she could see several of the boy soldiers huddled behind broken walls. She screeched – a screech owl's call – and had the satisfaction of seeing several of the soldiers jump.

'It be only birds,' she heard the sergeant say but his voice held a note of doubt. A blood-curdling shriek erupted at that moment from the ground under his very feet.

'Owls dinnae go under the ground, do they, Sergeant?' asked one of the soldiers, but the sergeant said nothing for a few minutes as he tried to recover his own somewhat shaken composure.

'There'll be rats and suchlike under the ruins, lads. Quiet now else the smugglers'll hear us.'

'Didn't sound like no rat to me,' muttered a trooper and once more silence fell. Not for long. Just as soon as the blood pressure and pulse rate of each trooper had subsided to a normal level, and each man, or boy, had relaxed sufficiently to be able to assure himself that there were no evil forces at work in Balgowan, the earth exploded beneath them. It seemed as if all the denizens of Hades were running along beneath the castle.

The whereabouts of the subterranean passages were unknown to the militia. They might well have suspected the existence of a smuggling tunnel, but that the ground was honeycombed, they had no idea. With humiliating screams of terror the soldiers fled. The sergeant, who would have stood alone against the entire crew of smugglers, was the vanguard. When the rumblings ceased Liddy and Keir were quite alone.

Seventeen

John and Charlie had sat uncomfortably in the midst of the ancient burial ground hoping for an opportunity to play ghost. It was denied them. They heard muffled bangs and then far from muffled voices as the soldiers were routed.

They climbed into a large tree and watched the stampede from the castle. The sergeant managed to recover his nerve before he hit the surrounding lands but the boys streamed through the fields and past the burial ground and their commander watched and gave up immediate hope of gathering them together. His would be the unenviable task of explaining the aborted capture of the smugglers.

John and Charlie remained perched in their tree until all the red dots had disappeared into the mists around Arbroath. Then they jumped lightly down and made their way to the castle. Lord Pittenmuir was waiting for them.

'Mission accomplished. Pate has gone home to roost. I suggest we do the same.'

'You routed them good and proper, Sir,' shouted John. 'They'll not stop running till they reach Montrose.'

'Aye, John, but mayhap they will turn themselves around and come back. They must find naught to make them suspicious.'

Quickly he explained how he and Pate had dispersed the troops. 'It was a trick Master Harry and I tried against Miss Carpenter many years ago. It failed miserably then.'

Old Charlie laughed. 'Aye, much easier to fool an entire troop of militia than Miss Lydia. Grand spirit she had as a child. Still has, I shouldn't wonder.' He looked at his young houseguest shrewdly.

'Enough of Miss Carpenter,' said Keir, carefully avoiding his eyes. 'We have work to do. They must find no trace of gunpowder.'

Dawn was breaking before Lord Pittenmuir deemed it probable that no vestige of earthly interference could be proved in the castle. No matter what the soldiers believed, however, their commanding officers would not be persuaded into a belief in the supernatural. They might well be convinced that smugglers did not use the castle. After all, smugglers were no more sophisticated than untried soldiers.

'Expect me sometime this evening, Charlie. No doubt Colonel Hepworth will call upon the Lord Lieutenant today. I must be available.'

Cushioned and protected by his staff, Keir was allowed several hours of refreshing sleep before he came face to face with the colonel.

That gentleman had been cooling his heels for nearly an hour before he was shown into a comfortable breakfast room where the Lord Lieutenant of the county invited him to share an enormous – if late – breakfast.

'I trust your Lordship will find your fields undamaged by the search for these smugglers,' said the colonel when they finally pushed their plates away.

'No doubt, but if there is to be much trespassing over my land, Colonel, damage is bound to occur. My man brought me news of some trampling last night. Not what I like to hear with my morning chocolate.'

'Indeed, my Lord. That is what I am come to report. It would appear that the ruins of Balgowan Castle represent an ideal hideout for this band, but the soldiers I sent – indeed I wonder if such untrained plough boys should be so termed – were routed by some, as yet unexplained, agency. Any damage done to your fields will be recompensed, I assure you, sir.'

Keir stood up to hide his face from his guest. 'Unexplained agency, Colonel?'

'My sergeant, at present cooling his heels in the guardhouse, would have me believe that denizens of the underworld chased an entire troop of militia out of Balgowan Castle. I believe the force to have been smugglers.'

'You and I, educated, cultured men, Colonel, do not believe in the forces of evil, but I have spent some time trying to uncover the identities of the smugglers and am forced to believe that they are my own tenants, farmers, fishermen, simple men, Colonel.'

'No doubt, m'Lord.'

'Not one of them would go within a mile of either the castle or any of the Danish burial grounds after dark.'

The colonel expelled his breath noisily. 'You are telling me you believe in the forces of darkness, sir?'

Keir threw himself into a chair and sat looking through lowered eyelashes at the colonel. 'My dear man,' he said in the supercilious voice that Liddy hated, 'all I am saying is that there are no strangers in the area. I would have been apprised of any arrivals long since. Ergo, my tenants are, at the very least, the land smugglers and none – let me reiterate, none – could be paid to visit Balgowan Castle in the dark.'

'I have sent for a troop of veteran soldiers, newly returned from Spain. The spectres of long dead Danish kings will not scare them. Every inch of Balgowan Castle will be searched.'

'How very wise of you, Colonel. I will commend the thoroughness of your approach.'

He rang the bell and Chalmers arrived to show the colonel to his horse. Major Fordyce came in time to watch His Lordship penning a note to Miss Carpenter.

'Henry, be the best of good fellows and ride over with this. I am off to Auchmithie. Tell Jamie to go ahead with his plans for his party. I hope I will manage to attend.'

Miss Carpenter was on horseback before His Lordship reached Auchmithie. Tam was delighted to earn a few extra guineas by sailing her out to sea to rendezvous with the *Shuska*. Here, however, she met a snag. Captain Visieux was awaiting a shipment of supplies and refused to sail without it.

'Very well, Captain. I will go below to rest. No need to inform the men of my presence. It will be interesting to observe them at work before I reveal myself.'

Several hours later she felt the bumping that heralded the arrival of other vessels. The loading was done in virtual silence and try as she might Miss Carpenter heard nothing. Later the boat containing the remaining members of the crew arrived and, as she had hoped, she soon recognized Keir's disguised voice.

If she showed her face she could not with any certainty say that he would not unmask her. Better to stay quiet. She wished she had thought to provide herself with food for it was hours since she had eaten and she could not demand a meal till the *Shuska* had set sail.

She dozed and woke and dozed again, but at last came the creaking and groaning that heralded the departure of the ship. Cautiously she opened the door of her cabin. The sailors were all too busy to take notice of her. She would prefer some nourishment before revealing herself.

Since Lord Balgowan had not considered the layout of a vessel to be an integral part of his daughter's education, it was as well for Liddy that Captain Visieux was, at that very moment, on his way to his cabin to dine. She required no second invitation to join him.

'If you will forgive my remarking on it, Monsieur, you are uncommon abstemious for a man of your class,' said the captain as his guest repeatedly refused to allow him to refill his wine glass.

'Not at all, Monsieur le Capitaine. If our enterprise were concluded I should quite happily drink you under this fine table,' lied Miss Carpenter without a blush while reflecting how easy lies came with practice. Conscious too that her interview with Lord Pittenmuir would be difficult enough without adding to his list of perceived wrongs an intimate dinner in a closed cabin with a man to whom she was not related, she brought the evening to an early close.

'Come, Monsieur Pate, a little of your own very fine cognac,' pressed the captain. 'How seldom it is that a man of my own class is aboard. I am loath to permit you to retire so early.'

'Ah, such temptation, Monsieur Visieux, but brandy muddles my head and I must be at the top of my form on the morrow.'

She moved to the door praying that the loquacious captain would stop short of accompanying her to her cabin and secondly that a certain member of the crew would be nowhere below decks until she was safely hidden again.

Luck was on her side and she was able to enjoy several hours of sleep before setting off to find Lord Pittenmuir. She saw him immediately she went on deck but was forced to hide in a hatchway until His Lordship was alone.

'Keir,' she whispered.

He turned from the contemplation of the mists hiding the coast of France and for a fleeting second she thought she might have seen joy writ upon his face. If she had, it was gone now. Unalloyed fury glared at her. His hands came up as if to lay hold of her but he controlled himself and merely hissed. 'You fool, what mischief are you brewing now?'

'No mischief, my Lord. I am come to find my father.'

He looked around and then his far from gentle hands hauled her along the deck to where there was little chance that they could be overheard.

'I told you that I would find His Lordship. You, Madame, will go below and you will remain there until I am able to return you safe to Scotland.'

She hit him with all the considerable force she could muster. 'You are the most insufferable man I have ever had the misfortune to meet.'

He looked at her, the marks of her fingers quite clear on his cheek, and for a second she was afraid. Then he gave a shout of laughter. 'Liddy dearest, if you must needs pretend to be a man, you must needs learn to hit with your fist. Behold, let me show you.'

He acted out the scenario. 'Now go below and practise and I promise to alert you when we reach France . . . Liddy, do not hit me again for I am losing patience and might well retaliate.'

She could not hit him again as she dearly wished to do. Noise would attract the other crew on watch and God alone knew what Keir Galloway meant by retaliation. She had to trust him and she went below to spend many boring hours waiting to disembark. Her mind was busy with plans to find her father, but the fact that she had no idea where he had been taken or whether or not he remained in France bothered her not at all. She would find him, they would return to Scotland and all would be well. She refused to think beyond that.

They reached France at sunset and the captain went ashore to arrange the exchange of cargoes. Once he was safely out of the way Liddy was rowed ashore by Keir.

'We will drift along the coast for some miles, Liddy, and go ashore where we can conceal the boat. I trust you can walk in those boots.'

Liddy looked down in dismay. Harry's boots were a good size too big for her, but she would suffer in silence.

'Will the spies be in the tavern?'

'Such a naive question shows how ill fitted you are for this undertaking, Liddy.' He thought for a moment. 'We can scarce go together for your clothes shout "nobleman". I will go ahead and settle myself near the fire. From there it is simplicity itself to observe everyone who enters. Should Lord Balgowan be within, he is likely to recognize you.'

'I will pull my hat down and my collars up.'

He sighed with the weight of the inevitable. 'Do and say nothing. When I leave, count – slowly – to one hundred before following me.'

They hid the rowing boat among the sand dunes and went over their plan once more. Then Keir sauntered off towards the village as if there was nothing on his mind but what he was to have for his supper. Liddy crouched down in the lee of the boat. She mastered an urge to run after him and instead set her mind to realizing that she, who had never in her life been farther than Edinburgh, was now in France. France, the land of her mother, the land where her father had spent most of his adult life. From where she sat it looked not unlike the beach at Auchmithie. Was there a message in that?

Time to follow Keir. Trying to still her beating heart, she reached the door to the tavern and went in. No one paid her the slightest attention. It was a totally unexpected, but very welcome reaction. She glanced around in what she felt sure was a non-chalant way and saw Keir sitting by the fire, a jug in his hand. How completely he blended in to the atmosphere and she almost smiled her approval of his cleverness.

She had absolutely no idea what to do. She moved to a table, sat down on a rough wooden bench and examined her surroundings. The room was small, ill lit and heavy with the overwhelming odour of garlic and wood smoke. It was also crammed with people. Obviously the tavern was the social centre of the area.

Liddy ordered the bouillabaisse – it was either fish soup or cognac – and was delightfully surprised. When she had finished the rich bowl of fish redolent with tomatoes, garlic, onions and wine she knew one reason why the tavern was so busy. She felt somehow that she too had blended into the haze and was thus more able to look around.

There were sailors and fishermen, probably smugglers, aplenty. Of Lord Balgowan there was no sign. Really, Liddy, did you expect to walk in and say *Good evening, Papa,* she scolded herself.

Suddenly she was filled with panic. She could not see Keir. Rather bosky sailors now occupied the seats by the fire. When had he left? It could not have been too long ago. The serving maid stopped her from fleeing for the door.

'Good, Monsieur?'

'What? Oh, the soup, yes, delicious, Mam'selle.'

Thank heavens she could think in French as well as speak the language.

'Monsieur would like a little more? You are new here, Monsieur. We have clean beds. One tonight that you could have all to yourself.'

Liddy looked up at the girl who smiled at her in an extremely friendly manner. Great heavens, I do believe that I am being propositioned. The serving wench was awarded Miss Carpenter's most brilliant smile. 'I regret, Mam'selle, but I am expected elsewhere tonight. Au revoir.'

'Another time, perhaps.' It was not a question, merely an acceptance.

Now to find Keir. No one heeded her departure. No cries rang out behind her, no scurrying figures sought to restrain her. Indeed spying was quite flat.

'Euan.' At first she paid no heed. Then the call came again, rather more imperative this time and in Lord Pittenmuir's unmistakable tones. There he was, skulking behind a cottage.

'Where in heaven have you been?' he demanded when she had hurried to join him.

'I did not see you leave,' she excused herself but he would have none of it.

'You gave too much of your attention to your stomach – pray don't argue, I can smell it. Quickly.' He grabbed her by the arm and pulled her behind the building. 'Now, follow me.'

They dodged in and out among the darkened cottages and stopped only when they had reached the end of the village. Liddy was content to lean for a moment against a wall to catch her breath. Keir was listening attentively to sounds from the street behind them.

'Liddy, listen carefully. Return to the boat, wait for me for no more than thirty minutes; an I fail to appear, row to the *Shuska*.

172

Needless to say, if anyone so much as approaches your hiding place before the end of the allotted time, leave immediately.'

He bent swiftly, gently kissed her lips, and pushed her away.

Almost in a daze she hurried back through the sand dunes to where they had left the rowing boat. She had to keep reminding herself of where she was and what she was doing in France, or she would have sunk down where she stood in the sand to relish what had just occurred. Everything else seemed suddenly unimportant. Her father, French spies, smugglers – how trivial it all was beside the fact that she had been kissed by the man she loved. There, it was said, it was acknowledged. She loved, indeed had always loved, Keir Galloway. And he had kissed her . . . he, who could have chosen from the richest and most beautiful women in the land, loved her too. He had kissed her.

Where was he? The time must be almost up. She would never leave him here . . . never. She turned back towards the village and began to run. She had almost reached the end of the beach when she heard the unmistakable sounds of an altercation. Keir was struggling with two men – two of the sailors, she thought that she had seen in the tavern. He managed to get his right arm free and felled one with an uppercut that must have come from the depths of despair and then he and the other man were wrestling on the ground. There was a flash of light in the moonlight and a gasp from Keir.

Dear God, he has a knife. Desperately Liddy looked round for a weapon. She snatched up a piece of driftwood, a perfect size for a cudgel, and hit the assailant as hard as she could just as he prepared to plunge the knife into his victim who lay still under him.

The sailor fell forward, the knife falling harmlessly from his hand. Liddy paid little heed to the injury she had inflicted but struggled to pull his heavy body off Keir. They had to get to the *Shuska*. No doubt the sailors had accomplices who would be coming to look for them.

'Look out, Liddy,' groaned Lord Pittenmuir and she turned to see the first sailor coming at her like a maddened bull. A shot rang out and he stopped, such an expression of amazement on his face, and fell to the ground.

'Not a bad shot,' smiled His Lordship, 'considering that I used my left hand.' He pushed the dead weight of the sailor from his

173

legs and still holding the smoking weapon, struggled to his feet. 'Come along, Liddy,' he ordered, taking her now shaking hand and pulling her after him on legs that threatened to collapse. 'Do you never do as you are told? We now have two dead spies – quite useless.'

The trembling left her to be replaced by sheer unadulterated anger. 'Were it not for me, my Lord, we would have one dead Scottish peer.'

'Nonsense,' he dismissed her action. 'Had you not been so precipitate, I intended to frighten them with the pistol.'

'A clever trick indeed, my Lord, especially for a dead man. The one I . . . hit . . . was about to plunge a knife into your heart.'

'My dear girl. Do you really think I should have allowed him to do so?'

'You were unconscious.'

'I trust you can still row, Madame,' he said ignoring her remark. 'I regret that, temporarily, I have lost the use of my right arm.'

She said nothing but helped him push the rowing boat into the water and got in, seating herself in the rower's place. He smiled and then pitched forward into the boat on top of her almost toppling them both into the sea. With frantic hands she pulled him upright. His shirt and jacket were saturated with blood and he was quite unconscious. His dark lashes fanned on his cheeks and his breathing was shallow. Again the years sped back and she was twelve years old. Keir had fallen out of a ruined window and Liddy and Harry were trying to smuggle him into Pittenmuir Castle without being seen by his father. In that instance Harry had been of invaluable help and Keir himself had not been completely insensible. How on earth was she alone to get an unconscious man on board the *Shuska*? Keir groaned again and attempted to sit up. She shipped the oars, dipped her handkerchief into the water, and pressed it to his forehead.

'Take that ghastly thing away, Liddy, it stinks of seaweed.' He was himself again or at least was in possession of his senses.

He said no more and she rowed to the ship. 'Can you board without help? I must hold the boat still.'

For a moment he looked as if he might remonstrate with her – every fibre of his being argued that it was he who should aid her – but he was sensible and knew that he had just enough strength left to climb into the *Shuska*. Liddy tied up the rowing boat and followed him as quickly as she could.

'My cabin,' she whispered and hurried below decks, praying that he would follow her.

Luck was on their side and they reached the cabin without being hailed by the watch. Once inside, Keir collapsed onto the bunk, and Liddy tore open his shirt to see the extent of the wound.

'Keir, I must ask Visieux to attend you. I have no basilicum, nothing that will do as a salve.'

He struggled to a sitting position. 'It is not a deep wound, Liddy. I am more exhausted than ought else. Bind it as best you can.'

'I will tell the captain that I have asked you to aid me in a private endeavour.'

He interrupted her. 'And no doubt you will tell him that you always play physician to your servants.'

'As you did to John.'

'I did not invite the lad to my bedchamber. There. Good girl, that should hold me. I must away. See if the way is clear.'

Liddy stood against the door. 'Keir Galloway, I am not a hysterical woman, but if you do not wish to be subjected to a fit of the vapours you will tell me all you have discovered before you move another step.'

'It is nothing good.' He hesitated a moment for he was quite sure that the realization that she had actually killed a man had not actually dawned upon her.

'You must tell me. Where is my father?'

'I met the man I had seen on the last trip. He said his masters were well pleased with the information I had given and were anxious to uncover more – mainly about troop placements. By dint of cautious questioning and liberal doses of a particularly potent rum, much admired by the locals, I heard that an English lord had come from Scotland – and that he was returned. His information and sources are so valuable that he has been promised the return of vast estates in France once belonging to his family if he plays upon the Jacobite sympathies of his neighbours and encourages them to welcome and even aid a French invasion.'

Liddy listened in growing horror. It was worse than she had

supposed. How could she ever ask for mercy from the government or for love from Lord Pittenmuir? Almost careless of his wounded shoulder she pushed him from her cabin and fell upon the bed. She was awake until dawn, not with crying, for she was past that now, but from a thousand thoughts running through her head with a desperation to find a way out of the predicament.

Eighteen

The *Shuska* anchored out at sea within sight of the tiny
fishing village of Easthaven. Liddy stood at the rail with
Captain Visieux while the signal was given to the land smugglers
waiting near the farm of Craigend. Liddy had arranged for John
to wait, in another clump of the great beech trees that supposedly
covered a Danish burial ground, for the signal that would tell the
smugglers that a cargo had arrived. John would then send a
message to Balgowan and the land smugglers would meet on the
wide sandy beach from where they would row out to unload the
Shuska.

'Ah.' The captain breathed a slow sigh of relief. The signal had
been received. 'Come, Monsieur Pate, a turn about the deck.'

'You are enjoying your participation, young sir.' He did not
expect an answer. 'Truth to tell, I had expected you to join us
long since.'

Liddy tried to sound bored and sophisticated. 'One has so
many other commitments, you understand.'

'*Exactement*, like the one which took you ashore last evening.'
He put up his hand as Liddy prepared to speak. 'Do not
misunderstand me, Monsieur, I have no political axe to grind
– France died for me over twenty years ago. Besides you hire my
vessel and may do almost what you will, but, you will forgive me,
you are very young and I could have been of help, perhaps of
more help than the sailor you chose to help you.'

Liddy essayed a nonchalant laugh. 'You are most kind,
Captain. But one hardly needs an experienced naval officer to
row a boat.'

He bowed and while they continued their stroll Liddy's mind
raced. How had the captain found out and how much did he
know? Was he simply being kind? Was he as disinterested in the
tense situation between France and Britain as he purported to be

and what did he do between smuggling trips for her? It could be that he also transported spies. Could Lord Balgowan have travelled on the *Shuska*? Does it matter? Liddy asked herself. More likely he is interested in making as much money as he can and what is wrong with that?

'We have our best cargo of all tonight, Monsieur,' the captain interrupted her thoughts, 'but I will be glad when we are unloaded. There are many troops in the area now.'

Since Liddy knew that that was why he had insisted on lying off from shore instead of anchoring near the cliffs at Auchmithie she said nothing and they stood watching the beach until the first of the land smugglers appeared. Even at this distance she could recognize John's red head.

Where was Keir? She had not seen him at all today. For a terrible moment she thought something ill had occurred until she heard his unmistakable voice hailing John. She had no chance to speak to him and she could hardly seek him out, but she must reassure herself that he was well. She needed to speak to him too about her father. Last night in the cabin had been so unsatisfactory.

The next few hours were too busy to think about anything other than unloading the *Shuska* and ensuring that their contraband cargo found safe hiding places until it could be delivered to its new owners.

'It'll be safe at Balgowan,' young John assured them. 'Seems like ghosts are walking again. Scared off an entire troop of soldiers if rumours be true.'

Since John had witnessed the flight of the militia, Liddy and Keir both felt that he was stretching the truth a little with his talk of rumours.

'No, we will bury some for a few days in newly ploughed fields and the larger part under the manure dump at Balgowan. They'll not think to look there,' ordered Liddy and saw Keir looking at her with a look of almost respect on his face.

The burying was done and inconspicuous markers left so that the smugglers could find their cache in a day or two. After all, miles and miles of ploughed earth would look remarkably similar in the cold light of day. The sailors would not forget the position of the manure.

'Now lads, home and to bed,' ordered Liddy as the *Shuska*

disappeared over the horizon. 'We will meet tomorrow night – that is this night in the keep at Balgowan. Wear your dresses and bring your creels. Charlie and Tam, can you provide enough herring to cover? Good. God be with you until tonight.'

She was alone and faced with a long hard walk to Balgowan House. She stood on the empty beach and her heart sank down into Harry's boots. With the work done, and without the stimulating presence of the men, she felt exhausted. Was she afraid? No, she assured herself bravely. What was there to fear on an isolated beach miles from her home in the middle of the night? Lydia Carpenter was made of sterner stuff.

A moment later the stern stuff quivered a little when she heard a muffled sound of hoofs. Hide, Liddy, hide. But where? She put her chin up. She would face them, whoever it was. 'Amber,' she almost sobbed with relief. But how and who? 'Keir!'

'Quiet,' he whispered. 'It was John's doing. The lad had her hid for you. I told Charlie I thought you too young to be alone and I met the boy on the way back.'

'Your arm?'

He shrugged. 'A scratch. Now go, and don't stop until you are safe home. I will find a way to talk to you at Jamie's party.'

He slapped Amber who responded immediately and Liddy was too tired to do anything but hang on to the reins. Lord Pitten-muir followed out of sight until he saw her turn into the grounds of Balgowan House and then he retraced his long painful route back to the sea.

Miss Rattray had been alerted to attend upon her arrival and when an utterly exhausted Liddy stumbled up the stairs of her turret after unsaddling the obliging Amber, it was to find Miss Rattray and a dish of tea awaiting her.

'Luckily His Lordship has retired long since, Liddy, for how we are to explain your arrival at this hour, I shudder to think,' she muttered as she almost pushed and pulled her erstwhile charge into her nightdress.

'Papa, oh thank God. But how did you explain . . .'

Rattles tucked her up under the embroidered sheets before replying. 'I am guilty of the most appalling falsehoods and – what is still more shocking – each and every one jumped effort-lessly from my lips. You have been in Edinburgh visiting the Lady Frazer. She was a friend of your mama and does not speak to your papa and, so I feel sure, my subterfuge will go unde-tected. It will not do for Charlotte, however, who knows that there has been no correspondence between the families since Lady Balgowan died.'

'You are clever, Rattles,' mumbled Miss Carpenter, already almost asleep.

The difficulties of her situation thrust themselves into the foreground next morning when Madame appeared with her morning tray.

'It really is not *comme il faut*, Miss Lydia,' she said in accents almost as fine as those of her employer, 'to arrive in the middle of the night and why her ladyship did not consider putting up at some genteel establishment when night was drawing in I cannot imagine. His Lordship will be justifiably annoyed that Lady Frazer's servants did not stay here for the night. This is a gentleman's residence after all and could easily cope.'

At first Liddy had feared that she need make some reply to this tirade but soon realized that Madame was like a burn in spate – she would not stop flowing until she dried up – and therefore Liddy need do nothing but lie back and let the tide wash over her.

'Of course, Miss Rattray has explained that there has been, shall we say, some tension between the houses and so, naturally, we could not expect dear Lady Frazer to make her first visit an overnight one, but now that we, that is, you and Miss Charlotte are to take your proper places in society . . . oh, Miss Lydia, it is exciting, isn't it?'

She looked at Liddy, expecting a reply but Miss Carpenter merely gazed back at her as she had listened to very little of the tirade.

'You won't know, of course, Miss Lydia, since you have been off on a visit, and why you did not ask me to pack for you . . .'

At this, Liddy's heart gave an uncomfortable leap. Pack? She had packed nothing but Harry's best shirt. Such things could not be explained away. But Madame was bent over an open valise. Rattles. Was there ever a more valuable friend? Not for the first time, Liddy vowed silently that, somehow, she would make life easier for their governess.

'You never took this old gown, Miss Lydia, and it with a tear, too.' Madame removed the offending garment from the bag and bore it off towards the door.

'I never wore it, Madame,' Liddy called after her truthfully.

Liddy had barely time to adjust the serviceable shawl around her shoulders when the door burst open to admit Charlotte. 'Dearest Liddy,' she said, enveloping her sister in a warm embrace and a scent of violets, 'it is so lovely to have you at home. You have been greatly missed, dearest, for we have had the most glorious time, practising our country dances, y'know, and I have told everyone the silly lie that Rattles bid me say, but I demand the truth from you now.' Suddenly she stopped being her idea of the proper young debutante and subsided onto the bed beside her sister. 'Liddy, I know you think me the merest child, always to be protected, but I am not, and I do wish you would tell me what has worried you so much and where you have been and . . . oh . . . everything.'

Liddy looked at the beautiful, troubled face. 'I will, Charlotte, I promise, but first you must prepare me for my meeting with Papa. When did he return and what did he say?'

'Say? Why, nothing Liddy, except that his business had gone well. Do you like my perfume? He brought lovely gifts again and was *desolé* when he found you from home, and so Miss Rattray concocted that story about Lady Frazer. He said then that soon grander ladies than any Frazer would be calling upon his daughters. Liddy, Papa says that very soon we will leave Balgowan and that he is to come into a great inheritance; his birthright. When I dared ask what inheritance he bid me not trouble my pretty little head about such things. Why do men treat us so? Will you explain, for I have such a strange feeling.'

Liddy slipped from the bed and went to the window. 'You have a strange feeling, Charlotte, because it seems set fair to rain for ever. Did you ever see such a morning?'

The view from the window was indeed dismal. On fine days Liddy could see the sea from the windows of the tower but this morning there was nothing to see but sheets of lashing rain. Even the fine tall trees around the house were almost hidden by the ferocity of the squall. She could hear them, protesting against their treatment.

'One day those trees will be tried too hard and will come out by their roots.'

'I am singularly uninterested in trees this morning, Liddy.'

181

'Apart from Balgowan, Charlotte, the only inheritance Papa might attain is in France.'

'I should not care to live in France, Liddy, there is no society there. Oh dear, how very shallow that sounds. In truth, Liddy, I like it here.' She blushed rosily and quite charmingly. 'Jamie came to the practices. Of course he danced with each one of us and he did not single me out . . . not exactly, Liddy but . . .'

'Jamie is all that a young man should be,' Liddy assured her and Charlotte needed no second invitations to extol his many and varied blessings. Considering that less than three months before she had scarcely noticed his existence, this was quite an achievement.

Liddy was forced to stop her in mid-flight. 'Charlotte, I must see Papa. Is he below stairs yet?' she asked and escaped once more without telling Charlotte anything. In truth she had to see what she would say to their father first. All subsequent action would depend on that.

She found him in the library.

'Lydia, my dearest child,' he exclaimed advancing upon her with outstretched arms and enfolding her in a warm embrace. 'You look *un peu fatiguée*. Too many frivolities with the charming Lady Frazer.'

Liddy looked at him and realized how very easy it would be to relax into the warmth of his smile and to pretend that everything was as it appeared on the surface but she could not disguise her withdrawal.

'Too grown-up for a hug from Papa, Liddy?'

'I do not know my papa, sir.'

Once more the cold, hard look was on his face. 'Come girl, this is a nonsense . . . not know your papa, indeed.'

'I have not been with Lady Frazer, sir. I am but arrived from France.'

The arms that had held her so lovingly were around her again in a grip like iron. He pulled her across the room and almost threw her down into a chair. 'France? What business had you in France, Madame? And unchaperoned?'

Liddy faced him bravely. 'I was most nobly chaperoned, sir, and my business was to find you.'

'Me? To find me? Insolent girl. Why should you look for me in France?'

'Suffice to say I watched you leave.'

At the expression of horrified parental concern on his face, she could have laughed had she not been so close to tears. For the next few minutes she was subjected to a tirade in English and French on her morals, her upbringing, her ingratitude, and anything else he could conjure up. It would have reduced a younger Liddy to a quivering mass of hysteria.

She let him shout and rant and then, when he was silent, she stood up. 'Thanks only to Mama and Miss Rattray my morals and my upbringing are both of them in excellent shape, sir. What Mama would think were she to know that her only son's father was spying for the monster who caused his death, I do not know.'

She had gone too far. With all his strength he slapped her and, tall as she was, Liddy fell to the floor. 'How dare you,' he almost screamed. 'England killed my son and ruined my family. What I do now I do for my daughters.'

He was talking almost as if to reassure himself as he strode around the room. He returned and looked down at her. 'It is almost finished and you will not interfere. You will go to your room and you will remain there until I am ready to remove you to France.'

Liddy stood up and, judging it best to say no more upon the moment, walked proudly from the room. She would go to her room quietly for if she defied him, no doubt he would lock the door and that did not fit in with her plans. As it happened the door was locked anyway.

Madame brought her a tray later; she was not the same excited happy woman who had been there in the morning, but looked unhappy and even frightened.

'I'm sorry, Miss Lydia, about the orders to lock you in. His Lordship is . . . I have never seen him so angry.'

She ignored the tray and sat by the window looking out at a landscape still lashed by rain. It suited her mood. She was resigned. By force, if necessary, she would prevent Lord Balgowan spying for France. She had stopped Lord Pittenmuir in his tracks – her stomach lurched as she remembered the sound when her cudgel had descended on his unprotected head – and now she would have to stop her father. But how? Should she contact Keir and allow her father to be arrested? No. There had to be some other way to prevent both treachery and scandal.

For two days she remained a prisoner visited only by Madame. Although her body was idle her mind was busily working out schemes to save her family honour, but each scheme seemed more ridiculous than the last. On the evening of the second day her father let himself into her room. Liddy stood up warily.

'Forgive me, child,' he said. 'I should never have struck you and cannot forgive myself. Your sister is most anxious to attend this dance given by young Pittenmuir and swears she will not attend without you. I wish you both to attend the party and to behave as if nothing untoward has occurred. Can you do that?'

Liddy had completely forgotten the dance but it was an opportunity not to be missed. 'I have nothing to wear,' was all she could think of to say.

He laughed. 'How very like a woman. The new dress is always the most important thing, is it not? Madame will bring you the gifts I brought you from France. Did you think I would neglect my girls?' He did not wait for an answer but continued, 'Come down to dinner, Liddy. We are reconciled, are we not?'

Scarcely had the door closed behind her father when it flew open again and Charlotte, closely followed by Miss Rattray, burst into the room. Charlotte threw herself upon her sister, half-talking, half-crying, and it was some minutes before she was sufficiently calm to speak.

'Oh, Liddy, we were so . . . it has been . . . Papa has been . . .' She could not finish a sentence.

'Silly puss,' said Liddy, 'did you expect to discover me chained to the wall and existing on black bread and water? No such thing. Mrs Harper has spoiled me immensely. I hope you ate down-stairs half as well.'

Liddy looked over her sister's bent head at the governess. 'I told him I knew, Rattles.'

'Not all, Liddy, surely. His fury would be insupportable . . .'

'No. He became so angry when I confessed to having been on the beach in the middle of the night that he quite forgot to question me closely. I think, however, that he will rectify that omission when he is calmer. We must tell Charlotte.' Her eyes said eloquently, but not everything, and Miss Rattray nodded to show that she understood.

'Tell me what?'

Before Liddy could answer there was a knock at the door and

Madame entered with her arms full of packages. 'Here we are, Miss Lydia. His Lordship asks that you wear one this evening to show that all is forgiven and forgotten.'

Liddy took the gifts and almost threw them on the bed but she was controlled again when she turned round. 'Thank His Lordship, Madame. Here are my sister and Miss Rattray come to help me select.'

Well satisfied Madame withdrew and Liddy turned with a shudder. 'I could not bear to touch his gifts – blood money. I should disgrace myself.'

In as few words as possible she told Charlotte as much of the truth as she felt the younger girl could assimilate this time. She said nothing of the smugglers or of her involvement with Keir Galloway, Lord Pittenmuir.

'So you see, Charlotte, we must do what we can to prevent Papa sending any more information. Lord Pittenmuir will, no doubt, do what he can to avoid a scandal. Father must be persuaded to go into retirement. I have it sure in my mind that, if someone Papa respects can make him understand the enormity of what he has done, he will see reason. It all hangs upon Harry's death – it has unsettled his mind. He is not responsible.'

'For now you must both dress for dinner,' said Rattles, 'and Liddy, I know your principles haunt you, but for the sake of the greater good, wear something your father has given you.'

Liddy wore the blue Lord Balgowan had brought upon his first return from London and dinner was thus a civilized occasion to which even the younger girls were commanded.

'Saving the pink for Pittenmuir's party,' smiled her papa.

Pink is purported to flatter dark women, but since it was not a colour Liddy could have been prevailed upon to wear even had Lord Balgowan earned the monies for its purchase by selling fish on the harbour at Arbroath, Liddy smiled archly but said nothing.

'Then we must look forward to tomorrow. Which of my girls will be belle of the ball?'

Nineteen

What a difference from the last formal party. There was no ransacking of old trunks to find fripperies, no trying to convert an old coach into a modern carriage. Just after a delicious luncheon had been enjoyed in the morning room, excited squeals from Alice and Marie-Claire alerted Liddy and Charlotte to the arrival on the carriage sweep of a magnificent coach drawn by four perfectly matched horses. On the doors of the carriage were emblazoned the Balgowan arms, and so Liddy's first hope that some unexpected guest had arrived was shattered.

'Papa promised his girls a surprise,' laughed Lord Balgowan and tossing little Alice up into his arms he led the way outside.

Liddy brought up the rear of the procession, her heart heavier than ever. How was he to pay for such an equipage or, worse still, was it already paid for with French money? It was no part of her plan that he should suspect that she was not all conciliation. ''Struth, sir, never have I seen such a fine carriage. Do you not agree, Charlotte? Shall we not be the envy of all tonight?'

Charlotte was speechless and this attitude pleased her father inordinately. He handed her up into the carriage, the better to admire the pale blue upholstery, and did not seem too distressed when Liddy refused to join her for a first short outing.

'Indeed sir, I must be dressed to do justice to it. I will wait till tonight. Take the babes, for I require all the time at my disposal.'

For once in charity with his oldest daughter, Lord Balgowan ordered the coachman to let the horses proceed. A smile fixed to her face Liddy returned to the house. She climbed the stairs to her room, but there was no spring in her step. A young girl going to a party should surely have danced. Liddy went to the window and looked out. Would this be the night? Would all come to a conclusion and, if it did, would she be able to hold her head up tomorrow? She tossed the selfsame head. Whatever happened she would stand tall. Well, tall as she was, she would have no choice.

She had heard nothing from Lord Pittenmuir and had decided against trying to send him a message. Memories of every moment they had shared on the *Shuska* had sustained her during these last days. Was he well? He had made nothing of his wound. She would not allow herself to think him unwell. How could he be? Tonight he was giving a party and perhaps he would dance with her and they could talk. She would not behave so foolishly as she had done previously. Her hands went to her lips and she leaned against the cold glass remembering. He had kissed her, a soft, gentle kiss. Oh, if only she had more experience or the wisdom of a loving mother. The kiss had meant so much to her and perhaps had meant nothing at all to him.

She turned almost violently from the window. Come, Lydia, behaving like a lovesick miss will avail you nothing. If he loves you he will tell you when the time is right. First we have to catch our spy. Our spy. Dear God, I am speaking of my father. There is no way out of this, no way. Completely overcome by the weight of her appalling problems, Liddy threw herself upon her bed but, almost as quickly, sat up again. To dissolve in grief was the easy way – the coward's way. She would fight and she was not alone. Keir is on my side and together we will find a solution.

By the time Charlotte returned Liddy was composed and seemed to have no more on her mind than what to wear at the dance. It seemed as if her entire wardrobe was piled upon her bed.

'Great heavens, Liddy, what are you doing?' Charlotte began to shake out the dresses and return them to their hangers. 'Surely you are wearing the pink Papa brought you from . . . well, wherever it was.' She sat down with complete disregard for that selfsame pink which she was clutching between her hands. 'Liddy. Do you know, I could almost swear our new gowns come from Paris. There is a *je ne sais quoi* about them. Think you not so?'

'Charlotte, but how naive; you must know there is a flourishing trade with France. Wear your new gown and enjoy the evening to the utmost. Has Jamie bespoken your hand for supper?'

Charlotte's blush was answer enough and Liddy thought how much more the pink would become her. 'I wish the pink were in your size, Charlotte. Will you take it and ask Madame to alter it for another occasion?'

Nothing she could say would persuade Charlotte, who was almost horrified that her sister could so casually toss aside such a beautiful dress and a paternal gift at that.

'Papa will be furious if you do not wear his gift.'

'He will not know until it is too late. I shall wear my cloak and afterwards it will not matter.' She could not tell her sister that she expected their father to have gone into voluntary exile before the night was out.

When Charlotte returned to Liddy's room, several hours later, it was to show off her finery, and indeed how very beautiful she was. Her dress was white, shot through with silver threads that caused it to shimmer in the candlelight. Silver rosebuds trailed under the bosom and rioted around the hem and more were caught up in her golden curls. She looked ethereal.

'Twelfth Night,' breathed the literary Miss Rattray who had followed her into the room.

'Liddy, is it not the most beautiful gown?' asked Charlotte as she pirouetted in front of her sister.

'Almost as beautiful as the girl wearing it,' smiled Liddy.

Charlotte stopped and stared aghast at her sister. 'You are still in your shift. The dinner bell has sounded. Did I keep Madame too long?'

'As if Madame had anything to do with the picture you present, Charlotte. Indeed I sent Madame away but she will return shortly. Go and excuse me to Papa. You too, Rattles. I will be dressed in time for us to leave, I promise.'

'Your new gown?' asked Rattles.

'Oh, dear, do you know I stepped on the hem, so clumsy am I, and no time for Madame to repair it.'

'Liddy, how could you?' began Charlotte, but allowed Rattles to lead her from the room.

'Come, Charlotte, the babes are waiting to see you and so lovely do you look that you will easily be able to deflect His Lordship's ire. We will leave you, Liddy. Here is Madame come to your assistance.'

Madame, too, was furious at Liddy's treatment of the pink

gown but since her tirade passed completely over her mistress's head, she contented herself with moaning continually about how much better Miss Lydia would have looked in the new dress and why should she worry herself over a young lady who made no effort to fix the attention of a young nobleman who – so far as Madame could see – was the embodiment of everything even the most selective of young women would wish to find in a suitor.

She stopped for breath and Liddy congratulated her upon Charlotte's appearance and was delighted to see that this took all Madame's unwelcome attention away from herself. Apart from sighing, 'Oh no, Miss Lydia, not that dress again,' she said no more.

An hour later she fastened Miss Lydia's new cloak – purchased from the profits from her enterprise – over the old yellow gown, and pronounced herself quite pleased with the results.

She looked coyly at her mistress as she gave a final pat to the brown curls. 'Did Miss Charlotte not say that His Lordship likes this gown, Miss Lydia?'

'Thank you, Madame. Indeed I am in my best looks this evening; you are a genius.'

But were her undoubted looks due to the ministrations of a competent dresser or did something else cause the glow that makes even the plainest girl into a beauty? Knowing that she looked her best made it easy for Liddy to deal jocularly with her father who had his suspicions about her continued compliance with his wishes.

'Come, sir. Do you not know that the Honourable Jamie Galloway will be in abject misery until he is granted a smile from Miss Charlotte? How can you keep the poor boy in anguish?'

Distracted, as she had hoped, from her non-attendance at his dinner table, Lord Balgowan handed his daughters up into the coach. 'I feel for Mr Galloway and pray that he has not lost his heart completely for I have other plans for my fairest flower.'

'The Regent, Charlotte,' laughed Liddy and saw the cloud, which their father's remark had brought, lift from her face.

History repeated itself. Liddy and Charlotte removed their cloaks in the withdrawing room and then went together to the top of the staircase. Below them, in the hall, Lord Pittenmuir and his brother stood in the entrance to the ballroom greeting their guests.

'Look, Charlotte, such magnificence outshines even you,' laughed Liddy to hide how her heart had leapt upon seeing him. For their country dance, His Lordship and his brother had elected to wear tartan. Their kilts were of wine and green plaid and their jackets were of deep wine velvet with falls of the finest lace at the neck and the cuffs. His clan tartan could have been chosen specifically to complement Lord Pittenmuir's dark good looks. Had he heard her joking remark to her sister, for he looked up and saw her. Liddy and Keir did not smile and they did not speak as he moved across to the stairs and she walked down to meet him. The precious moment could not last . . .

'My Lord Pittenmuir, how do you do, sir.'

'Lord Balgowan.' The gentlemen bowed, society smiles on their faces. Liddy marvelled at how Keir showed nothing of his knowledge of her father's activities but was able to sustain a conversation with the man he fully intended to apprehend at some point in the evening.

'You young ones must join in the dance,' suggested Lord Balgowan eventually. 'I am promised to engage with General Fairweather in the card room.'

He bowed to them with consummate grace and they watched his leisurely and elegant progress across the room. Lord Pittenmuir turned to Liddy for he still had her hand. He smiled down at her, making her feel small and protected. 'Save me a strathspey, Liddy, but may I take you to supper? Country dances do not allow for intimate conversation.'

Liddy kept the phrase 'intimate conversation' in the forefront of her mind for the next few hours. Her hand was sought for every dance and sometimes when she did dance the figures of the dance would bring them together. Then it would seem as if they were alone in the swirling colours. Liddy allowed herself to relax and gave herself up to the moment. The world of smugglers and spies no longer existed; there was only the touch of his hand, the intimacy of his smile, the messages she was certain she was reading in the depths of his eyes. She answered the messages boldly and cared not who else could read them.

Lord Balgowan saw them. 'She can look higher,' he said by way of excuse that he planned to take his daughter away.

Miss Fairweather saw them. She smouldered with jealousy.

'What can he see in such a longshanks? If that gown is not five years old I shall eat my own.'

Miss Fairweather accosted His Lordship as he looked for Liddy in the imposing marble-floored hall. 'My dear Pittenmuir, you have neglected me shamefully this evening.'

Keir turned and looked down into the pretty face held up so adoringly to his. He could scarcely believe that a mere five or so weeks before he had found her adoration a comforting balm applied to the wound his Liddy had dealt him. He had encouraged Miss Fairweather and he was not proud of himself.

'You are so elegant, Leonora, that every man in the room seeks you out. I can scarcely believe you have missed me.'

She laid a trembling hand on his arm. 'Indeed, sir, I feel like a very pariah. You have not sought my hand for *one* dance,' she said with an attempt at a charming pout.

He looked over her head in another attempt to find Liddy and saw her yellow skirts whisking behind a pillar. He smiled and Miss Fairweather thought the tender smile directed at her. She gripped his hands and stood on her tiptoes to plant a chaste kiss on his cheek and he stepped sideways like a startled pony.

'Leonora, Miss Fairweather, the eyes of every dowager are upon us.'

'Oh, dearest Keir, I was sure . . . Grandpapa was sure . . . and then, when you seemed to ignore me after such friends as we have been.'

Keir was in a quandary. To pull himself free would serve only to make them more visible to the elderly ladies seated like a row of tawny owls along the back wall of the ballroom. He left his hands in hers and thus they stood as Liddy, having safely avoided the young and arduous Mr Walker, came out from behind the pillar.

Keir did not see her. 'Miss Fairweather, we *were* friends and I had hoped that we might remain so. You do yourself no good service, Miss Fairweather. Allow me to escort you to your grandfather.'

Miss Fairweather saw Liddy and knew that she was defeated but decided to strike a last blow. She awarded Keir a dazzling smile, tucked her arm into his and allowed him to walk her into the ballroom. Behind them in the hall Liddy stood as still as one of the marble statues that graced the entrance.

191

Until that moment Liddy had been oblivious of everything but his presence in the castle. She had schooled herself to appear her usual light-hearted self, except for almost holding her breath with anticipation until supper should be announced. She had avoided the importuning of several young men, dancing only when she could do no other. Now to see him hand in hand with that woman, to watch her hold his arm so possessively and knowingly . . .

I am a fool, she decided. She remembered Mrs Wallace's wise words, '*Young men's careless kindness.*' Were ever truer words said? In a daze she went back into the ballroom. How could she avoid him if he did indeed recollect his invitation to supper? Never would he know how much he had hurt her.

She sat in the conservatory like Queen Elizabeth waiting to deal with Walter Raleigh. At last she saw him make his way to her across the floor but when he reached her there was no smile on his face.

'Quickly, Liddy, did you see him leave?'

Lord Balgowan was nowhere to be found. A broken heart would mend. Treachery was another matter.

'He has tricked me, sir. He thought me safe at the dance . . .' She stopped, realizing how right her father had been. She had been aware of no one but the man who stood before her now.

If Keir was surprised by her coldness and formality he said nothing. 'He has made fools of us both. What a perfect cover – a junket at the home of the Lord Lieutenant. I must go. Forgive me. I will send word through John.'

'I'm going with you.'

'Don't be a fool. Have you any idea of the gossip an we disappear together.'

She was running along beside him as he strode towards the stairs. 'No one will believe you invited me to a party in order to ravage me. Please, my Lord, I know where he will be. Will you send a footman for Rattles? I will pretend an indisposition and join you later.'

'Will you stop *my Lording* me. Damn all women,' he said but did as he was bid and a few minutes later Rattles joined Liddy in the hall.

'I've forgotten Charlotte,' said Liddy. 'You must stay to chaperone her. I will send the coach back for you.'

Miss Rattray understood immediately and needed no further explanation. When their coach was announced, she wrapped Liddy in her luxurious new cloak and solicitously helped her into the coach before returning to the party to smooth her passage. Major Fordyce was already at work explaining that their host, in his position as Lord Lieutenant, had been summoned on urgent government business.

Liddy sat back in the coach until it was through the old gates of Balgowan House. Then abruptly she knocked on the roof to tell the coachman to stop. When the door was pulled open she had already jumped out the other side and now stayed crouched among the bushes to see what her father's coachman would do. She could have laughed at the surprised expression on his face. He scratched his head and looked beneath the coach as if his passenger could conceivably have slipped under there.

'She were in the coach, Bob, weren't she? Then where the devil's she got to and what's to do now?'

Liddy did not wait to see but, fastening her cloak more tightly around her, hurried as quickly and as safely as she could back towards the ruins. Several times as she clambered and scrambled she thanked the prevailing fashion for flat shoes. She could have wished them sturdier but at least there were no heels to catch in holes and on stones. Where was Keir? She would not think of Leonora. She would think of nothing but the business in hand. She stopped to catch her breath and to listen. Nothing – and then, after a few minutes, the night birds calling to each other as they swooped across the fields.

She was staking all on Lord Balgowan's going to the castle. If she was wrong and he was heading for the sea, she was undone. She could never intercept him now, in a ball gown that was becoming more tattered and dirty with every step she took. At last she stumbled on to a track and was able to make better time. 'Oh, be there, Papa,' she pleaded, 'and be amenable to persuasion.'

By the time she reached the grounds surrounding the ruins she had a stitch in her side and grit ground into her palms from her repeated contact with the track before her. She wiped her hands on what was left of the hem of her gown, and taking a deep breath to ease her side, she slipped into the ruins.

Was there a light? Was it Keir or the spies? She stopped once more to listen. Breathing. Someone was breathing heavily very close to her. Liddy's heart almost stopped with fright. In her stupidity she had walked slap into trouble. 'Calaban,' she whispered in sudden relief, for it was Keir's stallion standing so patiently among the bushes beside her. She leant for a moment against his warm, strong side and he turned his great head to nuzzle her.

Pain, fatigue, worry; everything was forgotten. Keir had come. For a second her heart seemed to swell with pure joy and she dropped a light kiss on the horse and then she remembered his own treachery. With aching heart she hurried towards the tunnel entrance.

It is no easy thing to crawl through a dark, damp tunnel in a yellow ball gown and a satin cloak. Several times Liddy thought to dispense with the cloak but the moon peeped coyly through occasionally and the gown would be seen against the ruined walls. This tunnel would bring her into the great hall and she stopped a few feet from the end to think. Should her father and whomever he was meeting be in the hall they would both hear and see her as she emerged. Nothing for it, she must take the risk. Boldly she stepped out into the fireplace alcove.

Three men stood in the great window. They turned as they heard the scraping of stone upon stone.

'Father,' began Liddy and to her horror she sensed rather than saw the pistol and a shot rang past her ear. There was a shout – was it her father's voice – and she turned and scrambled back into the tunnel. She had to get away . . . her breath was coming in gasps. Were they following her? Were they hurrying round to catch her at the end of the tunnel? Stop, Liddy. Stop panicking and think. She stayed still for a moment and took a deep breath. Someone had shot at her. It could not have been her father, but he must have recognized her and he would protect her, wouldn't he?

I'm going back. They are not following and must therefore be intending to head me off. I refuse to fall into their hands like a plum from a tree. She could not contemplate moving backwards into known danger. By the time she had manoeuvred herself around she was exhausted and she hated to think what she must look like. Her cloak was gone, her dress was in ribbons, her hands were torn and battered and her hair had escaped from its elegant coils and was tumbling down her back.

'Let them have gone to look for me,' she prayed as she crept out of the tunnel and straight into iron hands that fastened around her and across her mouth so that she could hardly breathe and could certainly not scream.

'You are the most aggravating woman,' hissed a voice in her ear and her treacherous heart leapt joyously as she collapsed against Keir. He held her for a moment more gently and she had a glimpse of what the future could have held and then he released her. 'Thanks to your meddling, those men are gone . . .'

She ignored the criticism and the suppressed anger in his voice. 'No, Keir, they will have gone into the courtyard to catch me coming out.'

'Stay here. They expect an unarmed girl. What a surprise they are about to receive.' He turned, opened the hidden door and disappeared into the tunnel.

'But there are three of them,' she whispered, but doubted that he had heard or that he would have paid any attention had he done so.

No point in using a tunnel now. Boldly she fled from the great hall and hurried down the crumbling staircase to where huge doors had once stood and where there was a pile of masonry. Over this she climbed with further insult to her hands and her clothes and found herself in the courtyard. Moonlight shone on the pistol in the hands of a muffled figure too small to be her father. Where were he and the third man?

Slowly, the door of an outhouse opened. The gun was raised. Liddy stood transfixed – she could not move. A scream rose in her throat but threatened to choke her and refused to be uttered. There was a noise that shattered the moonlight and then another, this time from inside the tunnel. At the same moment Keir erupted from the doorway a smoking pistol still held in his hand. He saw her as she stood outlined in her yellow gown against the wall.

'Get down, Liddy,' he screamed and another voice shouted in French from the ruins as a third shot flew past Liddy and buried itself in what was left of the door jamb.

Released from her spell by Keir's voice, Liddy had thrown herself down behind a pile of rubble. Keir had shot someone – one of the men she had seen in the great hall was now lying in a pool of blood at the entrance to the tunnel and the other voice, the one that had shouted in French, that had been her father. Was he the one who had shot at her? No, he had ordered them not to shoot his daughter, '*Ne tirez pas. C'est ma fille.*'

She could not lie here all night. An unearthly silence wrapped itself around her. They were all waiting with bated breath. Who would move first? Who would dare to stand up in the bright moonlight and present a target for an enemy's weapon?

'Lydia, come, my dear. Where are you?' It was her father's voice. It came from outside the wall, a few feet from where she was lying.

Keir, too, was outside. What was he doing? And the third man, was he too creeping closer, a pistol ready in his hand? How many times had Miss Rattray scolded her for the melodramatic qualities of many of her childhood essays? Undoubtedly she would scold now. The pistols would require to be reloaded and therefore she was safe for the moment. Her father would never fire at her – would he?

She refused to lie there waiting to find out. Cautiously she raised herself up. She looked back over her shoulder and was afraid. Never before had she been truly terrified in the grounds of the castle. Those half-broken walls suddenly looked more threatening. What were they hiding? A sob escaped her and angrily she dashed away a tear that had dared to fall on to her dirty cheek.

There was a flurry of sound. A shot rang out and a dark figure threw itself over the wall and lay still.

'Keir,' screamed Liddy and, unconscious of everything but that still figure, leapt from her hiding place and ran to him.

'Get down, you little idiot,' said Lord Pittenmuir scrambling to his feet.

Liddy ignored this unloverlike speech. 'Oh, Keir, I thought you were shot.'

'Merely winded. You should try jumping over a wall that high. I misjudged the fall on the other side, but quickly . . .' He grabbed her hand and pulling her behind him, ran like a deer, for the castle. Once inside he stopped. 'They must return for they have left their papers. That was the only good thing to come out of your startling them. Then they will try to reach the cove. Dear God, where is your cloak?'

She was trembling with fear and cold and he shrugged himself, with some difficulty, out of his sadly torn jacket and helped her into it. In the moonlight she could see an ominous dark stain spreading across his shirt.

'You *are* shot.'

'No, 'tis the same old wound. I tore it falling over the wall. Hush, someone is coming.'

'Lydia, are you there? I will give you one last chance.' It was her father.

She made to rise but with a firm hand Keir kept her down beside him. From the shadows they watched Lord Balgowan walk across the empty floor to the window embrasure. A sheaf of documents lay on the sill. One man had died for them already. Liddy watched her father pick them up.

'I will take those.' A third man had emerged from the shadows. 'Come, man, give me the papers and I will return them to France.' In horror Liddy listened to the language she had learned to love. 'Your daughter and her lover are secreted somewhere in this mouldering pile and indeed it is fitting that they should die together.'

'What have you done?' It was a strangled cry from her father.

'Arranged to rid France of a nuisance, m'Lord. Now, give me the papers or I miss the tide.'

'These are to buy back my home, my property, my rightful place in society.'

'This,' said the Frenchman in a disparaging tone as he gestured round the ruined great hall, 'is where you belong. Give me the papers.' He lunged forward to take them just as a pistol appeared in Lord Balgowan's hand.

'You thought to double-cross me. Peasant.' He fired but the roar of the pistol was lost in a more deafening roar as the very walls of the great hall fell in around them.

Twenty

S he was numb, she could feel nothing. After her despairing scream when the whole window frame of heavy stones had come crashing down on her father she had been silent. Keir had pulled her up and away and they had run back towards the tunnel pursued by the appalling sounds of explosions and falling stones.

Only when they were through the tunnel and completely outside the ruins did they stop. They had looked back in horror; the ancient walls that had withstood the ravages of time were no match for gunpowder and had fallen in on themselves. A grey pall hung in the air and was joined by an unearthly silence. The countryside at night is not quiet; only city dwellers think it so, but now, every bird and scavenger held its breath and waited until the rumbling noises had died away and the choking dust begun to settle. Only then, as if inured to the strange behaviour of human animals, did the birds begin to call again.

'I must go back to him,' said Liddy at last and moved away from Keir's encircling arm as if unaware that she had been leaning against him, taking comfort and strength from the hardness of his body.

Keir restrained her. 'Liddy, my dearest girl,' he said gently. 'It will be impossible in the dark. Leave it. We will return to Pittenmuir and I will alert my men. Come, we need lights and ropes.'

It was as if she had not heard him as she was already walking with that long stride back towards the pile of rubble which had been her family seat for centuries. That was when the first flame licked up to touch the sky. The old castle was on fire. The lamp must have toppled over in the chaos, spilled its oil on to any wood that was left and ignited the remains of the castle. Liddy was running now and Keir followed her as more fires broke out

198

in different parts of the ruins. There was no way into the castle as the old doorway was now a pile of masonry and flames obstructed every other opening. Keir forcibly restrained Liddy as she attempted, tears streaming down her face, to scramble through the flames into the castle.

'Be sensible, Liddy. Must I knock you out and carry you?'

She slumped against him and he laughed harshly. 'Thank you, my dearest love, for I could scarce lift little Alice at this point.'

Fury gave her strength and she pushed him away. 'I am not your dearest love.'

Keir looked at her in surprise but stood quietly while Calaban came trotting over to them. He helped Liddy mount and then, exhausted, allowed her to help him climb up behind. 'Some knight in shining armour, am I not?' he said disparagingly but was distressed to feel how Liddy pulled her body away from him.

'Armour would have been vastly uncomfortable even for a knight with a clear conscience,' answered Miss Carpenter.

For a moment horse and riders stood quiet, the horse because he was waiting for instruction, its owner because he was wondering if perhaps his dear delight had been hurt. What else could account for her hostility? He reminded himself, too, that she had just seen her father killed before her very eyes.

Poor darling, he thought. He tightened his arms about her and coaxed Calaban into a trot. What time was it? He had no idea and he wished he knew whether it was better to take her to her own home and the comfort and care she would receive from Miss Rattray, or to proceed to Pittenmuir where there might yet be a house full of guests. He would spare her their stares and questions if he could. His heart ruled his head – he would keep her with him as long as possible – and he set out for his own home.

Their adventure, that had seemed to take but a few minutes, must have taken longer for, apart from courtesy lights left to guide the footsteps of the master of the house, all was dark. When he dismounted at the foot of the steps, however, the doors were thrown open and there stood Jamie, Major Fordyce, Tregarth and the butler all with lighted lamps held aloft. They rushed forward.

'My God, Keir, what's to do? We heard explosions and every man on the estate is alerted.' This from Jamie.

'I have sent for the militia.' Major Fordyce.

Liddy heard a confusion of voices but later she was never to remember whose were the arms that she slid into or how she found herself tucked up in a most comfortable four-poster bed. How could she have slept? Was it the brandy – 'unsmuggled, my love' – with which the warm milk had been laced, or sheer exhaustion and reaction to the catastrophic events of the night? When she awoke, not at first remembering the horror, it was to see Miss Rattray's dear kind face smiling down at her, and then full realization came rushing back and she started up in the bed.

'Papa,' she gasped. 'I must get up. The babes. Charlotte.'

Gently Rattles pushed her back against the pillows. 'Liddy dearest, indeed you must know that your papa died, but such a hero. Lord Pittenmuir has told everyone of His Lordship's bravery in apprehending two French spies,' she said firmly and clearly. 'It is too dreadful that Lord Balgowan died in the accomplishing of such a courageous undertaking.'

Liddy stared at her. Lord Balgowan a hero? 'But this is so wrong. I cannot accept this, Rattles, and I must get up and go home.'

She suited her actions to her words, threw back the covers and almost jumped from the bed. 'Oh, bless you, dearest of friends, you have brought me some clothes.'

A knock at the door heralded the arrival of a trim maid with a generous breakfast tray.

'Come, Liddy, so kind as His Lordship has been, you cannot leave without some nourishment. Lord Pittenmuir has arranged everything. Indeed, I do believe he has not yet sought his couch, so busy has he been. There are red coats everywhere and Major Fordyce busy with dispatches for London. He has left already and His Lordship will follow later today.'

That penetrated. 'Today? He is leaving?'

'Naturally, my dear. The Lord Lieutenant must report to the government. Never fret, Liddy . . .' Miss Rattray talked and talked, and as she talked she guided Liddy to a chair, wrapped her in the delicious confection of flowers so beloved of Madame Etienne, and handed her a cup of hot sweet tea. 'His Lordship's men had the blaze under control before the militia arrived, but the castle is quite gone. They . . . well my dear, they managed to bring out the bodies. Major Fordyce himself alerted me as they knew I would be most anxious and I have broken the news to your sisters. Charlotte has been quite wonderful. How proud of her you would have been. This morning His Lordship sent a coach for me – such a luxurious way to travel a few miles, I am quite spoilt, and the coach awaits you when you feel well enough to return home.'

Liddy said nothing but she did drink some tea and swallowed a few bites of toast. While she was dressing the same maidservant returned and informed them that His Lordship was anxious to have a few moments with Miss Carpenter if she felt well enough to speak with him.

'Please tell His Lordship that I am returning home and that I thank him for . . . everything.'

The girl curtseyed and withdrew and when Liddy had finished dressing she followed her downstairs – the same stairs that only a few hours ago she had walked down with such happiness. Once again Keir was waiting at the bottom. He had washed and had changed his clothes; only his eyes showed his exhaustion. When he heard Liddy approach he looked up and their eyes met.

He has done all in his power to protect me. He has lied for Papa, to save his name . . . for me perhaps, no . . . for Harry? But he encouraged me to love him, and now I can't stand the pain.

She did not smile politely. She could not. She offered him her hand. 'I thank you, my Lord, for your hospitality,' and then she broke and could say no more and Rattles ushered her to the waiting carriage.

He bowed. 'I will call, if I may . . . later.'

'Already you have been too kind, sir, too kind,' she mumbled and hurried into the coach.

She had to get home, away from Keir's disturbing presence. She needed to think, to grieve, and to comfort the little girls and Charlotte. She must send a messenger to her father's heir. Oh, dear God, legally they now had no home. Her father's solicitors must be informed. When would it all end?

Where to begin? A letter to the solicitors. A letter to her cousin, her father's heir.

Rattles showed Lord Pittenmuir in. He moved forward to take Liddy's hands but she knew that her carefully wrought control would dissolve an he touched her and went to stand behind her desk.

He looked down at his riding boots. 'Forgive my dress, Liddy.'

She said nothing.

He was not at ease. 'Dash it all, Liddy, I must go and I wished first to get things clear, but this is not the time. May I deliver any missive in Edinburgh as I ride through?'

'You are too good, m'Lord. John will deliver the letters, I'm sure.'

'Damn it, Liddy. I am too tired to try to follow your thoughts. If you have your business letters ready, allow me to deliver them.'

Still without looking at him she picked up a letter. 'This is for my father's man of business. If you could deliver it—'

He almost snatched it from her fingers. 'I cannot wait for more, my dear. The sooner I go the sooner I can return. Jamie, in the meantime, will do your bidding.' He stopped and his face softened. 'Liddy . . .'

'You have been all that is kind, sir,' she said dismissively.

'I thought . . . I hoped . . . oh damn all women,' said Lord Pittenmuir again and walked out of the room not forbearing to slam the door behind him.

Liddy looked at the door. She felt numb. Keir had been here and he had gone. She looked down at her ink-stained fingers. Yes, she had written a letter and he had taken it. Now John need not ride into the city. The new Lord Balgowan lived near the Firth. John should enjoy travelling on a ferryboat, he who had sailed with the smugglers. She smiled a little.

Later she wept for she could not remember what she had said to His Lordship. She remembered only that he had slammed the door. His papa had whipped him for slamming doors in anger. But we are not children, Keir, and everything is changed again.

The Honourable Lydia was become an automaton. She ate, she tried to sleep, she talked to her little sisters, she arranged the necessary ceremony and spoke sensibly and maturely to dear Mr Wallace. She felt nothing.

Being busy did help Liddy cope. If she filled her mind with all the details of the obsequies there was no room and no time to think about Keir. His brother, Jamie, was a frequent visitor and it was obvious that he came primarily to see Charlotte.

The new Lord and Lady Balgowan arrived two days before the funeral. Liddy met them at the door of Balgowan House. Since they had never been welcomed in the house before they were obviously ill at ease and Liddy set her mind to making them feel welcome in what was, after all, their house.

Mrs Harper prepared a delightful meal for them upon their arrival. His new Lordship relaxed a little. 'Naturally I am unaware of the contents of your father's will, dear cousin, or the extent of his private fortune which you must inherit, but we do want you to know that we will not seek to remove ourselves to Balgowan until such time as you are prepared to leave. We understand the difficulties and want you to know that you are most welcome to life tenancy of Ochil House – not so grand as this but pleasant I think, and it would not take a fortune to put in order.'

Liddy looked at their concerned faces and could have wept that their father's attitude to his only relative had made it so that she had not grown up knowing these kind people.

'You are generous, Cousin.'

'No indeed. An uninhabited dower house of modest proportions is scarcely right for the daughters of Balgowan. I had suggested leasing it from the estate once so that we might grow to know one another but . . . all that is behind us.'

If we take Ochil House we shall have a roof over our heads, but how can I play poor relation? She must decide what were best to be done and she must not include Pittenmuir in her equation. After all, he had betrayed her love, had he not? She would not think of him.

'It is most kind of you, dear William, and you too, dearest Maria, but it is too early for me to speak with any real authority. The will is to be read, as you know, after the interment and then I will make my decisions, but I do assure you that you are most welcome to install your family here in your own home as early as you wish.'

'Too, too kind.' Lady Balgowan almost wept and Liddy excused herself and took refuge in the thought of vigorous exercise. She could not ride – that would be unfitting – but she would walk and she found herself heading automatically for what remained of the old castle.

It would never be rebuilt now. The gunpowder had finished off the work of time's erosion and all that remained were charred piles of stone. There was no possibility of unblocking any of the tunnels and Liddy was sure that it was there that the trails of destruction had been laid. She must advise the new Lord Balgowan lest his own small children should attempt to uncover them.

She shivered in the cold air. The third man. How he must have hated Papa. But why we shall never know. Did he resent his birth and position or did he hold him in utter contempt because he spied against what was officially his own country? Honour. What was it?

Liddy groaned and sank down upon a stone. What will I do? Where shall I go? I hoped to marry Keir but he was jesting with me or perhaps it was such trifling as is done in society. How embarrassed he would be to find that I allowed myself to . . . It is over and it was never begun and now that I am penniless and almost homeless . . . As for Papa's will, if there is any money I shall use it for Charlotte and the babes.

The little girls had wept, but they had not really known their father and so, by the time the funeral cortège wound its way out of the grounds of Balgowan House, they were beginning to chafe at the restrictions on their activities. The service sobered them and reminded them of all that had occurred. Charlotte wept openly and Liddy had not the heart to prevent the Honourable Jamie from giving her his arm. Of his brother there was no sign, although at this funeral, unlike the last, there was a floral tribute from His Lordship.

'Such beautiful flowers,' wept Charlotte.

'I had expected Pittenmuir back by this time, Miss Carpenter,' Jamie confessed to Liddy as the mourners gathered in the drawing room.

She wanted to strike out, but she remembered in time that she had misjudged His Lordship before. Illness and the Prime Minister had kept him from Harry's funeral. She smiled now at the young man. 'I know His Lordship would have been here if he could.'

Charlotte looked relieved at her sister's gentleness and drew Jamie away and Liddy remained with her cousin, acting as hostess for the last time in her father's house.

Then it was time for the family to gather for the reading of the will and with mixed relief and horror Liddy discovered that Lord Balgowan had died a warm man and all left to his daughters. There would be money enough to purchase a suitable house where they might live modestly. Somehow she would yet contrive a coming-out for Charlotte.

'Ill-gotten gains,' muttered Lydia and almost earned a box on the ears from her sorely tried governess.

For the next few months better that they stay quietly at Ochil House. It would give her time to search out a suitable house, as far away from Forfarshire as could be managed. With a drawn face and controlled voice she told Miss Rattray of her cousin's very generous offer.

'How wonderful. Working hard to create a new home will help your sisters over their grief. Come, Liddy, let us visit the house on the instant to see how it can be put to your use.'

'I don't remember when there was last a tenant there, Rattles,' said Liddy doubtfully. 'It will need an army of workmen.'

'Since when are you afraid of dirtying your hands, Liddy? Today it cannot hurt just to look at the house. The little ones will enjoy to shriek at cobwebs.'

And so it proved. All four Carpenter sisters and Miss Rattray enjoyed a delightful afternoon. They peered into cobweb-shrouded rooms and discovered valuable oak furniture under accumulations of dust and neglect. The house was far smaller than Balgowan House, but it boasted four decent sized bed-chambers and a delightful sun-filled drawing room together with a sadly outmoded kitchen. There were overgrown but well-set-out gardens and a small stable for Amber.

Liddy was almost in a good mood when she closed the door behind them, but then realization dawned. 'Rattles, I have used the carriage all afternoon without a by your leave or one word to my cousin. When will I learn that I am no longer mistress of Balgowan House?'

'Don't dwell on it too much, Liddy. Indeed Lord Balgowan has no need of this carriage.'

'It has the Balgowan crest, Rattles, and therefore belongs to my cousin. Oh, how am I able to support the role of beggar, and indeed, it would be extremely charitable if the new baron does not tire quickly of indigent relatives on his very door?'

Miss Rattray said nothing, knowing that in such a mood of gloom there was nothing that could be said to cheer Liddy.

It was some days before all the guests from distant parts had departed and it was at dinner on the first evening when they found themselves alone, *en famille*, that Lady Balgowan in-formed Lydia that they too were returning to Edinburgh. 'For you must see, Lydia, that William had not expected to inherit for some years, and although we are anxious to pick up the threads of life at Balgowan, it will take some months to arrange matters in town. We would be happy, nay grateful, if you would consider remaining in residence here at least until the turn of the year.'

Later Liddy was to mentally chastise herself for the abrupt way she answered her gentle cousin. She felt that she was choking on cloying kindness and, instead of appreciating that the new Lord and his family felt badly about displacing them, she reacted negatively.

'Dear Maria, we could not possibly stay. In fact we will leave as soon as we can put Ochil House in order. Far better for the little ones to realize that this is no longer their home and that we are but pensioners. I will decide as quickly as possible about future plans and will write to you in Edinburgh. I suggest that you keep the house open with Mrs Harper. You may not need Madame, who is an excellent dresser, and her . . .' She didn't quite know how to explain that Monsieur Etienne had disappeared and Madame swore she knew nothing of her husband's whereabouts.

'But we should adore to hire her if you do not need her, Lydia. My own abigail has already told me she will not remove here and –' here she coloured slightly – 'we cannot blame Madame if her husband was not all that he purported to be.'

'Then all works out well, does it not?' smiled Liddy rather brightly and she retired in a fury but why she did not really know. She was furious with herself for wounding Maria and she had seen the look of horror on Charlotte's face. Charlotte. She had had very little private conversation with Charlotte recently – she must talk with her tomorrow. Thinking of Charlotte should have prevented other thoughts entering her mind, but they did not. She could avoid thinking of Keir throughout the day, but at night he invaded her mind and heart.

The next day she escaped from her worries and went off to the ruins. There she sat on a stone and let her memories invade her heart and mind.

'May I speak with you, Liddy?' Keir was there suddenly, tall and strong and so gentle as he looked down at her. 'I am but arrived from town and rode over with some fruit for Miss

Rattray from my succession houses. Charlotte told me I might find you here.'

Her heart was pounding but she willed it be still. 'No children will play here again, sir . . .'

'Of course they will. Their games will be different, that's all.'

She smiled wryly. 'Rattles will be delighted with your gift.'

He turned and stood looking down at the ruins. 'I did try to return in time, Liddy. When Harry died, I was too ill. I didn't even know he was dead for some time. You believe me?'

She nodded. 'Of course. He was your best friend. I should have known, I'm sorry.'

'You were my dearest friend, you and Harry together. Even when we were away at school I thought of you always together, Harry and Liddy, Liddy and Harry. But Liddy, I never *dreamed* of Harry.'

She stood up and held up a work-worn hand. 'Please, my Lord. Say nothing. I should hear your report?'

He did not answer for a moment as he marshalled his thoughts. At last he said, 'Very well. I reported on a successful conclusion to the enterprise. The French spies are dead and the Arbroath Ladies are disbanded. Mr Perceval will send the family his condolences on the heroic death of Lord Balgowan, together with his personal gratitude.' He looked warily at the Honourable Lydia. ' It is possible that the orphaned children of His Lordship will be awarded some small pension.'

She stifled a sound. He looked at her but could read nothing in her face, so still and calm as she was. Where was the old Liddy who had always made her feelings so painfully clear?

'Liddy, please speak to me?'

There was a quaver in her voice as she smiled brightly at him. 'But of course I will speak to you, My Lord. Do you wish me to say how grateful I am that you have made a hero of my father, or how grateful I am that our proud name will not be sullied? Right gladly will I do so. As to accepting a pension.' She drew herself up to her full height and looked him straight in the eye. 'You insult me, sir. Do you really think me capable of living such a lie? You think I can stomach to profit by my father's death?'

He groaned. 'It is not profit. What are you to do? Hire yourself out as a servant? Live a pensioner on your cousin? You could not stomach that. I want you to say that you will be my wife . . .'

No protestation of undying love. What had she expected or hoped for? She looked away from him out across the sea. 'You do me too much honour, sir. I thank you, no.'

'I had not meant to speak but given the circumstances—'

'The circumstance that Papa had the good taste to die,' she said flatly. 'So convenient for everyone. Please go away, Lord Pittenmuir, go back to your friends in London and tell them the Carpenters need nothing.'

She tried to prevent them, but tears started in her eyes. 'In truth, sir, I care not what you say.'

She turned and ran from him, down the hill. He did not follow her.

Twenty-One

Liddy reached Balgowan House with more colour in her face than had been there for some time. Miss Rattray saw it and commented.

'You were quite in the right of it to seek solace in vigorous exercise, Liddy. See how it has brought colour to your cheeks and a sparkle to your eyes.'

Liddy strode across the library to the windows. Since her cousins' arrival the family had once more tended to use this room and leave the drawing room free for Lady Balgowan's use. 'This is not exercise, Rattles, this is rage. He says he wants to marry me.'

Miss Rattray threw up her hands in joy. 'Why, how wonderful. Indeed I have been waiting for just such an eventuality. But why is your reaction one of fury?'

'You wouldn't understand,' was Liddy's cry, an age-old one had she but known it. 'He does not say he loves me. I saw him with *her*.' She spat out the word. 'They were holding hands . . . like . . . lovers, Rattles. She clung to his arm; so close were they. How she laughed at me as I stood gawping. But he says he wishes us to wed. It is to protect me as he has protected Father.' She sank down into a chair and covered her face with her hands. 'Mayhap he sacrifices himself for Harry.'

Involuntarily Rattles moved towards her.

Liddy forestalled her. 'Rattles, if you love me, say nothing. His Lordship has been to London and told some lie so that my father has become a hero and we have become pensioners of the government. I would hire out as as governess before accepting money for my father's hidden treachery. I must look to my sisters and their future.'

Miss Carpenter returned to her lists and her figures. Not a penny would she take from the government – not even to help Charlotte.

Later after the entire household was asleep she cried into her pillow for the hundredth time. 'I was in the right to refuse his offer. It was not really an offer, a few words blurted out in such a moment. If he had said one word, one single word of love then maybe I could have trusted him, but he did not because it would have been a lie and he is incapable of lying. Oh, was ever anything more vexatious. Of course he is capable of lying. He has been lying like a trooper for months and I . . . I am no better.'

Charlotte sought her out in the library the next day. Liddy had retired there immediately after their cousins had left, in order to finish up paperwork pertaining to the estate so as to leave all in pristine order.

'Liddy, I must speak with you.'

Charlotte was awarded a brilliant smile. 'Come in, dearest. I had intended to speak with you today. There is so much for us to discuss, for instance the removal to Ochil House. It is a small property but perfect for our period of mourning. If you dislike it too much, after Christmas we could take a house in Edinburgh or Moffat in the Borders which they say is almost as healthy and sociable as Bath. In a year we might even think of London.'

'A year?' gasped Charlotte as if her sister had pronounced sentence of a century's duration. 'Liddy, I love Jamie and wish to marry him.'

This impassioned announcement was not totally unexpected and so Liddy achieved a light laugh. 'Naturally you do, dearest, but only a few months ago you were quite *bouleversé* over his brother.'

Charlotte blushed rosily. 'That was a child's reaction to her first man of the world. Now I am grown up and wiser. Jamie is . . . Jamie is wonderful.'

'*Sans doute.* But Charlotte, Papa is just dead and you are still in shock. Forgive me, but you ought not to make decisions at such a time and Jamie had no right to speak to you at all.'

Charlotte stood up, suddenly much older and more mature. 'He did not intend to speak. It was the party. We danced. I wished it might go on for ever.' She stood lost in romantic reverie.

It was time, figuratively speaking, for cold water. 'And my Lord Pittenmuir? Has he given his blessing?'

210

'He does not know yet, but why should he not be pleased? Our families have always been friends and then, there is you.'

'Me?'

'Come, Liddy, he loves you. It is writ all over his face and your love for him on yours.'

'Nonsense. He was Harry's friend and I have had a certain . . . fondness. Now, no more talk of love and nuptials for the moment. I need your help in sorting furniture, linens and such-like. You have been overmuch in Jamie's company lately; I thought it would help you over your grief and so it has done. Better for all if we are settled before Christmas and Rattles and I cannot do it alone.'

Since Charlotte had always borne more than her fair share of the housekeeping duties, this was an extremely unkind and unjust remark but Liddy was unrepentant. Better to wean Charlotte from an unlikely alliance. She and Jamie were, after all, very young and would recover. This from the ancient Miss Carpenter who had not yet attained her twenty-fifth year.

For several weeks the house was in turmoil while she decided what belonged to the estate and must therefore stay and what was now or had always been their personal property. She was scrupulously honest in this undertaking and would not allow so much as an eggcup to be packed until its rightful ownership was ascertained. At the same time there were onslaughts into the dust and neglect of Ochil House. Liddy said no more about Jamie and forbore to comment when she saw his horse or phaeton in front of the house. If she wondered that his brother did not press his suit, she said nothing

She wished she knew how much Jamie had been told of the truth concerning Lord Balgowan's clandestine activities. Would he recoil in horror from Charlotte were he to discover the truth of her father's last hours? If only she could take Charlotte away so that she might meet other eligible young men.

Meanwhile Keir, Lord Pittenmuir, cursed himself for his stupidity and when he could no longer bear to be so close to Liddy and yet so far from her, he took himself back to London. While he lay back against the comfortable upholstery, he found himself going over his actions again and again. He remembered the disastrous meeting on the hill. Why had he blurted out his proposal? If only Liddy had known that he had practised several flattering approaches that paid tribute to her lovely eyes, the shine of her hair, her courage, the straightness of her delightful nose. Then he had coughed out bald words at the worst possible moment. Jamie had told him Charlotte thought him the epitome of sophistication. What price my sophistication now, Charlotte?

He had stood on the hill watching Liddy run, stifling the instinct that told him to run after her, sweep her into his arms, cover her face with kisses while cursing the impetuosity that had caused him to blurt out his proposal.

I meant to tell you how very much I love you, that I have loved you all my life even though I did not know it until I sailed for the Peninsula and knew that above all, I wanted to be wherever you are. I still do, Liddy. When I discovered that it was my brave reckless Liddy who scaled those walls . . . oh, Liddy my heart near stopped beating. Damn fool, you said none of it. You should have been on your knees, begging, praying that she would do you the great honour of becoming your wife.

He whacked the cushions across from him with his walking stick, stuck his head out of the window and yelled at his coachman to stop dawdling. 'Devil take it, man, I wish to get to London before Christmas.' He refused to feel ashamed of his bad temper, but by the time they had stopped for the night he was calm and, although he did not apologize, he thanked the coachman for the comfort and speed of the journey. A more than tolerable dinner did not push Liddy from his thoughts. He walked the floor of his bedchamber and ignored the angry thumps from below.

I could have told her that perfect happiness would be removing all worries from her lovely shoulders, that it would be an honour to take upon myself the upbringing and education of her sisters, the support of Miss Rattray, the boy John, even old Tom. But ah, Liddy, most of all I want to be with you, to love you, to be loved by you.

'I can live without you, my darling,' he whispered as he sought some refreshing sleep, 'but, oh, my dearest one, what an empty life it will be.'

The morning brought sunshine and a rise in his spirits.

He would stay away to give them both time to reflect. Liddy was in shock, still in mourning. She had scarce had time to come to terms with the loss of a beloved brother and now here was her father cruelly slain, before her very eyes. He would approach her more circumspectly. He would strive to recover the friendship, the affection that had surely existed during those last days on the *Shuska*. He laughed at the memory of her in her primrose yellow gown, torn and tattered and so stained. 'What a woman is my Lydia.'

He decided to buy her a gown and only after the most fashionable and expensive modiste had shown him several enchanting gowns that seemed perfect for Liddy did he remember that he had no right to give so intimate a gift. He took his seat in the House, he boxed with friends, he played cricket and was told to hie himself back to Scotland, so appalling was His Lordship's erratic fielding. He did as he was bid.

Liddy was engaged in cleaning the front hall and so involved was she in her work that she did not hear the front door open but remained kneeling on the floor, an apron around her trim waist and her hair hidden by a most unattractive turban. Her face was smudged and, had she but known it, a piece of spider web was caught in her left eyebrow.

Lord Pittenmuir thought she looked delightful.

'May I come in?' he asked at last and she started to her feet in surprise.

In the small hallway his tall figure seemed to loom over her as he stood outlined against the open door. She was aware of her oldest dress, a smudged nose and, good heavens, was this a spider web that she had brushed from her eyes. Why did he manage to look the epitome of elegance in his casual riding dress. Life was so unfair.

She was furious. 'How dare you walk in without being announced. I must look like a washerwoman.'

He examined her judiciously. 'No, Liddy. A washerwoman must, by virtue of her employment, be clean.'

She stole a peep at his eyes. Smiles danced there. So, he thought to be on their old footing did he? Did he think he could just leave and as casually return?

'Well, my Lord, you see how busy we are,' she said ungraciously.

He looked round. 'This is surely no work for a lady.'

'Dirt is no respecter of ancient lineage.'

So she had not forgiven him. He would be formal, too. 'I shall take but a moment of your time, Miss Carpenter.'

Her heart sank, so formal was he. Why had he not waited until she had returned to Balgowan House? Had she known he was come home she would have changed her gown. At least she would not have been caught wearing an unflattering turban.

'The drawing room is not yet prepared. Can you say what you have to say here in the hall?'

He laid his hat, his gloves, and his riding whip on a splendidly carved oak table that lurched drunkenly on its three good legs against a wall. 'Could we take a turn in the gardens? We might be overheard here.'

'There is only Miss Rattray here and from her I have no secrets,' but she was removing the turban and pulling on the shawl which had been draped over a banister. 'The gardens are overgrown but well laid out as you can see. I intend, however, to hire John to help put all to rights.'

'Impossible. John has agreed to work for me and, I assure you, I will keep that young man so employed that he will have no time to go adventuring with the gentlemen or should I say the Ladies of Arbroath, should anyone be foolish enough to resurrect them.'

Differing emotions warred within her breast. John of all people to desert her, but he was right to go to Pittenmuir. He would have a good home, decent wages, more than she could give him.

Keir knew full well what was going on in her mind and took pity on her. 'He did not want to come to me. Indeed I black-mailed him.'

She stopped and looked at him in surprise. 'Blackmail . . . you?'

'Indeed, Miss Carpenter, I find myself to be a most unsavoury character. He is pardoned by the Crown if he enters my employ.'

Contemptuously she looked at him. 'Unspeakable.'

'There is more,' he said calmly. 'I told him that you were going to marry me – quietly in the spring.'

Again she stopped. 'I could box your ears,' she said furiously while her heart beat a tattoo. 'How dared you say that. You, you Don Juan, you. I saw you hanging on to Leonora Fairweather, the overdressed – or no, should I not say underdressed – scheming old maid.'

He looked at her. Laughter, she pretended not to see, lurking in those brilliant eyes. 'Such words for a gently bred maiden, Miss Carpenter. I am deeply shocked. For a moment there, however, I thought I recognized my old friend, my best beloved of friends.'

'Miss Fairweather?'

'I blush to say it, Liddy, but it was she who was hanging on to me. I could not humiliate her before the whole of the county.'

'So you elected to humiliate me.'

He looked directly into her eyes. 'I did not see you there. Indeed I might ask why did you not rescue me?'

She turned away from him and whacked an unsuspecting and totally innocent flower. 'You did not appear in need of rescue, sir. Now, if that is all your business, my Lord, I would return to my work.'

He eyed her warily and then took his courage in both hands and put his arms around her.

She stood as stiff and still as possible. 'Unhand me, sir.'

'But I have no choice, Liddy. I am ordered to wed you, and you me, naturally.'

'Who dares to order me? Is it Perceval?'

'No indeed. He agrees with me that to shackle myself to a woman capable of scaling ruined walls in the dead of night, of leading a band of cut-throat smugglers, not to mention killing the odd spy with one blow, will be deuced uncomfortable, but I find myself obliged to make the sacrifice.'

Hope stirred in her heart. Was there a way out? This Keir was the Keir of her childhood, teasing, delightful, wholly dependable. She relaxed in arms that did not loosen. 'It will be a sacrifice for me, too,' she said mendaciously. 'Who gives the order?'

He pretended amazement. 'Why, the Regent himself. Visualize the scene, Liddy. I have gone to Perceval. All is understood and forgiven. Lord Balgowan's secrets are to die with him; no one else need know. But His Highness sends for me. I am commanded to tell the whole and when I confess that I, Keir Galloway, Lord Lieutenant of the county have joined a notorious band of smugglers . . . imagine the regal fury. I explain that I had need of the smugglers to get me to France. His Highness counters with a dozen honourable ways of entering the country. He is furious with you, too. Your Jacobite sympathies are well known. His Highness wants no scandals; all must be hushed up. Ergo we are compelled to wed so that each will stand surety for the continued good behaviour of the other.'

She whacked a second withered head from a sadly overgrown rosebush. 'How much of this faradiddle is true, Keir Galloway?'

'He *did* say that he wished he might meet a woman with just such spirit and that if she would lower herself to marry me I might count myself the most blessed of men.' He tightened his arms and turned her to face him. 'Oh, dear God, Liddy, I love you, I have loved you all my life and these last weeks out of the light of your presence have been unmitigated misery.' He bent and kissed her. Not a gentle kiss, but rough and compelling, a kiss that expressed all the pent-up emotion that he had tried to conceal and that seemed to draw the heart from her body so that she responded to him with all her love.

'That was all you needed to say. I love you too, my best of friends, and can think of no finer fate than to be your wife.'

Again he bent his head to seek her lips and then pushed her from him with a groan.

'We have wasted too much time, my love. Shall we obey the Regent's orders and wed in the spring?'

Demurely she slipped her hand into his. 'I am his Highness's most obedient servant.'